THE
PICTURE
BRIDE

BY LEE GEUM-YI

The Picture Bride
Can't I Go Instead

THE
PICTURE
BRIDE

*Lee
Geum-yi*

Translated from the Korean by An Seonjae

A TOM DOHERTY ASSOCIATES BOOK

NEW YORK

THE PICTURE BRIDE

Copyright © 2020 by Lee Geum-yi
English translation © 2022 by An Seonjae

A Forge Book
Published by Tom Doherty Associates
120 Broadway
New York, NY 10271

www.tor-forge.com

Forge® is a registered trademark of Macmillan Publishing Group, LLC.

Library of Congress Cataloging-in-Publication Data

Names: Yi, Kŭm-i, 1962– author. | Anthony, of Taizé, Brother, 1942– translator.
Title: The picture bride / Lee Geum-yi ; translated from the Korean by An Seonjae.
Other titles: Alloha, na ŭi ŏmmadŭl. English
Description: First U.S. edition. | New York : Forge, 2022. | Identifiers: LCCN 2022021137 (print) | LCCN 2022021138 (ebook) | ISBN 9781250808660 (hardcover) | ISBN 9781250808684 (ebook)
Subjects: LCSH: Mail order brides—Fiction. | Immigrant women—Fiction. | Koreans—Hawaii—Fiction. | LCGFT: Historical fiction. | Novels.
Classification: LCC PL992.9.K788 A45 2022 (print) | LCC PL992.9.K788 (ebook) | DDC 895.7/34—dc23/eng/20220608
LC record available at https://lccn.loc.gov/2022021137
LC ebook record available at https://lccn.loc.gov/2022021138

Our books may be purchased in bulk for promotional, educational, or business use. Please contact your local bookseller or the Macmillan Corporate and Premium Sales Department at 1-800-221-945, extension 5442, or by email at MacmillanSpecialMarkets@macmillan.com.

Originally published in Korea as 알로하, 나의 엄마들 by Changbi Publishers, Inc.

First U.S. Edition: 2022

Printed in the United States of America

0 9 8 7 6 5 4 3 2 1

*To my daughter, Noori, who always inspires me
with her fierce and fearless exploration of the world and life*

THE
PICTURE
BRIDE

Part One

1

1917, OJIN VILLAGE

"Miss Willow," the Pusan Ajimae said, "you'll be eighteen next year, won't you? What about going to Powa and getting married?"

At that, the eyes of Willow and her mother, Mrs. Yun, grew large. Although in fact she lived in Gupo, some miles away from Pusan, the "Pusan Ajimae" was a peddler who went about from village to village selling women's things like camellia oil, face powder, combs, mirrors, haberdashery, and matches, from a bundle she carried on her head. She had been visiting Mrs. Yun's family since she was a child. The Pusan Ajimae would visit Ojin Village once or twice a year, and always open her bundle, sell her wares, and stay overnight at Willow's house.

In the villages nestling in the valleys along the foot of Mae-bongsan Mountain, the sky was visible as if from the bottom of a well. Ojin, a small village of less than fifty households, was particularly remote. In order to reach the closest market, at Jucheon, it was necessary to cross the crests of three hills. Therefore, the village women waited impatiently for a visit from the Pusan Ajimae. Among the items in her bundle, they rarely bought anything but packets of needles or some matches, all the other things being too expensive for them, but still they were a feast for the eyes. And hearing news of the outside world from the

Pusan Ajimae, who journeyed all over the region, was a feast for the ears.

That evening, the women who had filled the room went back home, while Willow's younger brothers Gwangsik and Chunsik went across to their room to sleep. As she unfolded the bedding, Willow eyed her mother for some reaction to the unexpected talk of her marriage. She had never heard of a place called Powa. The same was true for Mrs. Yun, for whom the name was unfamiliar.

"Powa? Where's that?"

Her mother's expression was a combination of delight and anxiety. Willow knew the cause of her anxiety. No matter how good a marriage candidate the man might be, it was going to be difficult to find the money to prepare a new set of bedding to take as the bride's contribution.

Before she was born, her father, Schoolmaster Kang, had nourished the ambition of passing the state examination, restoring the fortunes of his impoverished family, and transforming the corrupt world. On passing the first part of the exam, he was entitled to be called Chosi Kang, but then the examination system was abolished. There could be no greater disaster for Chosi Kang, who had been doing nothing but preparing for the exam. Not only was the paltry financial aid he had been receiving from his family cut off, but his father-in-law also went bankrupt and could not help. A yangban without an official position and without money was like a tasty-looking, rotten apricot.

Chosi Kang set up a scrivener's office on the marketplace in order to earn a living, but they were so poor that Mrs. Yun was obliged to earn money with her needle. Then wealthy Mr. An invited Chosi Kang to become the schoolmaster in Ojin Village.

Eight years ago, when Willow's father passed away, a shadow

like that of a mountain fell over her family home, even on clear days, together with a heavy silence. When the eldest son died two years later, the shadow over the house settled on her mother's face.

"Well, it's a bit far off. Have you ever heard of America?"

"I've heard of it," Mrs. Yun replied. "The foreign pastor of Jucheon Church is an American. Is he from Powa?"

"Well, Powa is American land, but it seems it's an island that they call 'Hawai'i.' If you go there, they say you can sweep up money with a dustpan. I've been told that clothes and shoes grow on the trees, you only have to pick them and put them on. The weather is wonderful, too. Every season is late springtime, so you don't need winter clothes."

The Pusan Ajimae's face was looking more excited than when she was selling her merchandise.

"Outside of Paradise, can there be such a place?" Willow asked excitedly.

"Well, they say Hawai'i is a paradise. Once you go there, fortune will smile on you. If I were ten years younger, I might powder my face and get married myself."

At the wrinkled old Pusan Ajimae's words, Willow and her mother both laughed, and the atmosphere in the room, which had grown tense with talk of marriage, grew more relaxed.

"But are there men from Korea living there?" Mrs. Yun asked.

Willow was also curious.

"A decade or so ago, a large number of men from Korea went to work in Hawai'i. Now they've succeeded in life and want to find brides. One of my husband's relatives living in Pusan sent their daughter to be married in Hawai'i. When she went, she left in tears but after five years, she's helped them to buy land and build a house. And she felt it was too good to be enjoying life there alone, so she's sent her brother photos of would-be husbands, men wanting a bride from Korea. He's asked me to help find an especially good lady I know of. I even have a photo of the would-be bridegroom."

The Pusan Ajimae pulled a picture from her bundle and held it out. Willow was bashful about looking directly at it, as if she were facing a real man. Instead, Mrs. Yun took it and examined it closely. Willow scrutinized her mother's expression. She was curious to know what he looked like.

"Well, will he do as a son-in-law?" asked the Pusan Ajimae. "Does he look like a good man? He's not only a good person, he's a landowner who's farming on a really large scale."

On hearing that, the eyes of Mrs. Yun and Willow grew even larger.

"A landowner?" Mrs. Yun's voice grew louder. "In the United States? While the Japanese are taking people's land away from us, how could we become a landowner in a foreign country?"

It was the dream of everyone in Korea to farm their own land.

"That's right. If you're diligent, you can go to another country and purchase land. Why, you're holding a picture of a man who did this, aren't you? So, will you powder your face and set off?"

Mrs. Yun let the photo drop onto Willow's skirt.

Willow shyly picked it up; her eyes were already gazing at the man in a suit. He had dark eyebrows, big, bright eyes, a straight nose, and a tightly closed mouth and seemed to be staring at her. Her face turned red. Willow's heart began to race.

"On the back there's his name and age."

Willow flipped the photo over. On it was written in a neat hand, *So Taewan, 26 years old*. The name So Taewan was immediately imprinted on Willow's heart.

There was nobody else around, but the Pusan Ajimae lowered her voice. "If he's only twenty-six years old, that's young. It seems most of the men in Hawai'i looking for brides are older."

"If it's not a matter of a second marriage, what's a nine-year difference?" Mrs. Yun asked, indicating that she was half inclined to accept. "Where is his home and how large is his family?"

Willow's eyes were fixed on the picture. Even if she liked him, he was too far away. Even if he lived close by, it would be hard for her to visit her home more than once or twice a year, but if she went to Hawai'i, she might never see her family again. She didn't want to go that far, leaving her mother and younger brothers behind.

"His hometown is Yonggang in Pyongan-do, up in the north. His mother died a few years ago, his sisters are already married and living elsewhere in Korea. Father and son are the only remaining family. There will be no other family to care for. And just think, if you go there you'll be able to go to school."

Willow looked up. "Is . . . is that true?"

"Sure. The girl from our family was totally illiterate, but after arriving there she was able to study. Now she writes letters home, and she can speak English like an American."

Willow's heart pounded.

When a primary school was established in Jucheon, her father had sent her eldest brother to school. He reckoned that since the world was changing, his children should study the new subjects as they grew up. Two years later, he sent Willow, who had just turned eight. Hongju, her friend, pestered her own father, Mr. An, until she was able to enroll with Willow. Hongju's family had been commoners for generations, but Mr. An had earned enough money by buying and selling cattle and bought land in Ojin Village. He built a tiled house overlooking the fields and settled down, then bought a genealogy allowing him to be considered a yangban. The local people called him "Wealthy An" because they didn't think he merited any title.

Both girls were the only daughters in their families, the other daughters having died early. Willow was the second child among her brothers, and Hongju was the youngest, after her brothers.

It was much more fun for Willow to learn Hangul, Japanese, arithmetic, and gymnastics with friends at primary school than to study the *Thousand Character Classic* at her father's Confucian academy. Although she had to climb over three hills to reach the school, it didn't bother her. However, when her father passed away, her mother couldn't afford the monthly school fee for both children. If one of them had to quit, of course it would be the daughter.

Willow left school without completing her second year and helped with the housework, and taking care of her younger brothers. The following year, Mrs. Yun sent Willow's other younger brother Gyusik to school, but not Willow.

"What about me?" Willow argued and pleaded. "Send me back to school, too."

"It's enough if a girl can read and write her own name. What more do you need?"

At that, Willow threw a tantrum.

Mrs. Yun tore off her apron and stood up. "If you don't stop right now, I'm going up to throw myself over the waterfall in Maebongsan Mountain and die."

Frightened of being an orphan, Willow embraced her mother's legs as she prepared to leave the room and swore that she would never again talk about going back to school. After that, the only thing she could do was to comfort herself by writing on the ground with a poker so as not to forget the letters.

After graduating from the four-year primary school, Hongju had not gone on to the girls' upper school. She had no interest in studying, and her parents had no intention of sending their daughter to one of the new schools, the threshold of which none of their sons had ever crossed. After being in a place with a school and a market, Hongju returned to her mountain-valley home and felt bored, but Willow had been glad to have a friend nearby. While she was with Hongju, she could forget her situation, obliged as she was to help her mother earn a living. In the evenings, Hongju's house was the only place that Willow was allowed to visit. Taking her sewing with her, Willow would hurry to Hongju's place whenever she was free. Sewing was less boring when she was chattering with Hongju than when she stayed with her mother.

Hongju had a room all to herself opposite the main building. There, Willow had enjoyed snacks such as dried persimmons or cookies, and read novels that Hongju kept hidden in her clothes chest. After reading the books, they would talk nervously about free love, apply lipstick, and imitate the heroines.

The previous year, when Hongju had turned sixteen, her bridegroom had been chosen. He was from a prestigious yangban family in Masan. Her mother had taught her how to keep house lest her daughter be scolded once she was married. Most of all, Hongju had hated sitting quietly and sewing. Willow, who had acquired her mother's skill while helping with the needlework, spent the evenings embroidering the cushions and pillowcases that her friend would take to her new home.

When Hongju's mother left the room to tend to other chores, Hongju would lay aside her embroidery frame and chat away. While Hongju was thrilled to be leaving Ojin Village for busy Masan, Willow was already missing her friend. It would be different from when Hongju had been away at school. Then, there had been a time limit, she would come back after graduating, but getting married meant leaving forever.

When Hongju's wedding was celebrated in the yard of her home and she had left the village, Willow cried more bitterly than Hongju's mother. Now, there would be no one to open her heart to, no moments of respite with her friend. It seemed that Willow would never be able to cast off the shadow of her father's absence. However, two months after her marriage, Hongju became a widow. Rumors circulated that the groom's family had concealed the fact that he was sick, or that her father had been so eager to form an alliance with a yangban family that he had concealed the fact that a fortune-teller had said that their horoscopes showed that they were incompatible.

Tradition dictated that once a woman was married, she "buried her bones" in that house forever. When Willow thought of Hongju, she was reminded of an embroidery left bloodstained after her needle pricked her finger. No matter how well the embroidery was done, it was useless once it was stained. In a flash, through no fault of her own, Hongju's destiny had become that of a bloodstained embroidery.

Willow sometimes felt guilty wondering whether her friend's misfortune might have been caused by her own negative attitude, because she had disliked seeing her get married. "How will she spend her whole life in that household without a child?" Willow sighed as she sewed. Her mother had long been in the habit of saying that if it had not been for the children, she would have thrown herself over the Maebongsan Mountain waterfall long ago.

"Stop sighing," said Mrs. Yun as she cut a knotted thread. "That's just Hongju's destiny."

It turned out not to be the case. Hongju returned to her parents' house shortly after her husband died, thanks to a divination by the Surijae shaman, who declared that if a young widow remained in the house, a yet greater disaster might befall them. Not only Hongju's in-laws, but even her own family reckoned that her husband had died because of her. There was also a rumor in the village that Wealthy An had offered his in-laws a large sum, enough for them to live on, in return for bringing Hongju home.

On the evening she went to see Hongju for the first time after her return, Willow's heart and steps were heavy. Willow had grown up seeing her widowed mother. More tenacious than the suffering of the one who had lost her husband was the widespread gossip about the woman who had devoured his vitality. The title of "widow" that she would have to bear like a yoke all her life was like the name of a great crime.

As Willow made her way to Hongju's house, combining her own sorrow with Hongju's misfortune, she imagined all kinds of sad things. She prepared to hug her friend and cry. As she entered the gate, she could not help being struck by the sight of Hongju's mother's grief-stricken face. She seemed to lack the energy to say anything, merely greeting her with a look and nodding in the direction of Hongju's room. When she saw Hongju's elegant leather shoes lying on the stone step in front of the room, she felt tears rising. Willow left her straw sandals beside them and entered the room.

Hongju, wearing mourning dress and with her hair in a bun, sat in the darkened room with one knee raised. She didn't look around even though she knew that Willow was there. Her husband had died two months after the marriage. It was as though her whole world had collapsed. Willow, sympathizing with her friend's unfortunate situation, scarcely daring to breathe, sat down next to her. A housemaid, coming in behind her, put down a plate of dried persimmons and looked briefly at Hongju. Once she had left the room, Willow prepared to speak.

Just then, Hongju shook out her skirts and relaxed her formal posture, lowering her knee. With both fists resting on her crossed legs, she gave vent to her fury. "That guy had always been sick. I didn't kill him, so I don't see why I should stay locked in here like a criminal. If his family had not turned me out, what would have become of me? If I had to spend my whole life in that house, I would have suffocated to death."

Hongju was unlike any widow that Willow had ever seen. As Hongju spat out without hesitation ideas that she had barely dared formulate, Willow felt relieved. She was right. Even if someone became a widow, even if the children were left father-less, it was not their fault.

"That's what I think, too. They did well to turn you out."

Willow and Hongju hugged and laughed, instead of crying.

Without knowing that, Hongju's mother, fearing that her daughter might reach some bad decision on account of her changed situation, asked Mrs. Yun to let Willow visit her every day.

Once again, as before, Willow and Hongju sat embroidering or chatting together or reading novels. The only thing that had changed was that Hongju now had experience of a man, so her words were more forthright.

"I got through the first night as best I could because it was my first time. Having read love stories, I was better prepared than that sickly bridegroom smelling of milk. He was shaking so much he couldn't even undo my dress. . . . Really, it was so frustrating."

Willow listened with red cheeks and sparkling eyes.

The first rooster crowed. The rooster belonged to Jangsu, the most hardworking fellow in Ojin Village. Willow had not slept a wink, and not just because of the Pusan Ajimae's snoring. She felt that her beating heart was even louder.

Mrs. Yun had postponed giving an answer the previous evening, saying that she would think about it, but Willow inclined more and more toward marriage as time passed. "If you agree, the groom's family will send you all the wedding expenses, so you don't have to worry about money." She wanted to go to Hawai'i. She wanted to study. In the future, she didn't want to live like her mother, she didn't want to earn a living as a widow's child by sewing, then get married to a man in a similar situation. There was no time for herself in her mother's life. It was a world where it was natural for daughters to sacrifice themselves for their parents and brothers until finally they got married. But in Hawai'i, married women could also study. That alone made Hawai'i a paradise. Although it was a once-in-a-lifetime chance, she also knew she wanted to leave her family for the sake of her desires, and she felt ashamed.

If only Omma would send me to school, I wouldn't feel like this.

Willow braced her weakening heart and reminded herself that by getting married she would be helping the rest of her family. When she got married, that would mean not only a helping hand less but also one mouth less to feed. Then her mother would have fewer difficulties. Gyusik, who was working in a bicycle shop in Kimhae, was earning his own living, while Gwangsik and Chunsik were already fully grown. Rather than staying at home doing the cooking, it would be much better for her to get married and help her family live better, like the Pusan Ajimae's niece. The more she thought, the more she felt that there could be no better groom for someone in her situation, and felt impatient at the thought that they might miss the opportunity by putting off answering.

As usual, her mother rose before dawn, combed her hair and pinned up her bun before she went out to the privy. Willow, who had not slept a wink all night long, shook the Pusan Ajimae as soon as her mother went outside.

"Ajimae, Ajimae."

"What's the matter?" The Ajimae mumbled a reply, still half asleep, and turned toward Willow. Fearing that her mother would soon return, Willow spoke in an urgent voice.

"Is it true that I can study if I go to Hawai'i to get married?"

So long as she could study, it didn't matter if she didn't live in luxury. Even if she had a hard time, she wanted to do something for herself just once. As the Ajimae sat up straight, Willow did likewise.

"It's true. I told you, didn't I? My niece, who was completely uneducated, went and now she writes letters home and speaks American like a native."

"Ajimae, I want to go to Hawai'i and get married. Please, convince my omma." She seized the woman's hand and pleaded.

"You've made the right decision. Don't worry." The Ajimae rubbed the backs of Willow's hands.

Once Willow's decision was made, her mother agreed. But the marriage was not accomplished just because Willow had made up her mind. Willow also had to send a picture and receive the bridegroom's agreement.

"Don't worry," said the Pusan Ajimae. "There's no better bride to be found anywhere, I'll put in a good word for you. As soon as day dawns, let's go to the photo studio and take a picture."

"That's what you think," Mrs. Yun sighed, "but she has no aboji, we're hard up, nothing special . . . and she has nothing decent-looking to wear for the photograph."

Once she had decided to marry off her daughter, So Taewan became a son-in-law too good to lose. But her mother was right.

Willow spoke impatiently. "Omma, shall I ask Hongju to lend me some clothes?"

Mrs. Yun startled. "Are you asking for bad luck? How could

you even think of taking a wedding photo wearing a young widow's clothes? Do you want to ruin things from the start?"

As far as Willow could see, apart from not being able to leave the house, Hongju was better off than she was, being able to speak freely, eat freely, with no problems. At present she was worse off than a widow, but things would change once she got married in Hawai'i. Willow imagined herself as a new woman who had studied, beautifully dressed, coming home with husband and children. That was something that could never happen to Hongju.

"You're right, those clothes won't do," the Pusan Ajimae agreed.

After thinking for a moment, Mrs. Yun seemed to have come to a major decision. "We'll use a little trick. Willow, wear those clothes and have the photo taken."

The clothes she indicated were a set she was making for someone who was soon to be married, and all that remained to be done was to stitch on the lining of the collars.

"Oh, how could you propose such a thing?" said Willow, startled.

Her mother had never coveted so much as a grain of other people's barley, even if she was dying of starvation, and had taught her children to be the same.

Mrs. Yun spoke resolutely with a flushed face. "Do it. If we send a picture of you wearing a nice dress, the marriage will surely succeed. If you wrap it up well and wear it only when you take the photo, it won't show any sign of having been worn."

"That's right," the Pusan Ajimae agreed. "And since it's for a good cause it will be okay."

Mrs. Yun applied camellia oil to Willow's freshly braided hair. The Ajimae said she would go with her to the photo studio and apply powder and rouge.

Willow left the house with the Pusan Ajimae, carrying that other person's clothes in her arms. She felt a little awkward about deceiving the man she was to marry from the beginning, but even Willow was reluctant to send him a picture of her dressed in patched clothes. Willow wanted to please Taewan and go to Hawai'i.

The question of the clothes was solved, but there was another problem. It was the fact that Hongju knew nothing of this great event. Her mother had begged her to keep it secret from Hongju until the marriage was settled. If the word "marriage" started to circulate and then things went wrong, that too was always considered the woman's fault. Hongju had spoken to Willow frankly about everything in the meantime. She had not hidden the fact that her first love had been Willow's dead brother, or what happened on the first night of her marriage.

On the evening of the day when the picture was taken, Willow went to Hongju and told her the truth. No matter how hard her mother begged, she didn't want to have any secrets from Hongju, and the news was too daunting for her to keep it hidden in her heart. Hongju already knew about marriages between men living in Hawai'i and girls from Korea.

"I heard talk about it from my in-law in Masan and her neighbors. One neighbor's eldest daughter got married by a picture marriage then arranged for her younger sister to go too. At that time, I couldn't imagine going so far to get married, but now it looks a hundred times better than being a widow."

As soon as she heard what Hongju said, the anxiety that was lodged in one corner of Willow's heart vanished. The Pusan Ajimae was not the kind of person to lie, but there was the vague fear of an unknown place. But Hongju's neighbor's daughter wouldn't have called her sister to join her if Hawai'i wasn't a good place.

Willow even went so far as to tell her that the groom was a landowner, and that in the photo he looked manly. She couldn't bring the picture because she was not following her mother's request for secrecy. Willow was really worried. "What will I do if he says he doesn't like the look of me?"

"Then ask for another bridegroom. He's not the only one, is he? You have to be happy. I want to go to Hawai'i too. It's so boring, I can't endure staying cooped up at home any longer."

It was the first time Hongju had ever envied Willow.

But the next evening, Hongju's mother visited Willow's home.

"Go and fetch a bowl of water," said Mrs. Yun to Willow.

As she left the room, Willow felt sudden anxiety tugging at the back of her head. What was going on in the middle of the night? Had something happened to Hongju? Had she heard of the picture marriage? Had she come to complain that she had given Hongju false ideas? *Mother will scold me severely because I didn't keep the secret from Hongju.* Willow's hands trembled as she shut the door behind her. Just then, she heard Hongju's mother speaking.

Willow stopped and listened hard.

"I've heard about picture marriages. We'll send Hongju too. Her husband died before he could inscribe her name in his family register, so she's free, but there's no thought of deception in any case. There must be a widower like Hongju. Tell me where the Pusan Ajimae lives." Her voice was also trembling.

Willow went to the kitchen and drew a scoopful of water from the jar. Her hands were shaking and the precious water spilled. More overflowed when she poured it into the bowl. Willow sat down for a while on the stove to calm herself.

When she had thought that Hongju couldn't go, she had wanted to brag about her great good luck, but hearing she could go too, there was nothing better than that. If her friend was

there too she wouldn't feel lonely and would be much more as-
sured. Since it was a paradise, there would be no difficulties, but
it would be much more fun being happy together. Just as Willow went back into the room, Wealthy An's wife was suddenly
startled.

"Oh dear. We're acting behind my husband's back."

Willow set the bowl of water in front of her.

"How are you going to win him over?" Mrs. Yun asked with
a worried look.

Hongju's mother gulped down the water, then put the bowl
down with a bang, and spoke determinedly. "He can only kill
me, can't he? If Hongju stays here, it's a living death for her.
Even if I die, I've had my life. It's better I should die than have
a young child fading away, trapped in her room."

"You're right. It'll be far better than staying here. That's
why I'm sending our Willow. I was worried about sending our
grown-up daughter all alone on a long journey, but if Hongju
goes with her, that's wonderful. You've thought of Hongju's future and made a difficult decision."

Mrs. Yun seized Hongju's mother's hand and the two shed
tears together. Willow too had a runny nose.

2

THE WOMAN IN
THE MIRROR, THE MAN
IN THE PHOTO

Hongju insisted on choosing her bridegroom for herself. Her mother told her husband she was going to their son's house and set off with Hongju to visit the Pusan Ajimae.

Willow felt jealous of Hongju. Taewan wasn't too bad, but she was not sure how she would feel if Hongju picked a better partner. "If I had known this was going to happen, I would have gone with Hongju to find out more," said Willow, her sewing needles still in her hands.

"Stop that. Why trust a picture? The Pusan Ajimae is a much more reliable guarantee than any picture." Her mother's words silenced Willow.

Two days later, after her younger brother said he had seen Hongju returning over the hill, Willow went running over without even drying her hands after doing the evening dish-washing. Hongju explained breathlessly how she had met the Pusan Ajimae, gone over to the matchmaker's house and picked a bridegroom. On her way back, she had visited the photographer in Jucheon market to have a photo taken to send to the bridegroom. Wondering what kind of man Hongju's bridegroom was, Willow impatiently snatched at the picture Hongju held out.

Unlike the photo of Taewan, which only showed his face, it showed a man wearing a suit standing with one foot resting on the running board of a car against a background of a house and trees such as she had never seen before. Willow focused on the trees rather than the person, the house, or the car. The Pusan Ajimae had said that clothes and shoes grew on the tree. She looked carefully at the tree in the photo, but all she could see was some kind of round fruitlike gourds hanging at the top. She wasn't sure if it was because the photo was too small for them to be seen properly, or if the clothes and shoes were inside the round fruit.

"What do you think?" Hongju spoke excitedly. "He looks manly and reliable, doesn't he? He owns a car, too."

Only then did Willow take note of Hongju's potential bridegroom, the owner of a car that she thought only kings and high officials could ride in. His face was too small to see properly, but the way he stood with his chin on his hand while his elbow was supported by the leg resting on the car looked very elegant. Willow returned the photo to Hongju and asked, "How old?"

"Thirty-eight years old. He lost his wife early on and has no children."

When she heard that he was Hongju's father's age, Willow's eyes grew wide. That made him twenty-one years older than herself.

"Isn't that too old?"

"I've seen what a young bridegroom is like. I don't want to have a young husband. Older men are the most reliable."

Hongju was ignoring completely the problems arising from his age.

"I'm sorry, but he's not even like an older brother, he's like your aboji."

Willow recalled the village men of that age. They were so

old, and it was creepy just to imagine being under the same blanket as someone like that. Willow grew even fonder of Tae-wan, with his twenty-six years.

Hongju, who had met the Pusan matchmaker in person, had learned a lot about Hawai'i. Hongju asked her, "Have you ever heard of sugarcane?"

Willow knew about sugar candy, which she had tasted once, and she knew the sorghum growing along the edges of kitchen gardens, but she'd never heard of sugarcane.

"It seems that powdered sugar comes from sugarcane. When men from Korea went to Hawai'i, it was to work in sugarcane fields, several thousands of them."

"Are there so many sugarcane fields in Hawai'i?" Willow's eyes widened. When they were younger, Hongju had once been given some Japanese sugar candy that her older brother bought in Pusan. Hongju said it was incredibly expensive and precious, as she broke a piece of candy with her teeth and gave one half to Willow. Whenever Willow ate anything outside her home, she would usually think guiltily of her mother and younger brothers, but it was such a shame that the candy melted away in her mouth and disappeared so quickly, and her only thought was that she wanted to eat more. How expensive a field that made such precious candies must be. If Taewan was a landowning farmer, she could easily believe that he could "sweep up money with a dustpan."

Once the photos taken at the studio arrived, Willow and Hongju wrote letters to send with the photos, as the match-maker had instructed. When it came to writing skills, Hongju, who had graduated from primary school, and Willow, who had only attended school briefly, were pretty much equal. Willow sometimes wrote letters to Gyusik or her mother's parents. Willow and Hongju wrote painstakingly, line by line, all the time consulting one another. It was only a brief self-introduction, but they were as excited as if they were writing love letters.

Although Willow and Hongju had not yet received replies from the men, they still imagined life there as if they were already married. There was no comparison with the marriage of their parents or the people around them, or the marriage that Hongju had experienced so briefly. In Hawai'i, where food and clothing hung from trees, and women studied to their heart's content, marriage too would surely be very different from in Korea. Hongju, who had previously married a man her parents had chosen without her ever seeing his face, was excited about Jo Doksam, as if he was her first boyfriend. She said choosing each other and exchanging letters was as good as getting married by free love. When Willow said she would study when she arrived in Hawai'i, Hongju looked dumbfounded.

"What? Why study?" Hongju dreamily held the picture of Doksam to her breast. "You're really weird, but okay, go ahead and study. I'll wear pretty clothes, and drive about in my husband's car and enjoy sightseeing."

Willow didn't mean that she would do nothing but study. She wanted to study while living happily with Taewan. They would not be like the couples in Ojin Village, indifferent to each other as if they were cows or chickens, they would also love and cherish each other like lovers in a novel.

Letters between Korea and Hawai'i took over a month. A reply reached Hongju first. The letter said he was glad to have found a pretty bride with neat handwriting, and he would be waiting for the day when they could meet, with every day feeling like three years as he craned his neck and gazed across the white surf toward Korea. With the letter came a hundred dollars in American currency to cover expenses. He said the boat fare from Japan to Hawai'i would cost fifty dollars. Money would also be required to prepare documents and to travel to Japan. Hongju was delighted with the letter, more than the money.

Hongju smiled broadly as she showed Willow. "Why, I'm so embarrassed."

Willow hoped that the letter from Taewan would be sweeter than that from Doksam, for whom this was the second marriage. However, Taewan merely sent one hundred and fifty dollars through the matchmaker with a formal notification that he would marry her. Willow was disappointed, but comforted by the extra fifty dollars, which she gave to her mother.

"He must be shy," Hongju said, comforting her. "He's a bachelor, after all, so wait. It'll be different when you meet."

Hongju wrote back to her bridegroom saying that she dreamed of him every night. Willow envied Hongju, who impatiently awaited a reply starting from the very next day. Willow regarded Taewan as someone serious and deep-hearted and comforted herself with that.

There was a lot to prepare before they set off for Hawai'i. Since picture bride marriage was a legal formality by which a husband invited his homeland bride to join him in Hawai'i, the marriage had to first be officially registered in Korea. As soon as the marriage registration was finished, Willow considered Taewan her true husband. Once he sent the passport he obtained from the Japanese consulate in Hawai'i, she would have to obtain a travel permit, and even if she had all the documents, she would not be able to board a ship to the United States unless she passed a medical examination in Japan.

Willow secretly looked at Taewan's picture every evening. More often still, she looked at herself in a hand mirror. She had been given the mirror, and her mother camellia oil, as gifts by the Pusan Ajimae. Among all the desirable things in the Ajimae's bundle, the hand mirror had been the thing she had desired most of all.

"This is my last present. I'm going to stop this business. I'm aching all over from a life spent walking about carrying a heavy bundle on my head. My son is pestering me to stay home and look after my grandchild."

"It looks as though his brewery is doing well enough," Mrs. Yun said, looking lonely. "You'll have to do as your son says. But I'll be sad not to see you anymore."

Willow looked at herself in the mirror several times a day without her mother's knowledge. She hoped that the face in the mirror was pretty enough to be loved by a man. As the days went by, Willow was often embarrassed on waking from a dream in which she had become a lover in one of Hongju's novels. The main characters in the dream were the man in the photo and the woman in the mirror.

It was at dawn, on the seventeenth day of the first month of the year known as Muo (1918), the year in which they turned eighteen, that Willow and Hongju left Ojin Village. The date had been fixed so that they could celebrate the lunar New Year and the first full moon at home. After the departure date had been decided, Willow had set about mending her family's clothes and threadbare boson socks. On New Year's Day, she went to pay her respects at her father's grave, and on the day before she left, she went to the well several times and filled all the jars with water.

"You'll be leaving soon?" a neighbor asked when she met her at the well.

"Yes, I'm leaving tomorrow."

Since there are no secrets, the news that Willow and Hongju were going to Hawaiʻi for picture marriages spread widely across the neighborhood. Some people who also wanted to send their daughters secretly visited their home. On the one hand, there were those who criticized Wealthy An's wife for allowing her daughter to remarry less than three years after she was widowed, while others whispered that Mrs. Yun, who pretended to be a yangban, had sold her daughter for money.

"How will your omoni live after sending you so far away?" The woman clacked her tongue.

Now that it was time for her to leave, Willow's heart was heavy. Who would sit sewing with her mother, and who would take care of her younger brothers Gwangsik and Chunsik? Thinking of those she was leaving behind, Willow felt guilty for having been so excited about getting married.

On the last evening, Willow took a bath in the kitchen, then went to lie down as usual beside her mother. Normally, Mrs. Yun snored loudly as soon as her head touched the pillow. However, that night she seemed unable to get to sleep. Willow sensed that her mother was sobbing in the dark. Feeling a lump in her own throat, she took her mother's hand. The hand, chapped by cold winds and callused from sewing, felt like a tree stump.

"Omma, just hold on a bit longer. Then I'll make sure you're comfortable."

"Willow, I hope you realize I'm doing you a favor, sending you far away like this. I don't want you to spend your whole life here and grow old as a maiden ghost."

"Why should I grow old as a maiden ghost?" Willow asked, thinking it a joke, but Mrs. Yun sighed heavily.

"You don't know what I'm talking about. With the Japanese in control, who would ever marry the daughter of a righteous army member? You've had it hard thus far thanks to your unfortunate parents, so things will be better with that man in Hawai'i."

It was the first time that Mrs. Yun had ever used the term "righteous army." Willow had never heard from her mother exactly how her father died. When Japan was about to swallow up Korea, her father, who had sometimes gone away for a time, disappeared for good. Willow remembered when her mother had been taken off to the police station. She had lain ill for a few days after returning and had said nothing about the reason. Soon after, her father came back as a corpse.

Willow had heard from others that her father had been in an anti-Japanese righteous army. After the visit by Japanese police, for a while nobody came to visit them, as if they had the plague. If wealthy Mr. An had told them to get out of his house, they would have been on the street. Instead he allowed them to go on living there and secretly provided food.

Willow's brother, three years older than herself, was attending school in Kimhae at the time. Full of resentment, he had died standing up to a Japanese policeman, harassing people on the street, kicked in the head by the policeman's horse. Willow recalled what her mother had told Hongju's mother, wailing, the night she came back from the funeral.

"How can they talk of vanquishing the Japanese when even our king couldn't do it? That's how their aboji died, and now they've killed my son, but I won't hate them or blame them. And I'm not going to tell my remaining sons to take revenge on the enemy."

Her goal was to ensure that the children did not hold resentment against the invincible opponents. Subsequently, Mrs. Yun never mentioned the death of her husband or her son. Yet now she had spoken the name of the righteous army.

"For me, Korea is the enemy. Because our land is powerless, I lost my husband and my child. But Hawai'i is not Korea, there you'll have no country to protect. Once you're there, just forget us here, be happy with your husband and children, and enjoy life. That's my only wish."

Her mother's bitter voice was engraved on Willow's heart as she fell asleep.

At last she was in Hawai'i. The trees and buildings that she saw for the first time in her life were dazzlingly bright, like a paradise. As the Ajimae had said, food and clothes were hanging in clusters from the tree. Jo Doksam came to meet Hongju, driving his car. However, there was no sign of Taewan. Instead, a message came that he had canceled the marriage. Willow could not get off the boat, she would have to go back home. On the boat, as it sailed away from Hawai'i, she cried and shouted, stamping her feet, at which she woke up, relieved to find that it was a dream. On the one hand, she felt anxious that the dream might come true, but also hopeful since dreams often foretold the opposite of what happens.

Hearing rattling noises in the kitchen, Willow got up and opened the door leading to the kitchen, where Mrs. Yun was making rice balls. Willow rushed into the kitchen. She had vowed to prepare a meal for her mother before she left, but she had overslept.

"Omma, let me do it."

"Never mind, dear. Wash your face and get ready. I've put water on the fire to heat."

Before the meal, Mrs. Yun undid Willow's braided hair and tied it in the bun of a married woman. It would be safer to undertake her long journey as a married woman rather than an unmarried girl. Besides, the documents showed that she was leaving as the spouse of Taewan. Willow looked at her new hairstyle in her hand mirror. The front was not much different from when her hair was braided, but now there were no curls hanging down at the back, so it looked light and empty. Willow wore a cotton skirt and blouse made by her mother, the first new clothes she had had since her father died.

Mrs. Yun had used the money Willow gave her to make the new clothes. A skirt and jacket made of crimson silk for the wedding ceremony, a set made of cotton for everyday wear, two light summer jackets since it seemed the climate was hot, two slips and two loose drawers, and three pairs of boson socks. In addition, she made a pillowcase for the father-in-law, a pair of pillowcases embroidered with lovebirds for the newlyweds, and even a jacket for a not yet born grandchild.

There was only one spoon on the table where there was a dish of steamed eggs and roasted seaweed, in addition to the usual rice mixed with millet, bean paste soup and salted radish. Willow looked at the table, then at her mother. "Am I to eat alone?"

"I'll eat with the boys later," Mrs. Yun replied. "They said goodbye yesterday evening, don't wake them up."

Willow understood why her mother said that. If her brothers were watching, Willow would not be able to eat as much as she wanted. For the first time since she was born, she ate alone. Willow's throat tightened as she held back tears. Soon, she would be in Hawai'i and eat delicious food, while her family would not be able to eat their fill even of the millet-rice, hard as grains of sand. Despite her mother's urgings to eat everything, Willow left half the food uneaten.

After the table had been cleared away, Willow curtsied deeply before her mother. Mrs. Yun sat turned to one side, tight-lipped, saying nothing.

"Don't worry, Omma. I'll write as soon as I arrive. Just stay healthy until I can provide you with more comfort. My brothers, too."

Swallowing her tears as she took her leave, Willow leaned on the door for a while. The smell of the sesame oil mixed in with the rice balls emerged from the bundle she was clutching. Inside, there were the clothes her mother had packed, a menstruation cloth, and a pair of decorated shoes. Willow had put the hand mirror in her mother's sewing box. She longed to take it, but more than that she wanted her mother to look at the pretty mirror and remember her daughter.

Willow hugged tightly the bundle full of her mother's love. Willow stepped onto the creaking wooden floor and went to open the door of the room where Gwangsik and Chunsik were sleeping. A sound of snoring emerged. She resisted the impulse to caress the face of at least her youngest brother. Closing the door again, she vowed to give her two brothers a chance to study in high school. She would also enable Gyusik, who was working at the Kimhae bicycle store, to set up his own shop.

Putting on her straw sandals, Willow went outside. The flower buds on the plum tree planted by her father next to the privy were red and swollen. It was a pity she had to leave without seeing the plum blossom. Standing in front of the brushwood gate, she looked back at the house once more before departing.

Willow met Hongju at the entrance to the village. They had agreed in advance that they would say goodbye to their families at home. Instead of straw sandals, Hongju wore leather shoes, but she was dressed simply, although the bundle she was holding was larger than Willow's. When Willow saw her friend's swollen eyes, the tears she had been holding back burst free.

"Don't cry. It's a long way, it'll make you tired." Hongju took hold of Willow's hand. Whirlwinds of emotion passed from one to the other. Together, they took their first steps toward a new world.

After walking all day without rest, Willow and Hongju reached the Pusan Ajimae's house at nightfall. It was a thatched house behind the market. Apart from being located in a busy area, it was just as shabby as Willow's family home. The Ajimae came out barefoot to welcome them.

"Why, young ladies, come on in. You must be tired. Aren't you hungry? Songhwa, bring some food!" The Ajimae shouted toward the kitchen as she ushered Willow and Hongju into the room like a mother hen driving her chicks. The moment they entered the room, Willow and Hongju collapsed onto the floor like ripe persimmons. They no longer had the strength to bend a single finger, let alone a leg. It was amazing that they had been able to walk such a long way. A girl briefly put her head out of the kitchen, but Willow didn't get a good look.

Expressing pity for Willow and Hongju, the Ajimae brought out pillows. Willow's weary body lay flat on the floor, until it could fall no further.

"Ajimae, that girl in the kitchen, isn't she the granddaughter of Kumhwa in Surijae?" Hongju asked, as she lay on her back with arms spread wide, struck by a sudden thought.

"Do you know Songhwa?" Willow and the Ajimae asked at the same time. There was a shaman's house on Surijae, one of the ridges going from Ojin to Jinyong. People in the neighborhood went to Kumhwa to have their New Year's fortune told, for charms and talismans, and for shamanistic kut ceremonies. Kumhwa had a daughter named Okhwa, who had given birth to a daughter whose father was unknown. She was named Songhwa. There was no knowing if the madness came first, or the birth of the child, but Okhwa always carried Songhwa about with her. Every one of the children in Ojin had joined in throwing stones at Okhwa and her daughter.

Willow remembered Okhwa, who used to laugh lightly with a frightened face, more clearly than Songhwa, who would follow behind her mother looking terrified. Although Okhwa was crazy, she was the prettiest woman Willow had ever seen. After rumors circulated that Okhwa had fallen into a pond and died, there was no sign of Songhwa. People said that the elderly Kumhwa was having a hard time caring for her granddaughter.

"I saw her when I went with Omma for a ceremony not long ago." After Hongju decided to marry Doksam, her mother went to Kumhwa and had her perform a ceremony to appease the spirit of Hongju's first husband.

"Has she come to live here? To work in your house?" Willow asked.

"No. She's going to Hawai'i to get married, too."

Willow and Hongju abruptly sat up.

"What? Is there a man who would marry that girl?" Willow asked, looking incredulous. At some point, the boundary between yangban and commoner had begun to collapse, but it wasn't the same for a shaman or a butcher. Dongbuk the butcher, who lived in an isolated house, was obliged to bow low even before the young children of the village, despite being a white-haired old man. The same was true for the shaman Kumhwa, who had passed sixty, then seventy, long ago.

"Indeed, there is," the Pusan Ajimae said with a smile. "She's a good-looking girl. It's just been settled."

"It's unheard of. She's not even that pretty." Hongju pouted.

"But how did that girl hear about Hawai'i?" Willow asked, unable to hide her dismay.

"Old woman Kumhwa heard about it from Hongju's mother

so she brought her to me. She asked me to help Songhwa leave
Korea and live in a world different from that of her kin."

"The shaman kept asking questions at the ceremony, she
must have been planning this even then," said Hongju.

"The situation of Songhwa is very like your own. Who would
ever marry the granddaughter of a shaman without even a
known father? Either she would have to become a shaman like
her grandmother, or be sold off to become a gisaeng, an entertainer." The Ajimae sighed.

Willow could not agree that her situation was similar to that
of Songhwa, even if Hongju had already been married once.

The Ajimae went on, as if she could read Willow's mind.
"I've been roaming the world with a bundle on my head since
before you two were born, there's nowhere I've not been. I've
seen people living in every kind of house. And do you know
what I've concluded from that? It's that people are all the same,
everywhere. Yangban, commoner, rich man, beggar, they're all
the same. The yangban does not feel more pain, nor the butcher
less. When it comes to their children, every parent's heart is
the same. Kumhwa's concern for her granddaughter is just the
same as your omoni's concern for you. If you could live better
lives here, why would you go far away from your parents and
siblings? Aren't you setting off for a new world because you
can't live decent lives at home? Feel sympathy for Songhwa, and
accept her as your companion from here to Hawai'i."

Although the Ajimae spoke with intense sincerity, Willow could not help feeling uneasy at the thought of eating and
sleeping together with Songhwa over the entire journey.

Hongju, who had been silent, asked, "Did the man in Hawai'i
really think that girl was pretty?"

Just then, the door opened and Songhwa came in carrying
a tray table. They looked up at her as she entered. Compared

to her grim childhood, she looked very different, but her face, with eyes round as the snails in paddy fields, projecting nose, and pointed chin, could certainly not be called pretty. Perhaps intimidated by their piercing gaze, Songhwa placed the table with chipped corners before Willow and Hongju and went to sit down in a corner. She looked frightened, but didn't seem slow as the rumor said.

The moment the tray table was set down, Willow's interest shifted from Songhwa to the food. On the table was rice mixed with millet, radish-top bean-paste soup, shrimp sauce and marinated dried radish.

"Eat up, you must be hungry. Hongju, you must have eaten well at home, I don't know if this will suit you."

"I'm so famished I'd eat anything, even horse droppings," said Hongju as she turned to the table. For a while the only sound in the room was that of people eating. As soon as they finished, Songhwa left the room and brought in bowls of scorched rice soaked in water, just like Willow would do at home.

Willow turned her attention back to the Ajimae. "Are you living alone? Doesn't your son live with you?" Willow remembered how, whenever the Ajimae came to her home, she would talk about her son and grandchildren.

The Ajimae's face was clouded with sorrow. "They left for Manchuria just after New Year's Day. They urged me to go with them, but if I went I'd only be a burden and it would soon have been the death of me." The Ajimae smiled sadly as if she was forcing herself to be cheerful.

"Why did they go? Didn't you say that the brewery was doing well?" Willow recalled the people she had seen on the road. They were on their way to the train station, carrying not just bedding, but even cooking pots. They were all looking very shabby.

"The Japanese brutes demanded huge taxes, so he closed it down. They had an ax to grind about selling their own liquor. Unable to get back a penny of the money that went into it, he ended up ruined, with nothing but debts. He left because he couldn't stand the constant harassment. In Manchuria there's plenty of open land. He left saying that if he only cleared some stony ground, they could survive. When I think of what a hard time they'll have so far from home, my heart aches." The Ajimae used her skirts to wipe away tears and blow her nose. "Whereas, once you've suffered a bit, you'll prosper in later years. You'll be able to live comfortably watching your grand-children's cute tricks."

Everyone slept in the main room, where the fire was lit. The Ajimae took the bedding and spread it on the floor. "Tomorrow you leave for Pusan right after breakfast, so we'd better sleep early." With their feet on the warmest part they lay down in order: the Ajimae, Songhwa, Willow, and Hongju. One quilt covered the Ajimae and Songhwa, the other covered Willow and Hongju.

When the lamp was extinguished, the room became dark. The Ajimae fell asleep as soon as she lay down. Willow had been awake since dawn and had walked a long way, but she was still wide awake. As her eyes adjusted to the darkness, she could see the shapes of the clothes hanging on the wall. It seemed like several years had passed since the early morning.

Hongju prodded Willow. "Are you asleep?"

"I can't sleep. I'm used to sleeping alone."

"Not me. It reminds me of a school trip to Pusan when all the children slept together in one inn room. The first one to fall asleep got charcoal smeared on her face."

Willow remembered hearing about it from Hongju. Nothing made her heart ache like the story of the school trip she had missed. But now that was all past. Once she got to Hawai'i, she'd be able to do whatever she wanted.

"Songhwa, when did you come here?" Hongju asked, speaking to Songhwa for the first time.

The room filled with a silence denser than the darkness.

"She's asleep," Willow said, although she knew that Songhwa was not asleep. She no longer had a problem with going to Hawai'i with Songhwa, but she never wanted her to become a close friend.

"Are you really sleeping?" Hongju asked again.

"Just after the winter solstice." In the dark, her slightly hoarse voice echoed. It was similar to the voice of Kumhwa when she was telling New Year's fortunes for the neighborhood women.

"You mean you've been here ever since?" Willow asked. That was more than two months.

Songhwa sighed. "Grandma told me not to come home again . . ." Songhwa's pain was plain even in the dark. They could understand without her needing to say anything more.

"What have you been doing for two months?" asked Hongju.

". . . Just . . ."

Hongju gave up waiting for her to answer and instead asked, "What kind of person is your husband? Do you have a picture? Let us see it."

Willow was also wondering who might have chosen Songhwa.

After a moment's hesitation, Songhwa stood up with barely a sound and lit the lamp. Willow and Hongju, who were by now sitting, screened the light with their hands as the Ajimae murmured something. Once the Ajimae turned over and resumed snoring, Willow and Hongju giggled in relief. Seeing that, Songhwa also smiled, and carefully opened the overhead cupboard to retrieve a picture from her bundle.

Hongju, who had been watching her slow movements, snatched the picture and held it up to the light of the lamp. Willow pushed her head closer to get a good look. The man, who was also wearing a suit, did not look much different from Taewan or Doksam. On the back, the photo said *Park Sokbo, 36 years old*, three years younger than Doksam.

"Did you get a letter?" asked Hongju.

Songhwa shook her head.

"Can you write?" Willow asked. Songhwa shook her head again. It wasn't a big deal, because there were fewer people who could write than couldn't, but Willow felt sorry for this Park Sokbo, who would find himself with a bride who was not only the granddaughter of a shaman but uneducated to boot.

3

ALOHA, HAWAI'I

Willow, Hongju, and Songhwa arrived in Shimonoseki the morning after next from Pusan by night boat, where they took the train straight to Kobe, Japan. From there they would take a boat to Hawai'i.

Hongju, who knew Japanese, both spoken and written, reasonably well, took the lead. Willow was vague even about hiragana and katakana, though she was able to read Chinese characters thanks to the *Thousand Character Classic*, which she learned from her father. Previously, she thought that she sewed better than Hongju, did housekeeping better, and was more mature, but now she saw that she was only good at splashing about in a narrow, shallow pool. Songhwa, who was totally illiterate, never let go of Willow's or Hongju's skirts, like a child afraid of losing her mother.

"Come on, don't keep staring about like country bumpkins, just follow me."

Willow felt bad when Hongju treated her and Songhwa condescendingly, as if they were on the same level. When she was living in Ojin Village, it was enough that she could read and write. It was only now that she realized how good a decision it was to marry Taewan, in order to go back to school and master the power of words and writing.

Willow found comfort by imagining herself as she would be when she became proficient in English. In the meantime, the biggest change to these three was the relationship with Songhwa. Hongju was the first to fall sick. It was an indigestion caused by some rice cakes she'd bought at Pusan before boarding the ferry to Japan. As Hongju squatted, cold sweat dripping from a darkened face, Songhwa pulled a pack of needles from her bundle. Willow gazed in amazement at Songhwa's agile movements, so different from usual. Songhwa calmly tied thread round Hongju's fingers, then pricked them with a needle until drops of black blood rose from her fingers. Then, after she located the acupuncture points on her solar plexus and feet and pressed them hard, Hongju hiccuped, burped, and regained some color in her face. Back in Ojin Village, if someone had an upset stomach, their grandmother or mother would prick them with a needle, but Songhwa was like a doctor.

"Where did you learn this?" Willow asked curiously.

Songhwa simply muttered, "Collecting herbs . . . I learned from Grandma . . ."

"Songhwa," Hongju said with an encouraging expression, "you must stop using formal-style language when you speak to us. We're on our way to a new world, where there are no high- and low-class people."

"Right. That's true." Willow had also felt awkward being addressed in formal style by Songhwa. As soon as Willow and Hongju began to treat her as their equal, Songhwa gradually lifted her wariness. While they stayed at the Pusan Ajimae's house, she kept talking to Willow and Hongju about Songhwa whenever there was a free moment, begging them to help Songhwa, who had only ever lived in the mountains, to get to Hawai'i and to adjust properly. But in the end, it was Hongju who was helped by Songhwa, and later Willow with her severe seasickness.

At the inn near Kobe Harbor which had been recommended by the Pusan matchmaker, they found over a dozen Korea women, all on their way to be married in Hawai'i, waiting for the physical examination, where they would be tested for eye disease and parasites. The eye tests were made once a week and the parasite test once in two weeks. If they failed the parasite test, they had to wait another two weeks before being tested again. Willow, Hongju, and Songhwa all failed the parasite test, which meant their departure was delayed. The three pledged to take the same boat, no matter how long it took. The moment they left Korea, being three made them feel safer, and the mere fact of having all lived at the foot of Maebongsan Mountain made them feel like hometown friends. Other people envied them for having each other to trust and rely on.

While they awaited the day when they would leave for Hawai'i, the time they spent in Kobe was infinitely enjoyable. In the inn, there were women who couldn't leave because their parents had taken and spent all the money sent by the bridegroom. Hongju had brought additional pocket money from home, and even Willow and Songhwa had enough money to spend without worrying. For Willow, who had grown up so poor, it was fun to spend money, although she trembled over every penny. She couldn't believe she could just enjoy herself like that, and felt obliged to pinch her thigh every morning, in case she was dreaming.

When Willow and Hongju talked about Hawai'i, Songhwa would sit there blank-faced as though it had nothing to do with her.

Willow sighed. "That girl doesn't even know what getting married means."

"Do *you* know?" asked Hongju. "Willow, Songhwa, I'll tell you what marriage is, so just listen carefully." Hongju told them what the husband would do on the first night of marriage and what the bride should do. Willow blushed and giggled, while Songhwa stared at them with a dull expression.

Ever since she first learned how to cook rice at the age of nine, kitchen work had been Willow's lot. However, on the morning she left home, her mother had prepared the food for her, then Songhwa had done the cooking in Pusan, and now in the Japanese inn the maids prepared meals. She had been told that she would have a hard time after leaving home, but Willow was so comfortable and happy that she felt guilty about her family she had left behind. If the journey to Hawai'i was so good, it must be a paradise beyond all imagining.

The three of them wandered around every part of Kobe, day after day. Although all were ports, Kobe, with great ships coming and going from all over the country, was very different from Pusan or Shimonoseki. It was in Kobe that Willow and her companions caught sight of a dark-skinned person for the first time, one of the sailors unloading cargo.

"How can anyone be that dark?"

They had seen people with faces white as calico in Korea, but it was the first time for them to see a man with skin so brown.

It wasn't just the people that amazed them. Seen for the first time, the fruit, trees, houses, streetcars and motor vehicles, rickshaws and bicycles, the crowded streets, everything fascinated them. If Japan was already this different from Korea, what must Hawai'i be like? Willow most enjoyed seeing the Western-style houses built on the hillside. As she admired the colorful decorations glimpsed through the sparkling glass windows, she imagined the house she would inhabit.

Willow was satisfied by simply imagining things, but not Hongju. As soon as she arrived at the inn in Kobe, Hongju wrote a letter to Doksam, saying that she was embarrassed because he had sent less money than the other brides had received. Doksam quickly sent another ten dollars.

"I thought he would send fifty dollars, at least," Hongju grumbled. "What can I buy with just ten dollars?"

But she still went to a boutique and spent all ten dollars on Western-style women's clothes, shoes, and a hat. At first the Japanese shop owner ignored them, but once he realized that Hongju was really going to buy something, he hurriedly offered tea to Willow and Songhwa. Willow was proud to be made welcome by the Japanese owner, even though it was thanks to Hongju. Dressed in her new clothes, Hongju looked as smart as any Western lady. If she was carrying the suitcase bought in Pusan, she would not fail to attract attention anywhere she went.

"If you squander all your money like that, how will you manage?" As she spoke, Willow could not help fingering the soft hem and sleeves of the blouse Hongju was wearing. The owner kept taking out and showing Willow mouthwateringly elegant dresses, all made of lace.

"If you're going to live in America you should wear clothes like this. You should write to your husband asking him to send you more money. In Hawai'i, this much money means nothing," said Hongju as she viewed herself contentedly in a large mirror.

But Willow had only received a formal notification of their marriage, with no exchange of personal letters, so she could not send such a request to Taewan. Even when writing a letter saying when she expected to arrive, at the suggestion of the innkeeper, she had said nothing about money.

Willow bought a wicker suitcase at a stall because she had begun to feel shabby, as if she were Hongju's maid. Even if she could not afford to buy clothes like Hongju, she wanted to stop carrying a bundle on her head. As soon as Willow bought the suitcase, trembling at the expense, Songhwa bought one too. Once Willow returned to the inn, she excitedly transferred her clothes from the bundle into the suitcase, and Songhwa did the same. At Hongju's command, the two of them walked back and forth in the room carrying their suitcases. Willow felt like a character out of a novel, going abroad to study with just a suitcase.

"Now we can throw these things away." Hongju pushed aside the cloth wrappings from the bundles that were lying on the floor.

At that, the smile faded from Willow's face. All day long she had not once thought of her family, even while she was putting the clothes that her mother had made into the suitcase. Day by day, as she entered into her new, joyful life, thoughts of her mother and brothers were fading. Once the things that had been so carefully wrapped and embraced were taken and put into the suitcase, Willow sat down guiltily, hugged the empty wrapping cloths, and burst into tears.

"Let's have our picture taken together before we get on the boat," Hongju said, after they had all passed the physical exam and the date of their departure was settled. Willow was also in favor. Once in Hawai'i, all would become their husbands' wives. Before that, she wanted to have a picture taken as friends who had made the long journey together. Hongju wore the Western-style clothes she had bought previously. Willow took out the pink jacket and skirt that she had brought for the wedding ceremony, and she told Songhwa to do the same. Songhwa had so far kept her hair tied in tresses, but now Willow helped bind her hair in the bun of a married woman. Then the three of them headed for the studio.

The photographer offered them a bouquet, a parasol, and a fan. Willow preferred the parasol to the bouquet of artificial flowers and the fan that seemed more suitable for a gisaeng entertainer, but Hongju picked it up first. Willow did not really care what she held, so she let the others choose first, and Songhwa picked up the fan.

The photo came out a few days later, one copy for each of them.

"Hey, we look better here than in the pictures sent to Hawai'i. What do you think?" asked Willow.

Hongju agreed.

There was no knowing whether it was because the technology was better than in Korea or whether it was because their complexions had benefited from them enjoying themselves and eating properly. The bouquet, which had looked poor, looked real in the picture. It was a pity that Willow couldn't send this picture to Taewan. Maybe then he might have written a warm reply.

In addition to the women at the inn who were going to Hawai'i to be married, there were a number of others who wanted to go to the United States for other reasons. Among them, there was a woman named Esther Kim, who had graduated from the Ewha Hakdang. Esther said she was on her way to study in the United States, but she had waited a long time due to passport problems. The girls who were on their way to be married learned English from Esther. She said that they ought to know at least some simple English in order to pass the immigration test in Hawai'i.

They started with "ABCD." Soon, Willow was able to read the English alphabet used in her passport and travel documents haltingly. She didn't know what the words meant, but it was a new world opening before her.

Esther told them, "In English, you call women getting married like you 'picture brides.' "

"Picture bride, picture bride." Willow repeated the words to herself.

Esther was fond of Willow, who studied hardest among the picture brides.

Once, when they happened to be alone together, Willow asked Esther, "Why do you have that name? It's the first time I've ever come across a name like that."

"My given name is Butduri, 'Hold-on.' I was born after two older brothers died. I hated the name that my haraboji chose for me, meaning I was to hold on firmly to a younger brother when he was born. The name was not for me but for a younger brother, who still hasn't been born."

"Then who gave you the name Esther?"

"I chose it when I was baptized in the church. Esther is a queen who saved her countrymen. I'm going to America to study and save our compatriots."

Fascinated, Willow gazed at her friend, who was so dignified and self-confident. To Willow, Esther choosing her own name was more remarkable than saying she would save her countrymen. Some of the girls in Ojin Village were also given names meaning they should look after their younger brothers or that they were unwanted daughters. Names like Sopsopi, Souni, Tosobi expressed sorrow at having a girl, while Kutsuni, Maksuni, Malsuni, and Yumjon were expressions of hope that there would be no more girls born. There were also children, usually girls, without any name.

Willow was given her name because she was born when the pussy willows were blooming, and she had never thought that her name was any better than the names of other girls. The names of sons were often composed following ancestral tradition of the wishes of the family or parent, but the name Willow did not contain any expectations. Perhaps because a daughter was destined to leave home and become a stranger on marrying, nothing was expected of her from childhood. If that were the case, why did her father make her sit at the back of the room, behind the boys, and learn the *Thousand Character Classic*, and later send her to school?

With such questions remaining in her heart, Willow longed to choose a dreamed-of life, and a proper name for herself, like Esther. She decided that once she was in Hawai'i, she would study hard and do so.

The people in the ship cabin began to stir. Songhwa, who had just returned with rice balls served for breakfast, said they would soon reach Hawai'i. It was the twelfth day since they left Kobe, three months since they left home. They were nearly at their destination, but Willow could not so much as lift her head because of seasickness. For the first day or two after boarding the ship, she had forced herself to go up on deck, to watch the people and the sea, and to vomit over the side. She had felt nauseous if she so much as lifted her head, so she stopped going out, and was obliged to stay lying down with her eyes closed. Finally, Songhwa had managed to press the sharp tip of a bamboo comb into an acupuncture point, and her head ached less after that.

In addition to Songhwa and Hongju, two other women took turns caring for Willow. Jang Myongok from Jinju and Kim

Makson from Suwon were both picture brides too. Willow and her companion addressed Myongok, who was two years older, and Makson, who was one year older, as Onni. At first, they were all so worried about Willow that they clustered around her, but that only made her feel sorrier for being such a burden. The cramped, smelly third-class cabin was a space nobody wanted to stay in except for sleeping. Hongju longed to buy a second-class ticket, but she had run out of money, while the others wanted a third-class cabin to save money.

"I'm better on my own. Don't worry, go up and look around. I can care for myself."

The four of them gradually went out more often at Willow's insistence. Even with her eyes closed, Willow sensed when people left the cabin. Willow lay there, her eyes closed and teeth clenched, telling herself that she must not vomit up what she had eaten for breakfast. She couldn't meet Taewan for the first time tottering along with a sickly face. She had to conserve her energy. In the hope of alleviating her seasickness, Willow thought of all the things she'd experienced for the first time since leaving home, but found this so overwhelming that they left her dizzy as the sea.

"Willow, Willow, we're arriving at Hawai'i. They say there'll be another physical examination here. If you fail, you'll get sent back. Quickly, get up and get ready!"

At the sound of Hongju's voice, Willow opened her eyes with a start. From the look her friend gave her, Willow knew she must look seriously ill, and it would be terrible if she were sent back after making it this far. Willow hurriedly rose to a sitting position. The ship was still rocking, but far less than when it was speeding across the open sea. The cabin was crowded with people who had come down in order to prepare to disembark. There were about ten Korea women on board. The rest were mainly Japanese, and there were many picture brides among them, too. They had heard that picture marriages had been started by the Japanese, who had gone to work in the sugarcane fields earlier than men from Korea.

Songhwa brought a moist towel, then Myongok and Makson fetched Willow's suitcase. Willow wiped her face with the towel.

"You're so thin." Hongju clacked her tongue and held out a hand mirror.

Because of her hollow cheeks, Willow's cheekbones stood out sharply while her eyes looked smaller. There was nothing left of the pretty, plump face shown in the picture taken in Kobe. She suddenly remembered dreaming that Taewan had canceled the marriage, and so she could not leave the ship. Anxiety that the dream might become reality was more frightening than her nausea. Clenching her teeth and resisting the impulse to vomit, Willow changed into her pink skirt and blouse. Then she removed her straw sandals and slipped on the leather shoes she had carefully stored away in her suitcase. Using a little of Hongju's rouge, she concealed her pasty cheeks, and then tidied her hair.

Once they were ready, the picture brides climbed up onto the deck with their luggage, Hongju and Songhwa supporting Willow. After being so long in the dark cabin, her eyes were dazzled by the bright sunlight, while the breeze sent her hair aflutter. The scene spread before her found its way into Willow's squinting eyes. The sky held clumps of cumulus clouds, cascading as they touched the sea. The port was obscured by the crowd of people clustered at the bow of the ship, but the city and mountains were visible to the right. Although the shape of the hills was a little different from Korea, when she saw them, her mind began to calm as she thought that this too was a place where people live.

"Here it's warm all year round, with this kind of weather all the time," said Hongju excitedly. Dressed as she was in the clothes she had bought in Kobe, there was no sign of the widow who had left from Pusan. Likewise, Songhwa, who had rubbed off the mountain dirt and grown fair-skinned as time passed, showed no sign of being the granddaughter of a shaman. Willow stood straight, so as not to be leaning on Hongju and Songhwa.

The inspectors came on board with an interpreter, did a simple health check, then verified passports and travel documents. Since it was the United States, she had thought there would only be people with white faces, but already among the three officials each had a different skin color and appearance. As the inspectors came closer, Willow's heart began to pound. On seeing a few people being pulled out of the line and led away, she felt increasingly frightened.

During the eye examination, when the examiner raised her eyelids, Willow was unable to breathe properly. After checking her passport and travel documents, the inspector returned them with a kind smile.

Fortunately, all the picture brides from Korea passed. A stair that was like a ladder linked the ship to the pier over the open water below. Willow, carrying her suitcase and still unsteady, barely managed to cross the ladder, her blouse and skirt fluttering in the breeze. She had thought that once she got off the ship, she would start to live again, but when her feet touched the ground, it too seemed to be heaving.

The wharf was full of people from the ship, people come to welcome them, sailors, and merchants. Willow was overwhelmed by the strange sound of the voices emerging from people of such varied appearance. There were lots of hawkers selling garlands of flowers that they carried in baskets or on their arms. She wondered who might want to buy a garland when you could not even eat it, but many were buying them and hanging them on the necks of the new arrivals. It seemed to be a way of welcoming visitors.

Looking around, Willow hoped that Taewan might have come to welcome her with a garland, but she could not see him. It was not only Taewan. None of the other bridegrooms could be seen, either. Amid the uproar, the call of "Aloha" stood out. Myongok had heard from someone that in Hawai'i you only had to greet someone with "Aloha" and all would be well. Willow mouthed the words "Aloha, Hawai'i."

Five of the Korea picture brides went to the immigration building with the Japanese brides they'd met on the boat. For lunch, they ate Japanese-style miso soup with rice offered by the Immigration Service, then went to rest in a large room with shelflike beds. They were told that they would only be allowed to leave the room after their husbands came to collect them. After listening to the Japanese picture brides talking among themselves, Hongju told them that there was one woman who had been waiting for her husband for a week.

The brides from Korea sat close together on the edge of a bed and waited for their names to be called. Watching the Japanese brides being called in a steady stream, they dared not talk for fear of not hearing their names. The first of them to be called was Hongju, who made such a fuss that everyone in the room looked over. Willow picked up the hat she had dropped and handed it to her friend, saying, "Off you go to meet your husband. See you soon."

The next was Myongok, whom Willow had grown closer with on the ship.

"Have a good meeting with your bridegroom and see you later."

It was already evening when Willow's name was called, and

a sense of relief swept over her that Taewan had come to collect her, and she was excited at the thought of meeting her bridegroom for the first time.

As she walked down the hallway, she saw a Japanese picture bride crying outside the window. Beside her, an old man was smoking a cigarette and looking at the sky. The guide said something to Willow that she couldn't understand, but she could read her pitying expression.

As Willow continued along the hallway, she found Myongok crying and muttering, "But I can't be married to a man like him." Next to her, completely at a loss, stood a more than middle-aged man, clutching his hat, his deeply tanned face covered with wrinkles. Willow let out a sigh and said nothing.

In Kobe, the brides had passed around the photos of their future husbands. She could not clearly recall Myongok's bridegroom's face, but he had certainly not been as old as the man standing there in front of her. Perhaps something had happened to the husband so that he had sent his father or uncle to meet her instead? At the sight of Willow, Myongok wept even louder, her face full of despair. No, that man—so different from the picture—was her husband. He had obviously sent the photo of another younger man. Her heart fell. What if Taewan had done the same, or worse? Willow's legs shook at the possibility.

The guide stood at the door and beckoned for Willow to come quickly. Willow hurried after without saying anything to Myongok. She could see through the open door into the room beyond. A man sitting with his back to the door, another man standing facing the door, and a woman who looked to be from Korea were talking together. The man facing her wasn't Korean, so the man who was only showing the back of his suit must be Taewan. Her heart skipped a beat. Fortunately, his hair was not white. Seeing Willow, the woman, speaking Korean, told her to come in.

The man slowly turned. His face was familiar, though darker than she expected, but not that different from the face in the picture she had so often looked at and memorized. Willow was so happy he wasn't an old man that she barely noticed the cold expression on his face. If she hadn't seen the Japanese picture bride or Myongok's groom while coming to the room, she might have been hurt by the fact, but her eyes brimmed with tears at having arrived safely next to the man in the picture.

Willow sat down on a wooden chair next to Taewan as the interpreter directed. The official looked at her passport and documents and asked a question, which the interpreter repeated in Korean.

"What's your name?"

"Willow Kang."

"Your age?"

"I'm eighteen years old."

When asked if she had ever attended school, she said that she had stopped attending primary school. Willow tried to glance at Taewan, worried that he'd be disappointed, but he had his head down and was picking his nails. His thick hands looked reliable.

The official asked Willow the name of her bridegroom. "Taewan So," she said clearly. Finally, the official asked Taewan if it was correct that Willow was his wife.

"That is correct."

Willow heard Taewan's voice for the first time, and wished he'd say more.

As she left the office behind Taewan, Willow passed an old man with a bent back and white hair standing in front of the door. He looked much older than Myongok's middle-aged husband. Willow's heart sank. This must be Songhwa's or Makson's husband. The old man looked at Taewan and spoke delightedly.

"My, look who it is! Aren't you Supervisor So? Have you also made a picture marriage?" The old man's eyes turned toward Willow. In his face she recognized Sokbo, Songhwa's bridegroom. Goodness, how could this be? On the back of the photo it was clearly written "thirty-six," but the man before her looked to be well past sixty. Taewan ignored Park Sokbo's joyful greeting and walked around him, saying nothing. Willow was disappointed in Taewan's rudeness, but it was nothing compared to the disappointment that Songhwa would feel. Once they were a little way beyond Sokbo, Willow confirmed his identity with Taewan.

"Wasn't that Mr. Sokbo Park just now?" It was the first words she had spoken to Taewan.

"How do you know him?"

"He is to marry my friend. How can such an old man claim to be thirty-six?"

Instead of answering, Taewan merely laughed.

As they made their way out of the hallway, Willow saw two more Japanese women crying because of their elderly bridegrooms. Willow realized how lucky she was to have met a bridegroom who resembled his photo. She admired her mother's insight, when she said the Pusan Ajimae's guarantee was more reliable than the photo. As they left the immigration building, Taewan glanced down, and took the suitcase she was carrying.

"It's, it's not heavy," she said softly, worrying that he might be disappointed at how small and light her luggage was.

Again, he didn't reply.

She wondered if Taewan was someone who showed his sincerity through actions, not words or writing, and followed him with an overflowing heart. Her stiff leather shoes, which did not fit on her feet, kept slipping off.

A Western couple walked along arm in arm. At Kobe, she had even seen couples embrace and kiss. She guessed that it was a Western custom, even for strangers, to kiss one another on the cheek in greeting. Willow liked it, even if it *was* indecent. She wished that Taewan would do the same to her, and blushed, but Taewan was striding ahead of his bride, like the men did in Korea. Willow was happy enough that he was carrying her bag.

The pier was lined with shops and opened onto streets where horses, carts, and motorcars were coming and going. As they entered the bustling streets, the wind fell slightly. Carefully following behind Taewan, she glimpsed her reflection in the shop windows and adjusted her dress. Stores such as vegetable shops, tailor shops, shoe stores, and restaurants had signs in English and in Chinese characters, and there were more Asians than Westerners on the streets.

Willow had been expecting nice houses and well-dressed people coming and going like in the Westerners' neighborhood on the hills of Kobe, and was amazed at the street's turbulent, messy appearance. Most of the people seemed to be sloppily dressed. What if Hawai'i wasn't the paradise that the Pusan Ajimae said it was? As for sweeping up money with a dustpan, the street was littered with horse droppings and garbage. Willow realized it had been rather ridiculous to believe that clothes and shoes would be hanging from the trees. However, she saw the same kind of trees as she had seen in Doksam's photograph here and there, so she did not immediately give up all hope.

At the top of these trees, things round like pumpkins hung

in clusters. Willow hurried to overtake Taewan and asked, "What's the name of that tree?"

Taewan glanced at the tree. "It's called a coconut palm."

"Might there be clothes and shoes inside those round things like pumpkins?"

He gave Willow a pitying glance. "Is that what the match-maker told you? If you go to Hawai'i, clothes and food will be hanging on the trees? Did you hear her say that you can sweep up money with a dustpan?"

"Yes, that's what I heard. Is it really true?"

Instead of answering, Taewan threw the butt of the cigarette he had been smoking onto the ground and stepped on it.

Taewan took Willow to an inn beside a small stream. At the entrance to the two-storied wooden building, there was a sign written in Hangul, HAESONG INN. Willow stopped at the door. Even though they were a couple on paper, they hadn't yet been properly married.

"Why are we going in here? Aren't we going home?" asked Willow, grabbing his sleeve.

"We'll be going home after the wedding ceremony tomorrow. Come along, if you don't want to sleep on the street."

Willow had no alternative but to follow.

An elderly woman welcomed Taewan.

"Oh, so at last you're getting married? Your bride looks lovely. Your aboji will like her." When the innkeeper mentioned her father-in-law, Willow greeted her modestly. Anyone who knew Taewan was like part of his family. Taewan smiled as he talked with the innkeeper, the opposite of how he'd talked with Willow, but she listened with delight, as if he were smiling at her.

"Dear me," said the innkeeper, "just look at me chattering away, holding up the new bride. You must have had a hard time coming all this way on the ship, you should go up and get some rest."

The woman took out a towel from a cabinet, then pointed out the dining room, the toilet, and the communal bathroom on the first floor before leading the way upstairs. Willow, who had spent more than two months in Kobe, was familiar with inns, but the thought of sitting in the room alone with Taewan set her heart racing and her legs wobbly. She climbed the narrow, steep wooden staircase and found herself in a corridor lined with doors. Only then did she realize that she hadn't washed properly since Kobe. *I must smell terrible . . . how disgusting. What on earth will he think?* Willow blushed and felt dizzy, unable to think straight.

The landlady opened a door at the end of the corridor. "It's a nice, quiet room."

Willow blushed even further at the sight of the bed; she'd never slept on one before. It looked tall and narrow, and she reckoned she might fall off if she didn't hold on. She would be ashamed to cling to Taewan, and ashamed to fall onto the floor.

"Is this your first time seeing a bed? I brought it in last month. After sleeping on a hard floor, being in a bed is like lying on clouds. I hope you enjoy it."

"Yes, thank you. The bedding is pretty, too."

"It's a new blanket. You're the first to use it, so have sweet dreams. It's so good to see a young bridegroom after all those brides sobbing because their groom is so old. Take a rest, then come down for dinner when you hear the bell."

The innkeeper put down the towel and turned to leave. Once she had gone down the stairs, leaving them alone together,

Taewan, who had been standing two or three steps away, approached the door of the room. The sound of Willow's beating heart seemed to be filling the hallway.

Taewan put her suitcase inside the room, then turned to her. "I have to go out for a while, I have something to take care of. If I don't come back by dinnertime, eat without me." Without waiting for a reply, he quickly departed.

It was only after he was gone that Willow could breathe freely, glad to be by herself. She felt awkward being alone with him in the room before the wedding, and more than that, desperately needed a bath.

Crossing the room, Willow lifted the lace curtain, which was lighter than Hongju's sleeves, and looked out the window. It faced the road, but she could see the surrounding scenery, and the mountains. Willow sat down on the bed, but quickly stood up when the mattress, sinking under her weight, made her feel seasick.

Willow went downstairs carrying the towel. The communal bathroom was similar to that in Kobe, only with no large Japanese-style tub of hot water. As she was finishing her bath, she thought she heard a woman crying, and turned off the water. It was Hongju, standing just outside the bathroom. Willow quickly dressed and ran out. The innkeeper was holding on to Hongju, who was crying loudly and trying to leave the inn.

"Hongju. What is it? What's the matter?"

At the sight of Willow, Hongju collapsed onto the floor and cried even louder, striking the floor with her hands. Her eyes were swollen, and her hair and clothes were a mess.

"Is she your friend?" the innkeeper whispered to Willow. "Please, take her upstairs and calm her down."

"Where did the groom go?"

"He's in their room. Whenever he comes near her, she cries and makes a fuss so I sent him up."

Willow helped Hongju stand up and took her upstairs to her room. Hongju looked around with a tearful face.

"Why are you the only one with a bed?" Hongju sat on the bed, and even started bouncing around.

"Hongju, what's all this crying about? What's wrong?" asked Willow, already guessing the answer.

Hongju started to cry again. Grabbing Willow, she shook her, and spoke through her tears. "What am I to do? Jo Doksam is an old man. He's not thirty-nine, he's forty-nine. He's as wrinkled as a three-year-old salted cucumber."

Forty-nine was thirty-one years older than Hongju. No matter that she was a widow, it was terrible.

"What was the picture he sent you?" asked Willow.

"It was a fraud. He says it's an old picture. When I said I was going home, he said he'd spent a lot of money bringing me over, so I would have to repay everything before I could leave. What do I do? I can't live with someone like that. How could I ever sleep with such an old man?"

Willow silently patted her friend's back as she continued to cry, sitting on the bed with her legs stretched out like a child.

"What about your bridegroom? Is he the same as his picture?" asked Hongju after a long spell of weeping.

Willow nodded, controlling her expressions.

Hongju's eyes widened. "You mean So Taewan didn't lie about his age?"

"I don't know, exactly. He brought me here, then went away saying he had things to do, so we didn't have any time to talk."

"Did you see Songhwa's bridegroom?"

Willow nodded, and Hongju asked what he was like.

"He looks to be way past his sixtieth birthday," said Willow with a sigh.

"How on earth . . ."

Hongju started to cry again. Willow knew how much Hongju had been looking forward to a new life in Hawai'i. When she saw Hongju so desperate before her shattered dreams, she felt guilty that her bridegroom had not lied about his age.

"I'm going back," said Hongju in determined tones.

Willow's heart sank.

"Where? Back to Korea?" Willow was frightened that she might be left alone in Hawai'i, without her best friend. Yes, there was Songhwa, but she was someone who needed to be taken care of, not a friend to lean on. But it wouldn't be fair for Willow to ask her to stay.

"Do you have the boat fare?" asked Willow.

"I spent everything in Kobe. There's not a penny left." Hongju had used up all the money she had been given by her family, too. With Doksam demanding that she pay back all the money he had spent to get her here, he was not likely to give her the fare back.

"Then how can you leave? Will you ask your family to send the money?"

Hongju's face twisted. "No. Do you know what Aboji said to me? 'It's less than three years since your husband died, and it's a disgrace that you are remarrying so soon. You are never to come home again.' How can an aboji say such a thing? While he's supporting a mistress. Whose fault was it that I became a widow? I became a widow because I was married to a sick man because my aboji was sick to be a yangban."

Until then Willow had thought that Hongju's father had approved of Hongju's picture wedding. Although it was not considered a fault for a man to have a mistress, Korea was a place where it was a serious fault for a widow to remarry. Willow's heart ached at her friend's misfortune.

"Do you have any money?" asked Hongju. "Would Songhwa have any money?"

Willow had about five dollars left. Songhwa might still have a little, but it was far from being enough for a return trip. Besides, she didn't want Hongju to leave even if she had the money. While Willow was hesitating how to reply, a bell rang downstairs.

Dinner was ready.

"I've been crying so much that I'm hungry. Let's go and eat." Hongju stood up from the bed, thinking only of her stomach. Willow very much hoped that Hongju, who had been brave even when her husband died and she returned home, would overcome this difficulty and stay in Hawai'i.

Four bridegrooms were in the dining room, as were Myong-gok and Makson. Only Taewan among the men and Songhwa among the women were absent. Myongok and Makson were sitting at a different table from the men. Bottles of liquor had been placed on the bridegrooms' table, and the oldest of the men, Sokbo, was already drunk. Hongju went and sat next to Myongok without so much as a glance at the men. Willow sat next to Makson and asked if she had seen Songhwa. Makson and Myongok, whose eyes were red and swollen, shook their heads helplessly.

One of the men kept glancing at Hongju, and Willow realized it must be Doksam. For someone who had sent a sweet letter, and had willingly sent more money, he looked ungainly and impoverished, a far cry from what the photo had shown, and as for the motorcar his foot had been resting on, it seemed unlikely that he even owned an oxcart. Hongju was right to say she was going back.

Though she worried about her friends, Willow kept eyeing the grilled fish and meat, lettuce, green peppers, and bean paste set on the table. Since leaving Pusan she had mostly eaten Japanese food. Her mouth was watering at the sight of the plentiful Korea-style dishes.

The innkeeper, together with a girl who seemed to be her daughter, came in carrying trays of food. They set down a bowl of bean paste stew in the middle of each table, and placed bowls of rice in front of each one. It was pure, white rice! In Korea, only the rich ate white rice, and Willow could not tear her eyes away.

From the bridegroom table, Sokbo called out to the women, "Can you go up to room 103 and tell her to come down and eat?"

Willow and Hongju ran out of the dining room and up to room 103 when he was still midsentence. When they opened the door, Songhwa was crouched in one corner. Unlike Willow's room, this had a parquet floor, and there was a set of bedding folded up, lying to one side. They threw off their shoes before rushing in. Hongju hugged Songhwa and once again burst into tears.

"What a fate! How can you live with such an old bridegroom? I'd rather grow old and die a widow than live with Jo Doksam. Songhwa, let's both throw ourselves into the sea and die!"

Hongju sobbed as she held Songhwa, whose face was blank.

Willow embraced the two of them and wept. Until today, she had felt sorry for the man who would marry Songhwa, the ignorant-looking granddaughter of a shaman, the daughter of a madwoman, who didn't even know who her father was. But now, her feelings of pity had reversed. Most of all, what she felt right now was hungry for the food they'd left on the table.

Hongju wiped away her tears as she said, "Songhwa, let's go down and eat. We can think after we've eaten."

"Yes, the others are waiting," Willow agreed.

Together they led Songhwa down to the dining room. As Willow had said, Myongok and Makson were waiting for them. Meanwhile, the voices of the men, who had continued drinking, grew louder. Willow helped Songhwa sit down. As she sat down next to her, her eyes met those of Sokbo, who was smiling broadly. Willow stared daggers back at him.

Eyes downcast, the women began to eat without a word. At the inn in Kobe, and on the ship coming to Hawai'i, they had always had lively dinner conversation. But now they ate sullenly before the bridegrooms who had so deceived them. At first, Willow felt guilty at how much she was enjoying the food next to her miserable friends. But soon she was concentrating on how many pieces of meat she could eat, whether she could spear a fish head, and if someone had taken possession of the fish's eyes. She was not the only one. They devoured everything, to the last grain of rice and lettuce leaf. Encouraged by their drinking, the bridegrooms tried to talk to them, but the brides ignored them.

Willow went up to her room with Hongju and Songhwa, Makson and Myongok hurrying after them. With five people the room was full. The crying that had stopped for a while during dinner began again. Willow worried that Taewan might come back, but it seemed so minor a thing compared to the others who were in such despair. It was difficult to find a comforting word to say when she was so privileged.

After a while, the innkeeper brought up a sliced fruit she called "pineapple," set it down on the floor for fear it might leak onto the bed, and urged them to eat. The brides, sitting in the cramped space, still crying, ate the pineapple dripping with sweet, savory juice, even licking their fingers clean.

"I know how disappointed you must have been on seeing those old bridegrooms," said the innkeeper. "You probably feel like jumping into the sea. It's true that the men are older, but they also look older than they are because they work hard under the sun. They arrived here empty-handed and haven't had easy lives. You're already legally married, and you're stuck here, so I think you should take pity on them and just move in with them."

"Where are you from? Did you come as a picture bride too?" asked Makson, somberly. The innkeeper's dialect was similar to her own.

"I used to live in Incheon, until I came here with my husband and the children. I suppose you all came after hearing that Hawai'i is a paradise, and that if you come here, you'll never have to worry about starving?"

All of them nodded at her question and hoped that her next words might lighten their despair even a little.

"And we were told we would be able to study," Willow added quickly.

The innkeeper clacked her tongue. "Uneducated and simpleminded, and so you were deceived. Where in the world is there such a place? I came with three children because I was fooled by similar words . . . I came on the same ship as Taewan and lived on the same plantation. Aigo, I can't stand to think of those terrible years."

The brides were unable to conceal their disappointment. Willow alone struggled to hide her joy. If someone who had worked on the same plantation had become the owner of a fine inn, she was convinced that Taewan was indeed a landowner. Just as the lives of the people living in Korea were very different, so too the lives of the Korea people living here must be different.

"But you've succeeded in establishing this inn," Myongok said enviously.

"Success? How can I even begin to tell you what I went through when I first arrived? I've buried it in my heart to say things are fine now. It's been nine years since the first picture brides arrived. Most have stayed at our inn. Everyone cries at first, as if at a funeral. They make a fuss, say they're going back, but in the end they stay with their bridegrooms. Either they don't have the fare back to Korea, or they're not allowed back home, so they have no choice. You're here now, so even if your husband isn't up to your expectations, make the best of it. Then good days will come."

The brides, whose crying had stopped as they listened to her words, resumed their weeping.

MAY BRIDES

The picture brides did not leave Willow's room, although it was late in the evening. Their excuse was that there had not yet been a wedding ceremony. Willow relayed this to the innkeeper when she came to the door. "Since there has not yet been a wedding ceremony, we intend to sleep in this room tonight. Please tell the men."

"Very well. If you were to go to your rooms, the only thing we would hear would be wailing, so it's likely for the best. I'll tell the bridegrooms. If Taewan comes back, I'll tell him to sleep in another room. After the wedding tomorrow you'll be scattered, and I don't know when you'll see each other again, so you'd better be saying goodbyes, too."

"Scattered? Where are we going?" Myongok asked in surprise.

The brides were only just able to endure everything with each other's support.

"Two of the bridegrooms live on this island, but the other three are from Maui, Kaua'i, and Big Island."

Those were unfamiliar places with names that were difficult to pronounce. As the questions kept coming, the innkeeper sat down and explained about Hawai'i. It seemed that the same thing happened every time picture brides arrived, and she rattled off facts as though she had memorized them. First, she explained that originally Hawai'i was a kingdom, but more than twenty years before, Westerners had expelled the queen and made it into an American colony. The country they had been told was a paradise was just like Korea, a country stolen.

Everyone looked surprised.

"The queen, who was confined to her palace, died last year. When I saw Hawaiian people crying at the funeral, I cried too. They're gentle and generous, much better to deal with than haole."

"What's haole?" Makson asked.

"White people are called haole in this country's language. Whether it's sugarcane farms or pineapple farms, they all belong to haole. Originally, the land belonged to the natives, but now the haole own it all."

The plantation owners farmed on a large scale, exporting sugar and pineapple. They had made Hawai'i an American territory to avoid high export tariffs. They initially used indigenous people as workers, but the numbers were far from sufficient. So they had hired Europeans, but they couldn't stand the hot weather and hard work. Then the owners had looked toward Asia. The first to be brought in were Chinese, but the majority of them left the farms at the end of their contract and went to work on the mainland. The next to come were Japanese. They also went to the mainland after the end of their contract, and frequently held strikes, demanding increased wages and improved treatment. The first workers from Korea arrived in 1903. After that, more than seven thousand arrived prior to 1905, when immigration was banned, far fewer than the two hundred thousand Japanese workers.

"When did you come?" Willow asked, but what she really wanted to know was when Taewan had come.

"I came in 1905. Thirteen years ago, this year."

She explained that in Hawai'i people used the Western calendar. The picture brides had arrived on May 12, 1918, by the solar calendar. Willow was more interested in Taewan than in today's date, and counted on her fingers that Tae-wan must have been fourteen years old when he arrived, the same age as her brother Gyusik. Luckily, he had come with his family to this foreign place. The woman went on with her explanations. Hawai'i was composed of several islands, of which O'ahu had more than half the total population. Honolulu, where the inn was, was the busiest place in O'ahu.

"We call Honolulu Hohang, which is like Hansong, the capital city in Korea. Or rather, nowadays you have to call it Keijo, Gyongsong."

Japan had changed the name of Hansong, or Seoul, where the king lived, to Gyongsong, which they pronounced Keijo. Among the picture brides, Makson was the only one to have been to Gyongsong.

"Who are the two who'll be living here?" asked Hongju.

The innkeeper nodded toward Willow and Songhwa. Disappointment and envy showed on the faces of the other three.

"Both your bridegrooms live on the Kahuku Plantation in the north. You have to take a boat to reach the other islands, but Kahuku can be reached by train."

Songhwa smiled faintly on hearing that she would be living in the same place as Willow. It was the first time that she had shown any emotion since arriving in Hawai'i. Willow was also glad that she would not be parted from Songhwa, at least, and above all, she was relieved to know that she would not have to take a boat. The very thought of seasickness was terrible, and it was even more terrible to imagine Taewan seeing her in such a state. Willow was so happy that she unthinkingly seized Songhwa's hand, then, as Hongju began to shed tears, gently took her hand, too. Myongok and Makson wept alongside Hongju, and the smile faded from Songhwa's face.

The innkeeper left and returned with more bedding. "To-

them down to eat. They went to the dining room, still swollen-eyed and depressed by their situation.

Willow was startled to see Taewan in the dining room, sitting among the other men, looking like their son or grandson. He met Willow's eyes and nodded. Conflicting emotions of relief that Taewan had returned, and worry of her appearance, nearly overcame her. Like on the previous evening, the brides sat at a different table from the men.

Hongju, seeing Taewan for the first time, became noticeably cooler.

"Your bridegroom's just like in the picture. You're lucky," whispered Myongok, but still loud enough that all the men could hear.

Willow blushed, wondering what Taewan would think.

Rice and meat soup, kimchi and fried eggs, one egg per person. It was a wonderful banquet, the likes of which Willow had never enjoyed back in Korea, even on her birthday. The brides, ravenous after tossing and turning all night long, ate hungrily, while the bridegrooms, who had been so noisy when drinking the evening before, now ate quietly.

After breakfast, the brides packed their bags, then gathered again in Willow's room to prepare for the wedding ceremony. Instead of the Western-style clothes she had bought to wear at her wedding, Hongju was wearing the green jacket and red skirt her mother had packed for her. Her Western clothes were too crumpled to wear after she had sat on the floor crying the previous day. Willow changed into her pink jacket and skirt. After combing her hair, she reached out for the powder puff, but Hongju snatched it away. Previously, Hongju had generously shared her makeup with Willow and Songhwa, who didn't own any.

"How could the Pusan Ajimae do such a thing?" Hongju snapped at Willow. "How come you got a good deal, while

Songhwa and I were matched up to such old men? After my omma paid her a premium, too."

Willow blushed, abashed at the unfairness of it. Although she wasn't sure about Songhwa, Hongju had certainly chosen her bridegroom freely. She wanted to say that the person who chose Jo Doksam as her husband was Hongju herself, but tears came out instead of words. Criticized by her closest friend, her emotions rushed free. The moment Willow buried her face in her hands and burst into tears, the whole room became a sea of tears once again. Apologizing, Hongju offered her the powder puff, but Willow refused.

Eventually they were ready to go. After bidding farewell to the owners of the inn, the bridegrooms and the brides walked along separately. They had heard it would take about thirty minutes to walk to the church. The road was wet from the morning rain, and the brides walked beside a blackish stream with its pungent smell; their faces were somber, as if they were on their way to a funeral, rather than a wedding. They seemed to have calmed down the outbursts and tears, but Willow felt a subtle distance between her and the other brides. After seeing Taewan, Hongju had drawn closer to Myongok and Makson. Songhwa, who seemed dazed, was no comfort at all. Taewan, walking slightly apart from the other men, never looked back, and could do nothing to relieve the alienation and hurt Willow was feeling.

As they left the shade of the buildings, a blaze of warm sunlight struck them. The sea breeze did nothing to cool them, while their hair was blown about and their skirts billowed. The brides squealed, holding down their skirts. People stared as the group of women, each wearing a different-colored Korean dress, walked by. A Hawaiian woman selling fruit on the street greeted them with "Aloha," but none of them responded.

Beyond a small bridge over a stream, one- and two-story

wooden buildings continued, as on the street with the inn. The streets, full of people of varying skin colors, appearances, and languages, were untidy and messy. The wet road was slippery with a slurry of horse droppings and fruit peels. The picture brides sighed at the thought that if this was the neighborhood of Hawai'i that the innkeeper had boasted was like Gyongsong, what must the places where they would be living be like?

The men stopped in front of a church on the main street. It was a two-story building with a small courtyard. The brides followed the grooms inside. For Willow, it was her first time being in a church. Songhwa, who had grown up with her shaman grandmother, continued to look around, slightly dazed. The pastor's wife and two women who called themselves deaconesses welcomed them.

Veils and bouquets were available for rent or sale. The bouquets could be taken away afterward, but the veils had to be returned after the wedding. Makson shed more tears when her husband grumbled at the expense. Hongju looked at her bridegroom as if he were dirt, and picked the prettiest veil and bouquet.

The deaconess named Mrs. Kim powdered Willow's bare face and applied makeup to her eyebrows and lips. "You're marrying Supervisor So. We thought he would grow old like a ghost, and now he's getting married. Once you're married, you must coax your husband into attending church again. Together with you."

Park Sokbo had also called Taewan "supervisor" but Willow didn't know what that meant, nor how she might coax her husband to attend church. She finally felt like it was her wedding day after her face was made up and she put on the light veil that reached down to the floor. The other brides, caught up in the wedding atmosphere created by the veils and bouquets, seemed to have forgotten their husbands. Willow stared at Taewan. He had knotted a bow tie over the suit he was wearing and stood there looking awkward. He gave no indication of any excitement about being married.

"How pretty she is!" the pastor's wife said, looking at Songhwa, who had just finished dressing up. Park Sokbo, who had oiled and combed down his hair, making his wrinkles more conspicuous, was gazing at Songhwa with an openmouthed smile that showed his missing teeth. Songhwa, who was wearing the veil and carrying the bouquet that were left over after the others had made their choice, looked blank, as if she were a guest at someone else's wedding. If she could see Park Sokbo, Kumhwa, who had sent her granddaughter to Hawai'i in the hope that she would live the life of a respectable woman, would surely be heartbroken. Willow was more worried for Songhwa than for Hongju, even with all her crying and carrying-on.

After the preparations were complete, the pastor told the couples to stand together. Among the bridegrooms, Taewan seemed to be the only one indifferent to his bride, his face looking as blank as Songhwa's. Jo Doksam hovered over Hongju despite being blatantly ignored, while the bridegrooms of Myongok and Makson smiled at their dressed-up brides.

Myongok and Makson were in the front row with their husbands, while the other three couples stood behind them. Willow stood a little way apart from Taewan, holding a bouquet of flowers that had been picked for her. Deaconess Kim approached and had Willow stand closer to Taewan. The pastor presided over the ceremony, and the pastor's wife and two deaconesses were the only guests. A wedding ceremony, not only without guests but without her family!

Willow was overcome with sadness.

When the pastor asked if they took their grooms to be their husbands, Hongju burst into tears. At that, Myongok and Makson also started crying. Their weeping was louder than the bridegrooms' reply. The pastor continued the ceremony without pause, seemingly accustomed to such scenes. Myongok and Makson sang along to the hymns, through their tears. To Willow, who had never read a line of the Bible, never heard a single hymn, it was as if she were attending another person's wedding. Fortunately, she thought, Taewan seemed to be feeling the same.

As the pastor talked about love between husband and wife, harmonious families, the children they would have, and a future full of hope, the crying only grew louder. Myongok and Makson chanted "Amen" in response to the pastor's words while they wept, but Hongju went so far as to wail, "Aigo, aigo!," as if she were at a funeral. Tears flowed from Willow's eyes, too, as she thought of the mother and brothers whom she might never see again.

Then came the moment when the groom had to put the ring on the bride's finger. At the pastor's command, the grooms took the rings from their pockets. Taewan held a silver ring. Willow held out her hand, soft from months without heavy household chores.

Her heart raced. *It's because the ring is pretty*, she told herself. When Taewan took her hand, her heart raced even faster. Taewan slid the silver ring onto Willow's ring finger, but it caught on the knuckle, causing them both to blush.

Taewan tried to take the ring back. "I'll have it enlarged and give it to you later." It sounded as if he was saying the marriage should be postponed.

"Oh, no." Willow pushed Taewan's hand away, then forced the ring down, scraping the skin. She breathed a sigh of relief. The veil would be returned and the flowers would wither, but the ring would remain on her finger forever. It was proof that her dreams of studying and taking care of her family were coming true.

The newly wed couples had lunch at a Chinese restaurant near the church, together with the pastor and his wife and the deaconesses. Unlike at the inn, the brides did not enjoy the meal. The food was too greasy for them, and their imminent separation killed their appetite.

"I don't know where Maui is, but I'll run away as soon as I've paid back what I owe to Doksam. I want to know your address," Hongju told Willow when they went to the toilet together. Willow's hurt feelings from the powder-puff incident evaporated, and her heart ached at their parting.

"Could you give my friends your address?" Willow asked Taewan when they returned to the table. Taewan tore off the edge of a newspaper he had with him and wrote it down, which started an exchange of addresses. The other grooms did not know how to write their address in English. Hongju began to look suspicious, wondering to the others if someone else had written the sugary-sweet letter she had received. Willow shared the same question, but didn't think it was so bad. Even if he hadn't written it, at least Doksam had tried to win Hongju's heart.

The time came for Willow and her husband to leave for Kahuku. Myongok and Makson said they were staying in Honolulu for another day or two with their husbands as a honeymoon, while Hongju and her bridegroom were to take the night boat to Maui.

Hongju embraced Willow and Songhwa with a tearful face. "Willow, Songhwa, stay healthy, do well, and don't forget to write." When Hongju had become a widow, she had been angry but she hadn't once cried. But since she arrived in Hawai'i it was as if she'd never stopped crying.

Willow hugged Hongju hard. "Hongju, you do well, too. I'll write as soon as I've settled in."

Honolulu Station, near the harbor, was noisy, crowded with people, luggage, horses and carts. As the innkeeper had said, most of the haole living in Hawai'i were either high-class or wealthy, differing in dress and baggage. Willow was proud of her new husband, having become one of them, a landowner. Still, she wondered why he had chosen her as a bride, wondering if the Pusan Ajimae or the local matchmaker might have lied about her. To her, being seen as a liar was worse than not being loved.

After Taewan went to purchase the train tickets, Willow, Songhwa, and Sokbo were left standing in the sun. Travelers already filled the small waiting room, as well as the shade offered by buildings and trees. Willow and Songhwa were still wearing their long skirts, with the jackets, petticoats, even bloomers, and sweat was running down their backs. Their feet, too, in thick stockings and ornamental leather shoes, were feeling hot. At first, the local women with bare forearms or legs had looked indecent, but now Willow was envious of them. She longed to trade her leather shoes and stockings for straw sandals on bare feet.

Noticing that Songhwa's face was turning red as a ripe persimmon, Sokbo nervously took off his jacket and held it up as an awning. Songhwa pulled her underneath. Willow was surprised at how much cooler she felt as soon as she was in the shade. Sokbo grinned, reminding Willow of Jangsu's old father in Ojin Village, when he was wondering what to give a grandchild he hadn't seen in some time. Sokbo looked even older than that grandfather.

Taewan returned and distributed the train tickets. The long, rectangular card was in English, of course. She could only recognize the first letter, "A," of the English alphabet that she had learned from Esther in Kobe; the rest was a blur. In the middle, "MAY 13/18" was printed in slightly larger letters.

The conductor started punching the tickets. There were no empty seats on the train compartment for the four of them, so they would have to stand. The train was crowded, luggage and people, all of whom were Asian, crammed together. Willow worried that the bouquet she was hugging in her arms would get damaged. Some flowers were already drooping. Songhwa kept leaving hers behind, whenever she stopped for a moment, and Sokbo went looking for it each time, but finally she left it in the restroom just before boarding the train and by the time Sokbo noticed, the train had already left.

"Oh, what a shame, what can we do?" he asked.

Willow was a little sorry for him, but Songhwa didn't seem to mind.

The train rattled a lot. When it shook especially violently, Taewan grabbed Willow before she fell. Willow, with her nose suddenly pressed against Taewan's chest, immediately straightened herself and looked out the window to hide her red face. Whenever the train stopped at a station, people got off and fewer got on. At crossings, the people outside waved. At first Willow waved back, but quickly lowered her hand at a look from Taewan.

When there was an empty seat, Sokbo first made Songhwa sit down, then Willow. Reluctant to leave such an old man standing, and hesitating to leave her bridegroom, she only joined Songhwa when Taewan told her to go and sit down.

"Are you all right?" Willow asked.

Songhwa smiled faintly and nodded, looking much livelier than before, having improved considerably since leaving the bustling town. Willow had nothing to say to Songhwa, who turned to look out the window. Willow was already missing Hongju.

The train started running along beside the sea. At each station where the train stopped, towering chimneys and buildings could be seen.

"What are those chimneys?" Willow asked Sokbo, who was sitting in front of her. The age difference was so great that she didn't for a moment feel that he was a stranger from whom she had to keep a respectful distance.

"Those are sugar factories." Sokbo replied in a familiar tone, as if feeling the same. He even turned around and talked about things she had not asked. The railway line from Honolulu on the southeast of O'ahu to Kahuku in the northeast following the west coast had originally been made to carry sugarcane. The places where the trains carrying people stopped were mainly those with large farms and sugar mills. The factory-made sugar was shipped to the mainland or Europe. Willow saw Sokbo talking to Songhwa, who wasn't even listening, never taking his eyes off her. His face was full of warm smiles.

Willow looked back at Taewan, who was sitting a few seats farther back, reading a newspaper. After the wedding, the anxieties of the previous night disappeared, but disappointment at the way Taewan treated her began to replace them. Willow comforted herself with the knowledge that just as she had chosen Taewan, he had chosen her. If he didn't like her, he could have chosen some other woman. If he didn't like her, why would he pay one hundred and fifty dollars for her to come to Hawai'i, have a wedding, and take her home? It was several months since they had decided to get married, but yesterday was the first time they had actually met. It wasn't easy to be friendly and kind just because you were married, and was normal to be ill at ease and awkward.

Willow braced herself, her heart swinging between heartache and delight with each one of Taewan's actions, as if on a seesaw.

My heart feels so light. We are going to spend our whole lives together. Relax. Outside the windows, to the left, the sea stretched from the nearby coast and far away, and on the right a chain of mountains ran unbroken like a folding screen. The fields that continued up to the rugged hillsides were all sugarcane fields. People could be seen working in the fields, and piles of sugarcane rose everywhere, waiting to be taken to the factory.

Such extensive fields, with only one crop, made Willow ashamed to even give the name of "field" to the tiny fields in Ojin Village, with just a row of red peppers, a line of sesame, and a patch of cotton. How big was Taewan's land? How many workers might he have? Did the women take food out to the men working in the fields here too? With all of these questions and more on her mind, Willow fell asleep to the train's regular shaking.

"We're here," said Taewan, now standing beside her, touching her lightly on the shoulder. Willow opened her eyes then stood up, wiping away a dribble of spit. The bouquet she had laid on her lap fell to the floor, and she quickly picked it up. It had withered a lot, but still gave off a strong scent.

Kahuku was the final station. Outside, twilight was softening the landscape. Most of the people who got off the train seemed to be sugarcane workers, dressed in shabby clothes. Taewan took the lead, carrying Willow's suitcase. Willow held Songhwa's hand and followed, and Sokbo walked beside Songhwa. There were the same post office, grocery stores, and bars around Kahuku Station that she had seen at the other stations. In the yard of the sugar mill with its towering chimneys, sugarcane was piled up in mountains, and laborers were hard at work. More than the factory and the street lined with shops, what caught Willow's eye was the mountain that towered like Maebongsan Mountain back home. Sokbo told her that it was called the Ko'olau Range. Willow repeated the name silently to herself. The mountains she had seen from the speeding train had only been a distant landscape, but the Koʻolau mountain range towered in the distance.

Willow loved this boldly soaring mountain.

A man wearing a straw hat welcomed Taewan. He stood next to a carriage drawn by two horses. Willow's eyes widened. Two precious horses! The man looked at Sokbo and asked in amazement, "Mr. Park? Have you got married too?"

The man in the hat looked at Willow and Songhwa alternately, wondering what kind of woman could have married a man like Sokbo. Willow moved a little closer to Taewan.

"That's right. I'm going to be in debt now." Sokbo smiled broadly as he placed Songhwa's suitcase in the carriage.

The man in the straw hat placed a wooden footrest beneath the carriage. The women climbed on, and took their seats on the long wooden benches running along either side. After Sokbo got on, Taewan said something to the man in the hat before he too climbed onto the carriage.

Sunset was coloring the ground as the man pointed the horses down a red dirt road between the sugarcane fields, where the view on either side was nothing but sugarcane stalks. During the shaky journey, Willow began to feel sick, and hoped they would reach home before she vomited in front of her new husband.

After a while, houses appeared. They passed several clusters like a small village, and though the people varied in skin color and appearance, the small, shabby houses were the same. Very occasionally, a mansion like those she had seen in Kobe appeared, and Willow felt a thrill, despite her motion sickness, that it might be Taewan's home.

The carriage always continued on past the mansions.

When they finally came to a stop, Willow jumped out and ran to the edge of the cane field. It wasn't as far from Taewan as she wanted, but that was the best she could manage before she heaved and emptied her stomach. Songhwa, who had chased after her, patted firmly on Willow's back until everything was out.

The men stood together, smoking and watching from beside the carriage.

"Songhwa, am I looking okay?" asked Willow, feeling better. She adjusted her dress and sighed at how sickly she must seem to Taewan.

Songhwa only nodded.

When they returned to the carriage, Taewan stubbed out the cigarette and asked, "Are you all right?"

"Yes, I'm fine now. I'm sorry to be a bother. We can go on now." As she spoke, Willow prepared to get into the carriage with Songhwa, but Sokbo was taking Songhwa's suitcase down.

"We have to walk from here. It's not far," he said to Songhwa, who was looking confused. Sokbo pointed across the cane field.

"Aren't we living in the same village?" Willow asked in surprise.

"Our plantation is about three miles farther on from here," answered the carriage driver.

"What does that mean, three miles?"

Taewan explained that it meant about ten li in Korean distance. It wasn't that far, but it could not be considered the same village. Songhwa seemed to be on the verge of tears. Willow had not been as close to her as to Hongju, but still she felt terribly sad to be parting.

Fighting back tears, Willow embraced Songhwa and whispered, "Songhwa, I'll visit you when I have a chance. Your husband doesn't seem like a bad kind of person. Just imagine you're living with your grandfather."

Songhwa nodded, keeping her lips pursed, and Willow climbed back into the carriage. The bouquet had fallen to the floor again, and Willow picked up the flowers and sat down.

"Hey, Mr. Park," called the driver as they set off, "you're married now, so mend your ways, and don't do anything you shouldn't, mind."

Songhwa waved and burst into tears.

Willow contained herself and waved back, feeling as if she was all alone in the world. Willow hoped that Taewan, who got in after her, would sit beside her, but he sat opposite her as before. As they sat there facing each other, she felt more awkward than when they first met at immigration.

Willow looked back as the carriage moved ahead. Songhwa remained standing where Willow had left her until she was only a dot in the distance. Meanwhile, Taewan moved closer to the driver to talk about plantation work that didn't seem to be very urgent.

5

PLACE TO CALL HOME

The man in the straw hat brought the carriage to a halt in front of an open space where a crowd of people were gathered. There were several small houses nearby, and a large building like a community hall. At the sight of the carriage, the people cheered. Liquor and food were laid out on a long table in front of them, clearly a feast in honor of the newlyweds. Wide-eyed at the scene before her, Willow remained motionless. A whole pig was roasting over a fire. In Ojin Village, the only house where a pig might be killed for a feast was that of Hongju's wealthy family. Seeing Taewan standing beside the carriage, Willow stood up uncertainly.

"How come you don't help the bride down?" a woman called out.

Willow took the hand Taewan hesitantly extended and descended from the carriage.

Two children, who looked like sisters, hung garlands around Taewan's and Willow's necks. It was like the garlands she had seen for sale at the harbor. Everyone clapped and Willow bowed in their direction. She had thought the wedding was over after the ceremony at the church and lunch at the Chinese restaurant, and her heart warmed at this welcoming ceremony.

"Thank you," Taewan said to the girls. Willow stroked the head of the child who had given her the garland. Their mission duly accomplished, the sisters stayed close to the man with the straw hat, whom they addressed as "Aboji."

The man laid his arms round the children's shoulders and said to Taewan, "I'll take your wife's bag inside, go and greet your aboji."

Willow tensed at meeting her father-in-law for the first time.

"Follow me," said Taewan.

Willow smoothed down her dress and followed him through the people sitting on long, backless benches. They were darkly tanned, wrinkled men like Hongju's, Myongok's, and Makson's husbands. Here too, Taewan looked young by comparison.

Willow quickly realized that the old man sitting in an armchair at the top of the long table and smiling broadly was her father-in-law. It was clear at a glance that he was not in good health. Willow made her way onto a mat that people had prepared and greeted him, together with Taewan, with a deep bow. The old man held out a trembling arm, but it fell back onto his knees, unable to reach Willow. The man's awkward gesture was similar to that of an old woman back at home who had suffered a stroke. Willow, rising from her bow, approached the old man and took his hand.

"Welcome. You must have had a hard time on such a long journey." He spoke awkwardly, but with sincerity and affection.

Willow's eyes stung as her father-in-law's kind words wiped away all the sorrows accumulated in her body and heart since her arrival.

After elderly Mr. So, one man after another spoke a few words, all in their own regional dialects of Korea:

"Now I have seen your daughter-in-law, my wish is fulfilled."

"Sir, may you soon embrace a sturdy grandson."

"Taewan, starting tonight you must work hard to have a son quickly."

"Maybe he already started working hard last night, who knows?"

"Yeah. The groom and the bride are looking very pale."

Someone laughed loudly at that. Willow pretended to brush down her skirt to hide her blushing face.

The carriage driver with the straw hat formally greeted Willow. "I'm late in greeting you. My name is Hwang Jaesong." When he took off his hat, he looked older than she had thought.

Willow bowed in reply.

The feast began after Taewan and Willow were seated in the place of honor. On the table, Korean food such as kimchi, salted fish, pickled radish, and pancakes was laid out. The men started to carve the well-roasted pork, while the women were boiling noodles in a large pot in the yard. From the festive conversation, Willow learned that it was her father-in-law who had ordered this feast to be prepared.

As the sun disappeared behind the Ko'olau Range, an eyebrow-shaped crescent moon rose. Lamps were suspended here and there, and the children walked or ran around with the dogs. Hens pecked under the table until they were driven out by the people, while insects danced around the lamps. Willow's gaze sought out the women she would be spending the most time with in future. There were only five or six women present, and all seemed much older than herself. The youngest, who she learned was Jaesong's wife, was carrying a baby on her back.

Before she left home, her mother had said, "When you meet people older than yourself, say: 'I don't know, please, teach me.' Sometimes you are too much like me and I worry about your bluntness."

Jaesong's wife, who had introduced herself as Julie's mother, came up carrying a tray of noodles. When Willow rose and tried to take it, she refused. "Just you stay sitting quietly. Today's the only day you'll be served like this. My husband can take Tony for a while."

At that, Jaesong took the boy from his wife's back. The parents were from Korea, like their children, but the children's names were foreign. Willow was glad to hear friendly words from the wife of someone close to Taewan.

Julie's mother placed bowls of noodles garnished with strips of egg and pumpkin in front of Taewan and Willow, and said, "Enjoy the noodles. They say you have to eat noodles at a party in order to live a life long as a strand of noodles."

"Thank you. Where are you from, Ajimae?" asked Willow. "I'm from Kimhae."

"Our husbands are like brothers, so why call me Ajimae? Consider me your onni. I am from Masan," Julie's mother mock-scolded with affection.

Once noodles and meat were placed in front of everyone, Jaesong, holding Tony in one arm, offered a toast. At the urging of the hosts, Willow and Taewan filled each other's glasses with rice wine made especially for the party. Willow, who had never drunk any kind of alcohol, looked at her husband, who nodded, looking more relaxed than before. Her father-in-law also encouraged her to drink, with an awkward gesture. Willow respectfully turned her head to the side and took a sip, then began to cough as the liquid burned on the way down her throat. A flush of intoxication swept through her, on down until it tingled deep in her belly. Everyone urged her to drink up, to empty the first cup, so Willow drank the remaining wine. The warmth of the alcohol spread throughout her body, dispelling her worries. She smiled happily around the table.

In Korea, it would have been unthinkable for a newly

married bride to share drinks at the same table as the menfolk. At the sight of the other women sitting here and there freely consorting with the men, Willow realized that she had indeed come to a new world. Having arrived with an empty stomach after vomiting up her lunch, Willow made quick work of the noodles and pork. First, she tried to serve her father-in-law's food, but Julie's mother stopped her.

"From now on that will be your job day and night. I'll do it just for today."

Willow watched as Julie's mother tore the pork into fine pieces and placed them on a plate in front of her father-in-law.

"It's so nice to meet people from home."

"Thank you. I hope to learn a lot from you." Willow, who had been an only daughter, felt reassured at having a sister. When she lived in Korea, she thought that Kimhae, Masan, Jinju, and Pusan were all distant, different places, each with different dialects, but together in a foreign land, they all felt like a single family, just because they were from the same Kyongsang Province.

Willow asked about the names of the children.

"They're going to be living here, so they have to have American-style names. If we give them Korean names, no one will pronounce them properly. Jaesong was against it, but I won him over. When you have a child, you should give it an American name too."

As she imagined deciding with Taewan on the name of a child, Willow's face grew warm.

Willow also talked with the other women at the table, who were eager to share things that might help her transition to a new life in Hawai'i.

The villages where the sugarcane workers lived were called camps, the camps distinguished by numbers. Some of the camps housed people from a single country, while others were mixed. Camp Seven, where Willow would live, consisted entirely of Koreans. Willow wanted to ask if the field in front of them belonged to Taewan but thought it might be rude.

"What is life like in Korea nowadays?" someone asked Willow. Not knowing what to say, Willow looked around.

"I was told that the Oriental Development Company is grabbing all the farmers' land, is that true?"

Willow had heard the village men getting worked up about such things, sitting beneath the village tree, but it was not something that had interested the daughter of a poor family, with no land to be grabbed.

"I, I really don't . . ." Willow wiped her sweating palms on her skirt.

"Is it true that people in Korea have to use Japanese money now?"

"They say that even after the king was carried off to Japan and humiliated, the people of Korea stayed silent?"

"I don't really know anything about how the country is faring," said Willow in a faint voice. It was true. Whenever the children repeated things they had heard about the Japanese, their mother would scold them severely.

"It seems the townships are all under Japanese control?"

That was something she knew about for sure. "Yes, the head of our Jucheon township is a Mr. Nakamura." Willow was amazed. She wondered how they knew the news of faraway Korea better than she did living there.

"They want to take complete control of Korea," someone said excitedly.

"You did well to leave the world of the Japanese thugs."

Jaesong poured her another glass of wine.

Just as it was only after leaving Ojin Village that Willow

realized how small a place it was, she felt that it was only now, after she had left Korea, that she was learning *what* kind of place it was. Many raised their voices, saying that they could never live in Korea, and Willow suddenly worried that she had left her mother and younger brothers in a fiery pit and escaped alone.

Willow drank the wine and grew increasingly warm.

Once they were tipsy, people began to sing:

The wind and rain come blowing over towering Koʻolau
Mountains,
drying damp backs,
the waves of the ocean break on the beach
the sugarcane limply dances the exorcist's dance.
As twilight glows red, and in the clear sky the evening star rises,
I light a cigarette and stare at the northern sea.

The song expressed the feelings of immigrant workers. Three or four people got up and danced along to the melody. Food and joy were overflowing. It was a sight that could never be seen in Korea, suffering as it was from hunger and Japanese cruelty. Willow wished she could share this scene with her mother, and offer her brothers this delicious food.

After several calls for the new bridegroom to sing, Taewan reluctantly stood up. Willow, who was by now quite tipsy, watched in anticipation. Soon, a deep voice that seemed to rise from his very depths rang out. Under the moonlight, Taewan looked even more dignified and attractive. Willow gazed at him with all the pride she couldn't express when she was with the other brides. That man was her husband!

How lovely and beautiful our land, with its high mountains,
and sweet streams

Every mountain full of the spirit of independence, every stream
a thought of freedom!
Freedom! Independence! Holy ground! Oh, my love!
Great Korea peninsula! May your name never change for
eternity.
Though the ground may wear away, the sunlight grow old,
may the Peninsula of the East, the name of Korea our nation,
endure forever.

As the song progressed, the words "Korea," "freedom," and "independence" struck Willow's ears. Korea, freedom, independence. Startled, Willow looked around. She almost expected a Japanese policeman to come leaping out to arrest Taewan. None did, but Willow's heart continued to pound.

Her mother's voice was vivid in her memory, like a newly made embroidery.

"*For me, Korea is the enemy. Because our land is powerless, I lost my husband and my child. But Hawai'i is not Korea, there you'll have no country to protect. Once you're there, just forget us here, be happy with your husband and children, and enjoy life. That's my only wish.*"

But here was her husband, singing about the freedom and independence of Korea.

Willow gazed anxiously at the people. Everyone was carefree and enjoying themselves. This was American land, Hawai'i. They could cry out for Korea's independence to their hearts' content, and there was no Japanese policeman waiting to arrest them. That was why Hawai'i was called a paradise. It was also a place where women could sit boldly at the same table as their menfolk, eating and drinking together. Willow's heart grew calmer. Now, all that remained for her to do was to listen to her mother, to enjoy living with her husband, and to study. Across the road, in the field that must belong to Taewan, the sugarcane rose in row upon row, a sturdy fence protecting her happiness.

Willow woke with a sore throat, lying alone on the floor, under a mosquito net. She vaguely remembered that after she'd been offered three or four more glasses of wine by various people, the women had carried her up to the room and laid her down. What would her mother say if she knew that she had been drunk on the first day of her marriage? Sweat ran down her spine. From outside the window, she heard the voices of only two women, and realized that the party must be over.

Willow looked around the room through the mosquito net. Compared to what she had imagined, it was embarrassingly small and shabby, but since it was furnished with a chest and had a glass window, it was still far nicer than the house in Ojin Village. She also liked that there was a mat on the floor, not a bed. She noticed her wedding bouquet standing in a small jar on the chest. She recalled insisting on taking the flowers as she was being carried up. The garland that the children had given her was lying beside her. On the very first day, she had given such a poor impression.

From the bits and pieces of conversation coming from outside the window, it sounded like the women were tidying up. Willow quickly stood, intending to help them and make up for her irresponsibility. After rolling aside the mosquito net, Willow opened the door, but paused at the words "new bridegroom." Unthinkingly, she approached the window and listened. If people talked about the new bridegroom, they would surely also talk about the new bride? She was very curious to know what the women thought of her.

"The new bridegroom passed out. I wonder if he'll manage the first night properly."

It was the voice of the oldest among the camp's women, the Kaesong ajumoni. She was called that because she had lived in Kaesong before coming here. Willow blushed at their words, even though she was alone.

"I didn't expect Taewan to get married as meekly as this. He used to say he would never marry a picture bride."

Willow's heart sank.

"How could he refuse a marriage set up by his aboji after his stroke? The old man didn't even tell Jaesong because he was afraid the bridegroom might find out."

The marriage had been arranged without Taewan's knowledge? Willow's legs gave.

"So when did he find out?" Dusun's mother asked. She was the next oldest after the Kaesong ajumoni.

"Just three days before the bride arrived. He lost his temper, saying he wouldn't do it, then begged the old man in tears. But he said his only wish was to see grandchildren before he died. Julie's father calmed him down, and told him to think how Mr. So felt, having to act as matchmaker."

Willow sat on the floor. In Korea, it was normal to marry as the parents decided. Hongju, who was headstrong and assertive, had married her father's choice without ever once seeing the face of her bridegroom beforehand. In Korea, people often did not know they were being married until three days before. But this meant that while Willow was growing accustomed to thinking of him as her husband, he didn't even know that she existed. If Taewan was indifferent and curt toward her, it wasn't because he had only just met her, or because of his personality, it was because he was being forced into it, like an ox dragged along by a ring in its nose.

Willow's emotions were so confused, she didn't know what to feel.

"He chose a really good bride." The Kaesong ajumoni's words did not sound like a compliment.

"He even paid a premium to the matchmaker, and she found what was specially requested." Julie's mother sounded proud, but hearing that she had been chosen after a premium had been paid for her, Willow felt as though she had been haggled over.

"But still, does she fall that much short of Dari?" That was the voice of the woman from Wonsan, who was the same age as Dusun's mother.

Who was Dari? All Willow's attention focused on the next conversation.

"Who could follow her? When I think of how Taewan was like a living corpse after losing her, it's amazing that he's as fine as he is now."

Willow remained sitting on the floor, blankly listening to them.

"Who knows what changes time might bring?"

"I don't know. It's not so easy to forget your first love. Those two were as pretty as a picture."

"It's all over now." The Kaesong ajumoni warned them, "Don't breathe a word of this in front of the new bride."

Willow's ears seemed to be full of buzzing bees. First love, pretty as a picture, Taewan like a living corpse after losing the one he loved . . . It was all like something from one of Hongju's novels. It was like a knife plunged into her heart. It was not because he was forced to marry her that Taewan treated her as a stranger, but because his heart was already full of someone else. That was so much worse. Willow had left her family and traveled across the ocean to live with such a person.

Willow looked down at the ring on her ring finger. When

the ring didn't fit, Taewan had given up so easily. She had forced the ring on herself, and the place where her skin had peeled was still clear. She thought the ring was forever but now she saw it as a sign of a forced marriage. How foolish she must seem in Taewan's eyes. She longed to go back to that time and place and throw the ring down in front of Taewan. Willow tried to remove the ring, but the bulging knuckle held it like a great mountain. Had that other woman's hand been pretty? Willow began to beat at her breast as if trying to crush the thoughts as they came to her mind.

Willow suddenly realized why she had been so attached to the bouquet and had brought it all this way. It was to remind herself that she was Taewan's bride, an instinct she must have had on sensing Taewan's feelings. The bouquet was caught in a jar like Willow, like their marriage, wounded and withering. How was she to live now? Who should she look up to, hold on to in life? A feeling of despair swept over her. On the first day of her marriage, the newly wed Willow sat there as if she was all alone in the world.

At that moment, the door opened and Taewan staggered in.

Once the rooster in hardworking Jangsu's house heralded dawn, all the Ojin Village neighbors' roosters crowed one after another. Willow had to get up before the last rooster crowed, but Willow felt heavy and couldn't move. Today, she wanted her mother to go out to the kitchen first.

Sleepiness fled.

This was not Ojin, but Kahuku, Hawai'i. It was the dawn following her first night with Taewan. Gently opening her eyes, Willow could see the wooden walls and the window, which was propped open by a branch. Through the window she glimpsed the morning star, the same star she saw each morning in Ojin. But Willow was not the same. She had been transformed into a man's spouse.

She heard Taewan breathing behind her back.

Willow carefully turned over. Fortunately, it wasn't a bed, so she couldn't fall out. Taewan was lying at some distance from her, wrapped in the mosquito net instead of bedding, facing the opposite wall. She had a feeling he was regretting the first night spent with her, if not their marriage. She noticed a scar on his shoulder blade, like an earthworm crawling on his sloping shoulders as they rose and fell with each inhale and exhale.

The rooster crowed again, announcing that the new day had dawned. Willow climbed out of bed. As the Kaesong ajumoni had said, it was all over now. And like Julie's mother said, nobody is strong enough to overcome time. Willow, who had lost her father and older brother, knew that. She would never be able to replace Taewan's first love, but someday, it would become a faint mark like the scar on his shoulder.

Folding up the pink jacket and skirt that lay like a cast-off skin on the floor, Willow put them in her bag, took out her cotton clothes, and dressed. The party was over and her new life had begun.

I am the mistress of this plantation. I'm the only one who can bring together my father-in-law, suffering after a stroke, and my husband still cherishing his first love, and fill the yard with laughter.

Just as Willow was retying her bun, as her mother used to do each day at dawn, she was startled by a shrill sound and dropped her hairpin. It was the 4:30 A.M. wake-up siren operated by Julie's mother. Fieldwork on the sugarcane began at 6:00 A.M. and ended at 4:30 P.M., every day.

Willow prepared her first meal for old Mr. So after checking on him, as he was already up. In addition to breakfast, she packed a lunchbox for Taewan to take with him to the plantation. The kitchen was unfamiliar, but fortunately there was food left over from the party, so she didn't have to worry about side dishes.

After she served Taewan the breakfast she had prepared for the first time, he said:

"Take good care of Aboji. That's all I ask." He seemed to be drawing a line, indicating that he would only consider her as the daughter-in-law of the family.

Willow said nothing, but her heart felt bitter and hurt.

Taewan gave her five dollars. "This is housekeeping money for the week. Once you've gotten used to living here, I'll give it to you once a month. Ask the other women to explain things to you."

Willow had grown up worrying about where the next meal would come from, so the allowance softened the heart of his words, somewhat.

Finishing breakfast in less than ten minutes, Taewan donned his work clothes and left the house. Willow followed him outside to the gate, to see him off, where he turned back and said, "Please feed Aboji well."

"Yes, don't worry, come back safely," Willow said curtly.

Returning to the house, she went to her father-in-law's room and asked, "Work only begins at six o'clock, why is Taewan off so early? Is the field far?"

He answered that it took more than thirty minutes to reach the plantation, and that Taewan had to first check on the situation and tasks of the workers. Back home, wealthy Mr. An had a farmhand who was in charge of the work, but it seemed that Taewan did everything himself, which Willow respected.

There was a shop selling groceries and daily necessities at the Japanese camp about five li from Camp Seven. Also, once every few days, a Chinese couple came and sold food and goods loaded on their cart. For the first week Willow was afraid to spend the money that Taewan had given her. The weekly amount was the same that Willow received for two weeks of shoulder-wrenching, backbreaking laundry work back home. She didn't know the prices, and worried that she would be considered wasteful if she spent it all, so she made side dishes using only vegetables grown in the garden and eggs from their chickens. In fact, before she was married, Willow had barely seen food being prepared, let alone eaten it, so there were not many dishes she knew how to make. Though her cooking didn't seem to appeal to Taewan or her father-in-law, her husband ate and wore whatever Willow gave him, without asking or complaining.

It wasn't until Julie's mother scolded her that Willow first went shopping. "Look, dear, the old man may be one thing, but if you keep giving nothing but grass to your husband who works hard in the fields every day, what do you think will happen? Do you want to see your husband collapse?"

She had no sooner put stir-fry pork on the dinner table than Taewan emptied his rice bowl and asked for more. Her father-in-law also ate a couple more spoonfuls than usual. Willow asked Julie's mother what kind of food her family liked and learned new recipes whenever she had free time. When Taewan said it was something he liked, she bought pork bones and boiled them all day long.

The camp had a communal canteen and a communal laundry. Most of the unmarried workers lived in dormitories, and paid the camp's wives to take care of their meals and laundry. The cooking was done by the Kaesong ajumoni and James's mother, the laundry was taken care of by Dusun's mother, and the Wonsan ajume, together with Julie's mother. The Wonsan ajume left the camp with her husband only a few days after Willow's arrival, complaining that the workers kept bothering her. Willow offered to take her place.

When Willow got married, she had been expecting that a school would be nearby and welcoming with open doors. That proved to be as much a vain expectation as believing in the story of clothes and shoes hanging from trees. With no local schools, children were separated from their parents at a young age and went to study at the Honolulu Boarding School. Although she heard that a class teaching the Hangul alphabet was held every Sunday at the Kahuku Korean Church, it was intended for children. When the camp's wives asked her why she had come so far to get married, she couldn't admit to all the lies she had fallen for. With none of her picture-bride friends nearby, there was no one to complain to about how different things were from what the matchmaker had claimed. Unable to have an enjoyable life with her husband, and unable to attend school, she found that her only remaining desire was to serve her husband's family well.

"It's true we need help, but can you really do this kind of hard work?" said Dusun's mother, tapping her shoulder with a fist. To Willow it sounded as though she was wondering if the wife of the plantation's owner could do such work.

"I can do it. Once you teach me, I'll be fine," said Willow, all the more ingratiatingly because she dreaded anyone saying that the new bride was putting on airs as the owner of the plantation.

"You're right. While you don't have a baby, you should try to earn at least a few pennies. Working in the laundry might be hard for you but it's better timewise. In the canteen you have to prepare breakfast and evening meals as well as packing lunchboxes, whereas the laundry can be washed and hung out in the morning then taken down and folded before you prepare the evening meal. It brings in more than thirty dollars a month, we round that off and share it equally, ten dollars each per month. No one gets any more or any less."

The men worked for ten hours each day on the plantation for a dollar and twenty cents a day, six days a week, and the monthly salary was about thirty dollars. It was said to have increased significantly compared to the early days of immigration. It was only now that Willow realized what a large sum of money the one hundred and fifty that her father-in-law had sent represented.

Not wanting to ask her father-in-law to help her family, after he had already spent a lot of money to bring her to Hawai'i, and too proud to ask Taewan, Willow decided to earn her own money to send her family. Neither her father-in-law nor Taewan tried to stop her when she told them she would work in the laundry. The only idle people in the camp were babies like Tony. Julie's and James's younger siblings either took care of younger children or did some chores.

Doing the laundry was hard work. In particular, the dungarees thick with red mud were stiff and heavy when wet. For the initial washing they had to be rubbed with a brush, then beaten with a bat for a long while. After soaping, rubbing, and rinsing several times, her arms trembled and her back ached terribly. Sewing back in Ojin Village had not been so painful, after all. On the first night after working in the laundry, Willow was groaning with pain. The sound woke Taewan, who found some ointment for her to apply and told her not to do it if it was too difficult.

At his gruff tone, she bit her tongue and swallowed her groans.

Thankfully, doing the laundry wasn't all hard work. The

Kaesong ajumoni and James's mother would sometimes bring snacks. Willow enjoyed taking a break and listening to their stories. They had come to Hawai'i much earlier, and she listened attentively to their experiences. The women also ate lunch together, but because of her father-in-law, Willow would return home alone, though the Kaesong ajumoni often gave her side dishes to take with her.

One day, as she wielded the bat, bright red liquid began to spill over the working clothes. Realizing that her nose was bleeding, Willow dropped the bat and tilted her head back. Clouds just like the ones she used to see as she sat on the wooden-floored porch back home billowed across the sky. The pungent blood flowed down her throat.

"Is your nose bleeding? Oh dear, you're working too hard. Sit down here and rest a bit." Julie's mother helped Willow sit down close beside her. "It's all right now. Don't worry."

Dusun's mother handed her a wad of cotton wool.

Willow blocked her nose with cotton wool and deliberately smiled brightly as she spoke.

"It'll get better, doing laundry is nothing compared to working in the sorghum field."

"She's right, she's right there. When I was working in the sorghum field, I can't tell you how many people passed out," said Julie's mother.

Dusun's mother recalled her memories of working in the field. "I gave birth to my youngest, Dusun, after arriving here and I had no one to look after him, and so I took him with me to the field. I put him in a basket, laid it in the shade, and started work. By the time lunch came, my breasts were swollen and the front of my dress was all wet. Even when he was sick, I was too afraid of the foreman's whip to take care of him. When I heard him crying, I would cry too, but keep on working. Back in Korea we were poor as poor could be, but we only experienced such a hard life after coming here."

Willow looked at Dusun's mother's hands, swollen by the soapy water. The husband who had come to Hawaiʻi with her passed away five years before, and she had raised their six children after that. Her greatest pride was her youngest son, Dusun, who was attending middle school, while living at the home of her eldest daughter in Honolulu. Dusun's mother, who said she ached all over, often repeated that she had to keep working until he graduated from college. Suffering so without a husband, she reminded Willow of her own mother back at home.

"When I first arrived," Julie's mother said, "we had nowhere to live and stayed with some Spanish people. Julie's father couldn't afford a house for us when we got married. I used to cry every night until we moved to the Camp Seven. You were lucky to meet the husband you did. There's no one to equal him. He's good at running the plantation, and the owner says he'll renew the contract, too."

"The owner? What owner?" Willow asked, looking confused.

"The owner of the plantation, of course, who else?"

"You mean someone else owns the plantation? The Pusan Ajimae said that Taewan was a landowner."

"What?" Julie's mother jumped to her feet. "Who's the Pusan Ajimae? The matchmaker was told not to add or omit anything. Who on earth told you such a pack of lies?"

Willow said nothing more, not wanting to insult the Pusan Ajimae, who was almost part of her family, but she felt as if all the strength was draining out of her body.

"Then is Taewan *just* an employee?"

When Taewan came home soaked in red mud and sweat, looking shabbier than Hongju's family's farmhand, the only reason Willow did not feel disappointed was because she thought he was the landowner.

"He's more like a tenant," Julie's mother explained. "Julie's aboji and Taewan run the plantation according to a contract they signed directly with the owner. They receive money according to how much they harvest, pay the workers' salaries, deduct expenses and share the rest between the two of them. There is no interference from the owner, and they earn more than if they were mere employees."

It was difficult for Willow to free herself of her disappointment.

Seeing Willow stay silent, Julie's mother guessed what she was feeling and added, "I think maybe the matchmaker was told that the bridegroom was farming twenty acres and misunderstood that to mean he owned that much."

"How many majigi is that?" Willow asked. In Ojin Village, one majigi was two hundred pyong for a paddy field, and three hundred pyong for dry fields, eight hundred or twelve hundred square yards.

"Measured as a dry field it would come to about eighty majigi."

At that Willow's mouth gaped open. Back at home, even the richest family, Hongju's, had only thirty majigi in total, paddy and dry fields combined. Most independent farmers had just three or four majigi. If he and Jaesong were the only two farming the land, divided in half, that meant forty majigi each. Even for tenant farmers, that was huge.

"You shouldn't think of it as simply working someone else's land. Employees have to do as they're told, but it's not the same for your Taewan and Julie's aboji. There's nothing more difficult in life than being in charge of people. There are all kinds of workers here. There are those who get drunk and pass out at the least chance, some draw advance pay, gamble it away, and run off, and some get injured. There are a lot of people who are cowed by the haole foremen, while they despise and ignore Taewan or Julie's aboji. Out in the fields, it's Taewan and Julie's aboji who work hardest of all. Now that you're his wife, you have to take good care of Taewan. He depends on you."

Julie's mother spoke quietly. The last words weighed heavily on Willow's heart. She longed to ask how to open Taewan's heart to her. Ever since that first day, saying that she only needed to take good care of his father, nothing had changed. Nothing could be easier than that request. Her mother had said before she left for Hawai'i: "Obey your widowed father-in-law. If he tells you to climb up a wall, climb it. That's how demanding a widowed father-in-law can be. Once you're married, you must treat him as if he's your aboji come back from the dead. There's no man who will mistreat a wife who takes good care of his parents."

Even without her mother's or Taewan's words, from the moment she first saw him Willow felt a father's affection in her father-in-law, while he cherished Willow as if she were the daughter he had left behind in Korea. Despite being loved by her old Mr. So, Willow had an empty space in her heart, but it was difficult for her to talk to the other wives in the camp about her marital affairs. Willow was envious of Julie's mother and James's mother, who were of the same age and could speak freely to one another. The two were very close despite frequently quarreling. It might not be as bad as it had been for Julie's mother, living with people who spoke a completely different language, but Willow felt similarly suffocated and lonely being surrounded by people she couldn't talk to about the things that mattered most.

Willow missed Hongju, a friend she could unburden herself upon, while sitting in her room in Ojin Village. She longed to talk honestly with Hongju, who had more experience, about her relationship with her husband, and ask for advice on what to do. She was also curious as to how Hongju was getting along with the husband she so disliked. It was obvious that Hongju's husband would not have the house and the car shown in the picture. Her friend was sure to be suffering more than Willow, certainly not less. As for Songhwa, who was living with a bridegroom only one year younger than old Mr. So, Willow was more worried than curious.

"Julie's aboji told me that your friend married old Mr. Sokbo, is that true?" Julie's mother had asked soon after she started work at the washhouse.

"That's right. Do you know him?"

"Sure, I know him. Why, that worm used to live here until he got kicked out." Julie's mother explained that he was kicked out for gambling when out of funds, on account of his laziness, for drinking, and even for being violent. That explained how Taewan and Jaesong had spoken to him as they parted. Even though she was worried, Willow was unable to visit Songhwa. Although she lived not far away, Willow had to go to the laundry on weekdays, and on Sundays Taewan was at home, making it difficult to find time. Maybe it wasn't so much a matter of time, as of inclination. Willow was fully preoccupied with her own life.

6

THOSE WHO CAME BEFORE

More than three months after arriving in Hawai'i, Willow was picking lettuce in the garden for supper. Also growing in the garden were Chinese cabbages, red peppers, eggplants, and green onions, among other vegetables she was less familiar with. It always amazed her to see the seasonal vegetables that she had eaten in Korea grow here throughout the year. Standing in the warm sunlight, Willow gazed up at the sky. Clouds draped over the ridges of the Ko'olau Mountains. If there was a shower, it would feel cooler, but the clouds showed no sign of ever leaving the mountain ridge. After living here for a while, she now knew why the men working on the plantation looked so old and worn for their age. It was because of the sun constantly blazing down on the sugarcane field.

"Child, come into the shade." Old Mr. So spoke as he sat in his chair under the shade of a papaya tree. Willow pulled up a few more green onions, put them in the basket, and then went across to the old man, feeling cooler at once. When she started working at the laundry, it had taken all her courage to ask the old man: "I want to send the money I earn by doing the laundry to my family. Would that be all right?"

Her father-in-law gave his approval, saying that although she was married she was still her mother's child. Upon receiving her first salary, she wanted to prepare a special meal for him using her first earnings. She told her reluctant father-in-law that it was her treat, and grilled pork so that it would suit Taewan, who liked spicy food. She took pride in watching her husband sweat as he ate hungrily. After that, each time that Willow got paid, she would take a little of the money and go shopping. It wasn't that anyone told her to or noticed it, but it made her happy.

Willow grew accustomed to life at Camp Seven, adapting to the weather, and to the back-aching work of doing the laundry. However, she did not get used to her distance from her husband. Taewan was still the same. If he stopped using honorifics and switched to the familiar style of speech, it was because people kept asking him if he was being old-fashioned, not because they were closer. When they first met at the Immigration Service, it seemed that she was getting closer to him at a simple touch of the collar, but now she felt the deep gulf between them, regardless of whether they shared their bodies, or spoke familiarly.

So far as she could recall, her father and mother were not an affectionate couple. Rather, they treated each other like visitors, following the Confucian rule of maintaining a strict separation of the sexes. The other couples that Willow saw growing up were not much different. Even so, Willow longed for herself and Taewan to be a married couple who exchanged tender looks and expressed loving feelings.

What on earth do I like about Taewan? Why do I like a man who doesn't make it possible for me to study, or help my family, who's not a landowner, and who has another woman in his heart?

Willow kept asking herself this, but it was difficult to find any clear reason. In Korea, she had already liked the face in the photo. Arriving in Hawai'i, and finding he was not different from the photo, she liked him more still.

She seemed to hear Hongju's voice saying, *You should kick and sulk*. Willow swore that she would not beg for Taewan's heart, and tried to overcome her pride, but it did not last long. She wanted to know who Dari was, how they had met, and how they had parted. But she couldn't ask Taewan. If ever that name were to be uttered, she reckoned, the distance between them would only grow further. She didn't think she could ask old Mr. So, either. Instead, she asked him about the family's past.

He might have been a typical old man, but he never seemed as energetic as when he was talking about the past. Once he was immersed in his stories, he was no longer a man whose speech and movement were restricted by a stroke, waiting for the day he would die, but rather the courageous man who had embarked on a ship and emigrated, leading his family toward a new land with hopes of a better future.

In mid-March 1905, So Gichun boarded a steamship heading for Hawai'i, no longer so young at the age of forty-six. He was accompanied by his wife and two sons. The couple had had eight children, but only fourteen-year-old Taewan and twelve-year-old Taesok remained. Three had died in childhood of contagious diseases, and they hadn't heard from their three daughters in some time, who were grown up and married in various places.

Born in Yonggang, Pyongan-do Province, So Gichun had worked as a farmhand or as a tenant farmer all his life. The country's name had changed several times, but the hard, tiring life of the ordinary people did not change. Every year, Gichun worked until his palms were as hard as the soles of his feet, but instead of feeding his family properly, he had to use the rice to make payments on the loans he'd taken to work the land, and even then, the high interest only increased his debt. When even the land he was tenant-farming was confiscated, Gichun went to Jemulpo Harbor at Incheon in search of a job. There, he heard that people were being recruited to go to Hawai'i. It was like a lifeline descending from the sky when all was hopeless.

According to the recruitment advertisement, the Hawaiian archipelago, a territory of the United States, had mild weather year-round, and he would be paid seventeen dollars, the equivalent of seventy Korea won, per week if he worked ten hours a day six days a week. Seventy won was a tremendous amount of money for Gichun, who had never earned even one hundredth of that. It was a pity that it wasn't rice farming, and he wondered if sugarcane farming was more difficult than rice farming. Also, it said that housing would be paid for by the plantation owners, as well as firewood, and medical expenses in case of sickness. With these terms, Gichun reckoned he would soon be rich.

It was beyond his wildest dreams, even in his next life. Best of all, it said there was a school on each island, where English was taught for free. That meant that his children could be educated.

"How could I not be captivated by the idea of both earning a living and sending my children to school. Even if I went on living as an illiterate person all my life, my children would be able to live in a different world, so I decided to leave."

The old man spoke hesitantly but energetically and his eyes were shining. Willow could understand her father-in-law's feelings. Now that Willow's hopes for studying had disappeared, she consoled herself with dreams of the future of the child who was not yet born. *When I have children, I'll have them learn everything that I couldn't.* She had decided that even if it was a daughter, she would send her to college.

After leaving Jemulpo, the *Mongolia* arrived in Honolulu after a stop at Kobe, Japan. More than two hundred migrants from Korea were on board. The majority of them were single, no matter whether they were young or older, and there were only a few cases where the whole family came together. Very rarely, a wife brought children without a husband.

The previous wave of immigrants came out to the pier waving American flags and Taegukgi, their own national flag. The new arrivals were quarantined for a time by the Immigration Service on a small island in front of the port, unlike when Willow came. Gichun's family was assigned to the 'Ewa Plantation, not far from Honolulu. Single workers had to live in a dormitory, but any with a family were given a small house with a yard. Gichun's family received a shabby wooden house with one room and a kitchen. It was not as good as they had hoped, but since they had never lived anywhere better, they were satisfied. Willow understood how they felt. She had been disappointed about much of what the matchmaker had promised, but life in Hawai'i was still better than her life would have been in Korea.

"At first, all the family worked on the plantation. There was no help for it because we didn't know how things worked here. We worked without rest from six A.M. until four thirty P.M. Lunch was just thirty minutes, barely enough to finish a lunchbox. Strong youths were paid sixty-five cents a day, while women and children received fifty cents. I was a farmer by birth, so I could manage to endure it more or less, but it was hard for the educated people from the city."

The sugarcane, taller than a man, had strong, sharp leaves that often slashed their hands and faces and even cut through thick clothes. Hands developed blisters, while countless workers collapsed in the scorching sun. The foremen, called "lunas" by the Hawaiians, meaning "high, above," were merciless. As the name suggested, they watched the workers from horseback and if they saw any slack they galloped over wielding their whips, irrespective of whether it was a woman or a child.

"They treated the workers worse than animals. Treated so poorly after coming to a foreign land, we were furious and sorrowful, but what could we do? Once, Taewan couldn't stand it and stood up for himself, for which he was given a severe whipping. He suffered a lot when the wounds got infected. He probably still has the scar."

Sugarcane fieldwork was divided into weeding, cutting, carrying, and irrigation, with the women mainly engaged in weeding and sometimes carrying. Irrigation was the hardest, since it meant being waist-deep in cold water for long periods, but the pay was correspondingly higher. Gichun did that until he left 'Ewa Plantation. The old man said that it was the reason for his stroke.

"I went to the plantation church every Sunday for worship, and gradually began to see the light. The children attended the church school, where they learned to write."

Her mother-in-law soon began to cook for the unmarried men, together with two other married women who had come on the same boat. She had originally been a servant in the household where Gichun was a farmhand. She was called Onyeon, which simply meant "young girl," without any family name or proper name. When she filled out the passport paperwork to come to Hawai'i, that became her official name, and as she was married, they followed the American custom and she took her husband's surname, becoming Onyeon So.

Willow tried to recall the name of her mother, Mrs. Yun, but she couldn't. She had never heard it, and had never even wondered whether her mother had a name or not. Even though her mother was a yangban, she was always addressed as Mrs. Yun, or as Namsil's wife. At least Willow had a name that had been given to her, even if she didn't like it. Afraid that she might burst into tears at the thought of her mother, Willow changed the subject.

"The woman at the Haesong Inn said that she came on the same boat?"

"That's right. The Haesong innkeeper and Dari's omma did the cooking."

Willow started at the name. She very much wanted to know about Dari, but she hadn't expected the name to come up so quickly. At the same time, she very much did not want to know.

"And who was Dari's omma?" asked Willow with a trembling voice.

Old Mr. So was slow to reply. For once, it seemed not to be due to the stroke, but because he was reluctant to speak. Willow waited nervously for her father-in-law to speak.

"She came on the same boat as us, a young married woman with a daughter, and we became close from the time we were on the boat." The old man grasped his stick and stood up. "I haven't talked so much for a long time, I'm feeling tired. I need to go inside and rest."

This new information made Dari even more real in her thoughts. Even when she was with Taewan, Willow found herself wondering how he had treated Dari, what he had said to her. All those speculations and imaginings, to say nothing of the moon, Dari's namesake, that rose every night, troubled Willow. She had the impression that so long as the moon rose each day over the sea, shone on the sugarcane plantations, then set behind the Koʻolau Mountains, her husband would never be able to forget his first love.

It was a few days before old Mr. So continued his story.

In September, the year following their arrival in Hawaiʻi, a Korean boarding school had opened in Honolulu. The school was established by the Methodist Foundation at the request of the migrants, for which the workers had raised two thousand dollars. People with children, like Gichun, and even those without all donated with one accord, to educate their young.

"Two thousand dollars?" Willow asked, overwhelmed at the thought of so much money.

"People thought that the reason why our country was so powerless was because the people were uneducated and therefore ignorant. So the idea that the children could study here, even other people's children, gave the community a feeling of strength. In those days, there were not many children around, and in a way, they belonged to everyone."

Taewan entered the school at the age of fifteen. The Korea American School and Korea Methodist Church were located at the Korean Station. The school taught regular classes in English in the mornings, and Korean history and the Bible in Korean in the afternoons. As soon as he began to talk about the school, the elderly man's pronunciation grew awkward.

How old was Dari then? Willow wondered. *When did the two become so close? Was it before or after they began going to school? Or did it begin on the ship?* Such thoughts raked at Willow's heart like a plowshare.

When he said that Taewan's younger brother died in an accident, Willow returned to the present. She remembered vividly how her mother had taken to bed after her own brother had died. Willow held her father-in-law's rough, age-spotted, trembling hands. How sad Taewan must also have been.

Did Dari comfort him?

After a year or two, many of the workers left the sugarcane farms in search of other jobs, but Gichun continued, because although it was hard, he was accustomed to it, and Onyeon was also earning well.

Starting in 1910, the United States approved picture marriages for the Korean workers, since so many men were unable to get married. He explained that almost all the women were wives who had come with their families or children, with very few single women of marrying age. Very occasionally, one might marry a woman of another nationality, but most of the men were reluctant to marry a foreign bride, and so had no choice but to grow old in a harsh, lonely life. The government finally allowed picture weddings in the hope of curbing the alcohol and gambling addictions of many single workers. The already elderly men gave the matchmakers old pictures in which they looked younger, or pictures taken beside someone else's car, in order to attract a bride.

Willow thought of Jo Doksam.

"That was not all. Ignorant men who couldn't read a word lied about their jobs, claiming to be bank clerks, businessmen, or to work for the local Korean association. Even the newspapers reported on the problem. Julie's mother cried for days after she got married."

Willow had already heard about that from Julie's mother.

"I was nineteen years old, and my husband was thirty-five. He said he was an office worker for some kind of company when in fact he was a sunburned farmworker without so much as a single farmhand. I nearly died, it was so hard living with an affectionless husband, squeezed in among a group of foreigners. Even after we joined Camp Seven, I disliked my husband, and the work was so hard that I cried every day, until your mother-in-law hired me to look after the daughters."

Despite having such a husband, Julie's mother had four children and was living well. Willow smiled wistfully, thinking that such times would also come for herself and Taewan.

The old man shook a trembling hand, misunderstanding Willow's smile. "There was no cheating when it came to Taewan. The picture was taken when he entered the academy over the mountains, it wasn't an old one."

Willow changed the subject. "Yes, I know. But what kind of academy was that, over the mountain?"

"It was the military academy of the Greater Korea National Military Corps, established by Yongman Park. He was convinced that we needed military might if we were to regain the country stolen from us by the Japanese bandits."

"What?" Willow asked, looking shocked. "Taewan went to a military academy? Are we fighting the Japanese here?"

"The Japanese here are poor, weak workers like ourselves. Master Yun Chiho also told me when I first went to 'Ewa Plantation that I should get along well with the Japanese people. What the cadets at the academy over the mountain wanted was to train to fight abroad."

The old man's words only increased Willow's anxiety, and she forgot that he was talking about things that had happened several years back.

"They were recruiting cadets, and a teacher at the Korean boarding school recommended Taewan. Even Chairman Park said he liked Taewan very much." The face of the old man was full of pride.

Gichun gave almost all the money he had saved to his son, who entered the academy at the age of twenty-three. The cadets lived on a plantation, growing pineapples during the day, and receiving military training in the evenings.

"Because it was beyond Kahalu'u, it was called 'the academy over the mountain.' We called the cadets 'the children over the mountain.' A parade and the opening ceremony of the academy was to be held on August thirtieth, but the families and guests had gone there the day before. Since it lay some fifty li from Honolulu, Chairman Park chartered a dozen trucks and buses. Several hundred people went, setting off from the Assembly Hall of the National Association. People on the streets watched open-eyed, wondering what was happening. It was so spectacular to see the long line of vehicles that it felt as though independence was already in sight.

"After winding our way around the mountain, dozens of cadets were lined up applauding and shouting to welcome us as we arrived at the academy, to say nothing of the rolling of drums. I only had eyes for Taewan. Of course, I was thinking of his omoni, who had suffered and died without seeing her son in uniform."

The old man wept, overcome from the memories. Her mother-in-law passed away two years before Taewan entered the military academy. Willow had not yet been to visit her grave, which lay near 'Ewa Plantation. She had mentioned it once, but Taewan had merely said, "Later," and that was the end of it.

Old Mr. So gathered himself and went on speaking.

"That evening, we sang the national anthem at the inauguration ceremony with lumps in our throats. The next day, the academy opening ceremony was even more moving."

The cadets marched across the training ground carrying wooden rifles and sang the "National Military Song" written by Yongman Park loudly enough to make Kahalu'u ring.

They took the oath with firm resolve: "The cadets of the Greater Korea National Corps will receive military training with all their might until the people of Korea achieve independence. We vow before God that we will unite and endure all personal sacrifices."

"Dr. Syngman Rhee also gave a speech. Chairman Park had invited Dr. Rhee, who had originally been stationed on the American mainland. I am truly saddened that the way people who were trying to work in unity at the beginning are now divided and fighting with each other."

The old man sighed.

Willow could guess without asking whose side Taewan was on, having attended the military academy established by Yongman Park. He went on, telling her that the song sung by Taewan on their wedding night was the "Korea National Anthem" written by Yongman Park, which he had learned at the National Military Academy. Taewan had not made a long speech before the workers, but he was different from when he was drinking with Jaesong. There were those who said that the National Military Corps had been disbanded because Syngman Rhee and his followers had divided Korea society, and that military training should begin again. Willow was inclined to support Syngman Rhee's claim that independence should be achieved through education and diplomacy rather than by armed struggle in which lives could be lost. To be even more honest, she liked Jaesong's opinion best of all.

"Damn it all, what has Korea ever done for us?" said her father-in-law. "Nation comes after self and family. Just look at Yongman Park, Syngman Rhee, our so-called leaders. Far from setting a good example to their compatriots, all they do is slander and argue with one another. I hate both of them, I'd rather earn money and send my children to school so that they can succeed."

There were many reasons why the National Corps was dissolved. The whole world was at war, one side against another, and Japan, an ally of the United States, brought pressure to bear on the U.S. to put a halt to Korea's military exercises in Hawai'i. To make matters worse, the exports from the pineapple farms had been greatly reduced due to the recession and poor harvests, making the funds needed to maintain the corps tight. One of the reasons for the dissolution was that, as Tae-wan claimed, the migrants from Korea were divided, decreasing the support and sponsorship for the National Corps.

Taewan, more passionate than any other cadet, stayed with the academy until the bitter end. It was around that time that Mr. So suffered a stroke, so that Taewan remained in Kahuku to care for his father. Taewan reached an agreement with the owner of the plantation, who had signed a contract with the academy, allowing him to continue farming the land. Then he went to see Jaesong in Honolulu, where he was running a grocery store, and suggested that they work together. Many of the migrants who left the farms went into business without skills or capital, and consequently failed. Jaesong, who had run out of money, decided to close the store and join Taewan.

"The workers need people to cook and do their laundry, could your wife find some women for that?"

At Taewan's request, Julie's mother had gathered the women she had been close to since their days at 'Ewa Plantation, the women working in the camp now, and said to them, "Although your husbands work their fingers to the bone, they're barely able to earn enough to support Chairman Park. You should save as much money as you can. I'm doing the same, since we have no idea how long we'll be able to stay here. We have a lot to worry about. If we go on living here, we'll have to send our sons to boarding school, but that means we have to save the tuition fee."

When Willow was told this story, she didn't even know how much Taewan was earning, let alone how she could spend even less than she was. She was satisfied with the money for house-keeping he gave her, but grew worried on hearing that Taewan was giving so much financial support that he was unable to save anything. However, she didn't know how she could talk about it to Taewan, who barely spoke even a few words to her in a day.

A few days before Chusok, the autumn full-moon festival, Taewan spoke, suddenly, in the middle of dinner. "Aboji, we should visit Mother's grave this Sunday."

Willow, who was laying cooked fish on top of her father-in-law's rice, was startled, and looked at her husband. She had been feeling embarrassed that she had not visited her mother-in-law's grave, now four months since she had arrived. Chusok fell on Thursday, but most of the single plantation laborers said they would replace it with the Sunday church service. Those families that lived together said the same.

"Yes, that's a good idea. Your omma will be so glad to meet her daughter-in-law. Taesok will be glad, too. They'll be happy even in Heaven." Old Mr. So was moved to tears. Willow hadn't realized that Taesok's grave was also there.

After dinner, Taewan read the newspaper by lamplight as usual. He subscribed to the *Gungminbo*, the newspaper produced by the Hawai'i branch of the Korean National Association, as well as an English-language newspaper published in Hawai'i. Willow reckoned her husband was impressive to be able to read newspapers full of indecipherable letters, and envied him. It seemed such a long time ago that she had dreamed that she would do the same. Instead, Willow opened her sewing box and began to darn Taewan's working clothes. Every day, when she saw his clothes slashed here and there, it upset her as if it were Taewan who had been injured. The couple of hours she spent with Taewan before they went to bed was her favorite, most eagerly awaited time of day.

Willow repaired them using pieces of cloth cut from her

father-in-law's old working clothes, fixing patches skillfully over the frayed places. It wasn't merely a matter of sewing on buttons and mending tears, it was skilled sewing.

The only sound to be heard was the rustle of the newspaper. Taewan had spat out the news that they were going to visit his mother's grave on Sunday, but then resumed his general silence. It was during her favorite, most eagerly awaited time that Willow felt most disappointed and hurt. While they were together, she longed to talk about their days, but Taewan was incapable of talking about his work, or really anything at all. Willow learned belatedly what had happened on the plantation from Julie's mother.

"What on earth do you talk about every evening?" Julie's mother had asked, one time, embarrassing Willow that her quiet relationship with Taewan was so noticeable.

"Don't you know? Why ask?" said Dusun's mother. "Whoever heard of newlyweds talking together?"

Willow's face burned even hotter.

At first, Willow tried to talk to Taewan by bringing up things she had heard at the laundry or from the other women. "Today, Julie and James got into an argument. At first, they were joking about which of them were doing better in school, but then James said there was no point in a girl being clever, and they really began to fight."

Taewan would say, "Hmm," and turn over the newspaper, so that Willow couldn't tell if he was responding to what she said or to an article. But today, there was a shared topic, the visit to the graves, which Taewan had mentioned first.

Willow waited until he was about to turn to the second newspaper before speaking. "What food should we prepare for offerings when we visit your omma's grave?"

When Chusok was approaching, Willow's mother used to

prepare some simple food offerings and go with her children to their father's grave. During the visit, they also cut the grass. Her mother worried that if they didn't, the spirit would come to the ancestral rites in the house with grass on its head. Recalling that, Willow had mentioned grass-cutting to old Mr. So a few days before. Her father-in-law told her that American tombs did not need to have the grass cut, unlike those in Korea.

"Do as you like," Taewan replied without lifting his eyes. Once again, the couple's conversation was cut short by his blunt words. The room went back to being full of nothing but silence. Taewan's heart was harder to open than any door.

From the beginning, Willow was curious about her husband's newspapers. She wanted to know what the articles were about that absorbed him so. Leaving aside the English newspaper, the articles in the *Gungminbo* had the titles only in Chinese characters, but the contents were almost all printed in the Hangul alphabet. Willow knew Chinese characters as well as Hangul, but it was still difficult to understand. One day, old Mr. So asked Julie's younger sister Nancy to read from the *Gungminbo*. Nancy, who attended the church's Hangul school, admitted that she could not read the newspaper, but Willow was amazed to learn that her father-in-law, who knew so much, did not know how to read.

"Can I read for you?"

The old man was surprised that his daughter-in-law could read. Willow enjoyed reading to him and discovering the daily news. As the old man said, a newspaper allowed you to see across a thousand li while sitting at home, and a few small pages contained all kinds of information, about individuals living in Honolulu to independence activists around the world.

Willow had never been very interested in the war taking place in Europe, thinking it had nothing to do with her. But reading the newspaper, she realized that was not the case. The United States had developed into a powerful country thanks to the profits made by selling military equipment to the warring nations. But the previous year, a British merchant ship was attacked by a German submarine, killing over a hundred Americans aboard. As a result, the American government had entered the war, which led to an improved economy in Hawai'i, where there was an American base. Workers' wages increased and the Korean immigrants benefited. The newspaper also contained articles about compatriots opening new shops, and about successful businesspeople making large charitable donations. People were dying in the war, but on the other hand, their community was living better thanks to the war. In contrast, the news from Korea was uniformly bad.

"Because our country is helpless, the people are wretched. Look to the United States. Because their citizens died, the country declared war on their behalf. How mighty a people are with such a nation behind them."

As her father-in-law said, life was getting worse for the people of Korea under Japanese oppression, and if that was not enough, epidemics followed on the heels of poor harvests. In the last letter her brother Gyusik sent, he hadn't mentioned any problems, but there was no knowing what had happened to the family since then. Willow's heart ached for days after learning news of Korea. She was repulsed by the thought that knowledge could be like poison, but the newspaper also gave her the antidote, thanks to news of the independence movements underway in the United States, China, and Russia. Willow was proud that Taewan generously donated his money to the Independence Movement; it was like he was sending money to help her family. Still, she wished he wasn't doing it by supporting Yongman Park, an advocate of armed struggle.

Willow longed to share her thoughts and ideas with her husband, articles she had read in the newspaper about the war, the Independence Movement, childhood memories, wounds . . . not just talk about the day's events or practical details. She longed for them to lie in bed, talking softly to each other until they fell asleep. But when Taewan read a newspaper or a book with his mouth tightly closed, Willow lost the strength to start a conversation. Then, when the time came for them to sleep, as soon as the light was turned off, Taewan would hastily paw at Willow's breasts, finish, then pass out.

Willow felt mortified and angry that Taewan had given his affectionate, warm, sweet heart to his first love, Dari, and considered his wife as merely a release for his physical desire. She wondered how the other couples on the plantation lived, but she was too embarrassed to ask Julie's mother. When the women joked that she was looking more radiant every day, her husband must be taking good care of her at night, "You're in the prime of youth, you'll soon have a baby coming," she grew yet more desolate.

Willow wanted to have a child quickly. Once they had a baby, the distance between them would be sure to grow less. She also wanted a baby for her father-in-law to embrace, longing as he was for a grandchild, but there was no sign of a pregnancy.

7

GRAVES AT 'EWA

Even though it was a visit to the family graves, Willow was excited as if it were an all-day picnic with her husband. The only excursion she had made since the wedding was a visit to Kahuku Beach with Jaesong's family, which they had planned for when Julie came home on vacation. Something came up on the plantation that day, and Jaesong was unable to go, so Willow went instead, to help look after the children. Among the people on the beach, Willow couldn't help noticing all of the affectionate couples spending the day together.

Taewan sometimes went to Honolulu, but Willow went nowhere except to the laundry and the shop. Julie's mother urged her to come to the church several times, but neither her father-in-law nor her husband went, and it was difficult for her to go alone. It was also difficult for her to go because she knew that her mother was praying to Buddha for her children's welfare.

Old Mr. So had told her why he had left the church. "In those days as now, many people attended the church, because it was the center of everything. My family also attended regularly. The children learned to write at the church's Hangul school. But after my wife and youngest son died, I no longer felt like going to church. I felt resentful if such things were God's will. Perhaps I didn't have faith to begin with. Taewan was the same."

As the day approached, Willow went shopping at the Japanese store and from the Chinese cart, then woke at the first cock crow on Sunday and prepared the food for offerings. The weather was too hot for her to be able to do it in advance. Recalling her mother's recipes, Willow placed chives and young cabbage leaves on a thin layer of batter made with flour and fried them. In addition, she fried thinly sliced fish that she had coated in flour and beaten egg, and stewed some beef in soy sauce. Food that was fried in oil or boiled in soy sauce could be kept longer.

Willow prepared food for her father-in-law's lunch separately and put everything else in a picnic basket she had borrowed from Julie's mother. She added a cloth and dishes for the offerings, chopsticks, a bottle of Chinese liquor, and some boiled eggs. Finally, she took the lunchbox that Taewan carried when he went to the plantation and filled it with boiled rice, then filled a pot with water. Once the basket was packed, she grew restless at the thought of sitting with Taewan in the shade of a tree, eating lunch.

After clearing the breakfast table, Willow took out her pink jacket and skirt. It would be hot, but she couldn't go to greet her mother-in-law and brother-in-law for the first time wearing ordinary cotton clothes. Old Mr. So came to the door to see them off, walking with a cane.

"Aboji, we'll go now. You must get better quickly so that you can come with us next time. I've made your lunch, and it's ready for you to eat." Willow held Mr. So's hands as she spoke, but turned around when she felt Taewan's eyes resting on her. The moment their eyes met, Taewan quickly looked away. Willow was often conscious of Taewan's gaze when she was with her father-in-law. He seemed to be checking that she was performing her tasks properly as a good daughter-in-law.

They climbed onto the carriage that was already packed with people going to church, including Jaesong's family. Since early morning, bright sunlight had been streaming down.

"It's so hot, what will you do? You should ask your husband to buy you a parasol." Julie's mother tilted her sunshade to cover Willow and spoke aloud so that Taewan, who was sitting opposite, could hear.

Willow hurriedly replied, "What would I do with a parasol?"

The carriage went back up the road that they had taken when Willow arrived for the first time after her marriage. She thought of Songhwa, whom she had not once seen since they parted. If she asked Julie's mother, she might be able to hear some news of her. But even if Songhwa was having problems, she was in no position to help her. Whenever she thought of Songhwa, she merely prayed that Sokbo had mended his ways. It was the least she could do.

Willow and Taewan got out where the road leading to the church forked off. They would have to walk twenty or thirty minutes to reach the station. After the carriage disappeared, Taewan took the basket from Willow's hands.

"Why so much?" Taewan murmured to himself, only now realizing how heavy the basket was. He walked at a brisk pace, and Willow had trouble keeping up with him, even empty-handed. The silk jacket and skirt clung to her, and her feet burned in her thick boson socks. When they reached the station, Taewan put the basket down next to Willow and went to buy the tickets. Willow stood beside the basket and looked nostalgically around Kahuku Station. The four months since she'd first arrived here seemed very long, and at the same time very short. In that time, she had become a very different person, and yet she was still just the same as before.

The station was noisy and crowded with passengers getting

on and off the trains, and family and friends coming to welcome them or see them off. At a glance, it was clear that most of them were sugarcane plantation workers and their families. A small number of white people were first-class passengers, plantation managers and their families on their way to the scenic beach. The first-class fare was equal to the amount a field-worker earned for three days of work. It was also the money that Willow could make washing clothes for ten whole days.

They have a lot of money, so they can pay for it.

Willow, who was standing, looking in the direction of the first-class car, turned as someone shouted from behind a cart full of bags. She hurriedly picked up the basket and stepped aside. A native Hawaiian was pushing the cart, while a haole man, who seemed to be the owner, was walking beside him, giving orders. Behind him, his wife was holding a little girl by the hand while a nanny carrying a baby followed. Blocked by the crowds, they stopped beside Willow. The wife peeped at the baby and spoke to the nanny.

Willow's eyes were fixed on the little girl standing next to her, dressed so perfectly and standing so still that she looked like a doll. It was her first time being so close to a haole child. The curly-golden-haired girl stared at Willow with her green eyes. The moment their eyes met, the little girl stuck her tongue out at Willow, suddenly looking much more like the child she was. Willow playfully stuck out her tongue. Next, the child raised her hands and pulled up the corners of her eyes. Finding that cute, Willow pulled a boiled egg from the basket and offered it to the child. When the child looked at it without taking it, Willow put the egg into her hand. The child pulled at her mother's skirt and showed her the egg while pointing at Willow. The woman glanced at Willow, frowned, took the egg and threw it to the ground. Willow was startled.

"Oh, why? What a waste!" Willow was about to snatch up the egg that had fallen to the ground, when a familiar shoe crushed it. It was Taewan, looking very angry.

"Come on." Taewan picked up the basket and went striding off toward the train, leaving Willow on the verge of tears. She followed Taewan without a moment to think. The fare for the third-class car, where people and baggage were all jumbled together, was just over a dollar. This being the last stop, there were empty seats. Taewan let Willow sit next to the window, then sat down beside her. Taewan was about to stow the basket under his legs when Willow took it and placed it on her knees, worried that it might tip over.

"Why did that haole woman throw away the egg? Don't they eat eggs?" Willow also wanted to ask why Taewan had stepped on the egg, but stopped there.

"Because it was something you gave her."

"What do you mean? Did she think I might have poisoned it or something?"

Taewan interrupted her with a cold smile. "Those people don't think we're the same as they are. Don't waste your time on them."

Willow suddenly recalled Taewan's scar. It was caused by a haole luna wielding a whip.

"My goodness, even if they're that high-class, in Korea I'm a yangban. If my schoolmaster aboji heard what they did to me from his grave, he'd come back to life."

Taewan kept his mouth tightly shut, and Willow wished she'd bitten her tongue.

The train set off. The sea breeze blowing through the open windows cooled their sweat. Willow had fallen asleep on the first day, as she was arriving, but now she saw the landscape as they passed. Boats floated on the endless open sea and people were swimming off beaches that were lined with ironwood trees, which looked like the pine trees of Korea. When she saw the dim horizon, she remembered a conversation with Julie and her mother.

"If we set off from here, we'd end up in Korea. I want to be a fish and swim there," Willow had said with a sigh. At that time, Willow thought that the sea seen from Kahuku Beach was the sea she had crossed.

"What are you talking about?" said Julie's mother. "Do you think all the seas are the same? That sea is to the west. This is the sea that leads to the mainland."

Her words left Willow deflated, but Julie quickly refuted her mother. "Omma, it's not so. The earth is round, so you're sure to reach Korea if you just keep going. But if you want to swim there, Willow, you'd have to be a big animal, not a fish, more like a whale. Did you know that whales are not fish, but mammals that breast-feed their babies?"

After the vacation, Julie would be in the second grade of elementary school. Even though she had been corrected, Julie's mother looked delighted with her smart daughter.

"Now you know that her tuition is not being wasted," said Willow.

Willow was envious of little Julie, who could go to school and spoke English better than Korean. If she had a daughter, Willow wanted to bring her up to be a smart girl like Julie. But there was still no sign of a baby. If she never had a child, Willow knew she would lose the strength to stay with Taewan. As her thoughts led her to melancholy, Taewan's body slipped toward her. Willow stayed still so that Taewan could sleep comfortably leaning against her. However, Taewan soon righted himself and folded his arms. As the landscape continued without change, Willow began to doze, having risen earlier than usual to cook.

They woke at the braking of the train at 'Ewa Station. With its view of the sugar factory's high chimney, it was no different from Kahuku Station, but for Willow it was special because it was where Taewan first came and lived, as well as the place where her mother-in-law's and brother-in-law's graves were located. When they left the train, it looked busier than around Kahuku Station.

"Wait here a minute," said Taewan after a moment's pause.

Without giving her time to respond, Taewan disappeared into the crowd. Willow's heart fell. This was also where Dari had lived. Did she still live here? Was he going to meet her? Taewan had been going to Honolulu about once a month. Perhaps he got off at 'Ewa, not Honolulu, to meet her? Just thinking about it was enough to make the ground give way beneath her feet to an endless hell. Flames of jealousy and rage rose from the depths of Willow's heart as she sat crouched on the ground.

If that's the case, I can't stand it. I'll never look at him again.

As she pressed her lips together, a shadow fell across the ground. As she lifted her head, Taewan was holding out a parasol, panting as if he had been running. Willow stood up awkwardly. The parasol was light blue with a floral pattern, and a lace border. Julie's mother had mentioned a parasol, but she had never imagined that Taewan would buy one. Shyly, she accepted it, blushing at having imagined all those absurd thoughts.

They walked about thirty minutes from the station to the cemetery. The road lay in the opposite direction from the main street, and the sunlight was so strong that it was hard to keep their eyes open. There were no trees or buildings to offer shade. Willow proudly opened her parasol, and felt as cool as if she were in the shade of a tree. Taewan walked ahead, refusing Willow's offer to share the shade.

Taewan stopped when they reached the cemetery. While she

had been on her way to offer her first greetings to her mother-in-law and brother-in-law, all Willow's thoughts had been focused on the parasol. Willow carefully folded it up, and adopted a serious expression following Taewan's example. Inside the cemetery, instead of the grave mounds of Korea, tombstones rose above the level ground. Trees standing here and there provided shade. Taewan headed for a grave in the middle of the cemetery and stopped. Willow stood next to him and saw that on the tombstone a name was engraved in Korean and English.

SO ONYEON
1861–1912

Taewan coughed, and Willow, who had been absorbed in being in the presence of her mother-in-law, came to her senses and laid the food offerings on the cloth. Taewan poured wine into a small cup. Willow remained standing, thinking that Taewan would bow first. However, Taewan stood there looking at Willow.

"Shall we do it together?" he asked.

They bowed and Willow prayed sincerely to her mother-in-law in the world beyond.

Omoni, I am your daughter-in-law. I am sorry to visit you so late. Even if I do not satisfy Taewan, I will do my best. Omoni, please take care of me so that I can have sons and daughters and live well.

Now that she had paid her respects, Willow felt that she was truly part of the So family. Taewan drank the wine in the cup placed before his mother's grave, then filled and drank another cupful. Next, he ate some of the fried fish Willow had prepared. She was curious about whether he liked it, but Taewan said nothing.

Willow hid her disappointment and asked, "And where is your brother's grave?"

Taesok was buried a little way away from his mother.

SO TAESOK
1894–1910

Willow bowed to the brother with a reverent feeling. There, too, Taewan drank two glasses; then he left the grave carrying the bottle of wine before Willow had time to clear everything up. She assumed that he was looking for the shade of a tree to have lunch. Willow was in a hurry, like a Buddhist monk more interested in the food offering than in chanting prayers, but still she looked at Taesok's gravestone and prayed.

Brother-in-law, I'm sad never to have seen you. It is a great pity that you left this world so early. Rest in peace, and I will visit you again.

After hurriedly filling the basket, she followed after Taewan, then abruptly stopped. Taewan was sitting, not in the shade of a tree but in front of another grave. Instead of his normal hard expression, that never seemed to vary, he stared blank-faced. Willow approached, her heart trembling. Taewan seemed unaware the she was there, as he stared vacantly at the gravestone. After seeing the name on the stone, Willow froze for a moment, then collapsed beside Taewan.

DALHEE CHOI
1892–1911

It was Dalhee, not Dari. And she was already dead.

Taewan, noticing Willow, silently raised the bottle to his lips.

She felt more hopeless than when she thought Dalhee was alive. A dead woman still buried in a man's breast would never be forgotten until the day he died. Tears flowed from Willow's eyes.

"What's wrong?" Taewan asked, surprised by her emotions.

At that, she burst into a storm of weeping, like a dam collapsing. "I know who this person is. I know everything." Willow pointed at the stone, speaking in a voice mixed with tears.

Taewan's expression wavered. "We should be going." He threw the empty bottle into the grass and stood up. However, instead of following Taewan's words, Willow poured out all that she had kept locked in her inmost heart.

"I know you said you wouldn't marry me because Dalhee is in your heart. And even once we were wed, it's because of her that you've never considered me any better than livestock. I told myself I should believe that it would get better in the years to come, that I should wait. But now I see that those were false hopes. She is the only person in your heart, isn't she? But what about me? Is there no room for me?"

Taewan, who was plainly embarrassed, hesitated, then sat down again. "Who told you all that?"

"First, the matchmaker said you were a landowner and that if I came here I would be able to go to school. I admit that if I had disliked the look of you, I wouldn't have come, but after never having left our village, I left my family and crossed the sea in order to get here. Even if I couldn't study, or live in luxury, even if you weren't a landowner, that would not have mattered if we were a true couple. All I wanted was for us to live together, caring for each other, helping each other. But you can't give me as much as a fingernail's space, so what is to become of me? Tell me. Have you ever once thought of me as your beloved wife?"

The more she talked, the more she wept, until she was sitting with both legs out, sobbing. She cried like a child, tearing up clumps of grass and throwing them. Taewan bowed his increasingly flushed face and said nothing.

Having revealed all her worries and fears, Willow felt relieved in a way she hadn't since she arrived, and even ventured to think that she didn't care if Taewan disliked her more than ever. After kicking at her hem and blowing her nose, she asked one last cutting question. "If you feel so different, why did you pick me up at the Immigration Service instead of letting them send me back? Why did you go through with the ceremony and bring me home with you? To make your food and use my body?"

Taewan's expression grew stony. After a moment, he pulled out a cigarette, lit it with a match, and opened his mouth as if he had come to a decision.

Just as he was about to say something, Willow suddenly worried what he might say and nervously interrupted, "Let's eat before we go home. It's so hot that the food will soon spoil." She jumped to her feet and carried the basket into the shade of a tree. Taewan watched as she spread out the cloth and took out the food, laughed, and stood up. As Willow took out the lunchbox and opened the lid she grew tearful again. The rice was black with ants.

"Goodness, what's happened?"

Taewan sat down and took the lunchbox from Willow, and poured water from the pot into the rice, until the water overflowed, and the ants went floating away. Taewan scooped out the rice on one side, put it on the lid, and handed it to Willow. Then he blew off the ants that were still left in the lunchbox, put the rice into his mouth, and began to chew, as though everything were normal.

As she watched Taewan sitting in the hot, silent cemetery, eating the rice that had been covered in ants, Willow felt moved that she had seen in a flash all the time that Taewan had spent since he came to this foreign land and began to live here.

Willow hurriedly swallowed her tears, together with the rice he had scooped out for her. Deciding that before he spoke, she would tell him about herself, Willow put everything back in the basket, and began her story.

"Listen to what I want to tell you."

Taewan sat with his knees upright and smoked a cigarette.

"I lost two elder sisters early on, so that I grew up as the only daughter with three brothers. Aboji was the village schoolmaster, he made me sit behind his pupils and taught me the *Thousand Character Classic.* Then he sent me to the primary school to study further. We weren't rich, but we lived without being envious of anyone." Willow choked up as she recalled the long-forgotten times.

Taewan quietly listened to her.

"But when I was nine, Aboji joined the righteous army and lost his life. A couple of years later, my older brother died after being kicked by the horse of a Japanese policeman. After that I can't remember ever having enough to eat. We were lucky not to starve. Omma's only goal in life was to provide food for her remaining children. I had to leave school when I was Julie's age, to cook and care for my younger brothers. As I grew up, I helped Omma sew till my fingers were swollen. Every night I feared that she would run away, leaving us behind, or throw herself over a waterfall up in the mountains. So I lived as the filial daughter of a woman who regularly threatened to kill herself. I wanted to run away, to leave home and find happiness, and that is maybe why I chose to come here. It wasn't you I wanted, it was Hawai'i."

For a while, the space between them was full of silence and the shadow of leaves fluttering in the breeze.

"Why did you marry me?" Willow looked straight at Taewan. "If you didn't want to, you should have said so on the first day we met, if not three days before. Once you're married, you have to take responsibility as a man. To be a husband is not simply a matter of providing food."

Taewan bowed his head with a heavy sigh. After a moment's silence, finally he spoke.

"Dalhee died out at sea." His voice sounded broken.

Willow followed the direction Taewan was looking with her eyes. Only the sugarcane fields were visible, but the sea must lie beyond them, where the clouds rose.

"She ended her life because of me."

She took her life? Willow lifted her knees and held them with both hands.

Taewan raised his voice and continued, "I first met her on the boat to Hawai'i. She was sixteen and I was fourteen. We were assigned to the same plantation and lived in the same neighborhood. But my omma disapproved of Dalhee from the start. She disliked the fact that Dalhee's omma had been a gisaeng entertainer. As if we were any better."

Willow blushed at the thought that she had boasted of being yangban.

"You asked me once how I got the scar on my back?"

Willow knew that he had been whipped by a luna, but remained silent.

"It's because I stood up to a luna who was harassing Dalhee. From then on, Omma hated Dalhee, claiming that she would ruin my life. She told me I should give her up because she would never accept her so long as she lived. Instead of trying to convince Omma, I ran away to school, leaving Dalhee to suffer on the plantation. There was an accident on the plantation, and Taesok was seriously injured saving Dalhee's life.

"When Taesok died, she hated Dalhee even more, blaming her for the death of her son. There was nothing I could do to help, not wanting to choose between them, but I also couldn't let her go, either. Not long after, Dalhee took her own life. The next year, Omma died. I lost three people in three years. How could I ever forgive myself for not being there for them?"

Willow knew what kind of wound it was to lose those you love, the harder to endure if you think it was all your own fault. She felt sorry for Taewan. It was as if the door that Taewan had kept closed for so long was now opening to reveal him as he was, rather than simply revealing those whom he had lost.

It was this that Willow had so longed for from him. Talking freely about good things, bad things, sad things, soothing each other's wounds.

Willow suddenly rose to her feet. "I want to keep going."

Taewan raised his head abruptly and looked at Willow.

"Even if you've given your heart to another woman, I want to keep going with you. As we go on, there will be a day when your heart will come back. And you will do what you can, too. Promise me that before your omma."

A faint smile spread across Taewan's face.

"I know it's very sudden. You won't let me down, will you?"

Willow held out her hand to Taewan.

NEWS FROM A FRIEND

Hawaiian weather was warm throughout the year, it was simply divided into dry and rainy seasons, and the rainy season began in November. Although it was called the rainy season, it was not an endless series of monsoons, as it was in Korea. After a squall of heavy showers, bright sunlight would again soon shine out over the world. Then a rainbow would appear, like a bridge leading to the sky. Willow was thrilled every time she saw one.

A letter from Hongju arrived on a day when there was an unusually large, bright rainbow. Willow was as delighted as if her friend had come in person. Willow had begun to write to Hongju several times before giving up. When writing a letter home, all she had to do was write good news so that her mother and brothers didn't worry, but she didn't want to do that to her friend. If there was one person in the world from whom she should have no secrets, that person was Hongju. However, no matter what she might write about Taewan, it was bound to sound like boasting to her friend, who had cried so much about her unlovely bridegroom, so she had delayed and finally given up.

Willow hurried up to her room and opened the envelope. The jagged letters filling three pages were like Hongju's voice. From the opening greeting, she could hear Hongju's words.

"I'm working at the canteen of Kahului Plantation on Maui Island. People tell me it's better than working out in the fields, but you know

how hard it is for me to live here. If I ever go back to Korea one day, I'll kill that matchmaker. Even if I was a widow, how could she send me to be married in a place like this? I earn pocket money by writing letters for illiterate workers in the same camp. Jo Doksam is a terrible miser. He shudders if I so much as ask him to buy me one orange. He's so tightfisted, I don't know how he managed to send the money to bring me here. But at least he's sincere and kind. There are also men in the camp who gamble and beat their wives. If he were like that, I'd leave him in a flash. . . ."

Willow laughed until she nearly cried, for reading Hongju's letter was like sitting together and talking, like they used to. After two and a half pages full of her misfortunes, she sent her love to Willow and Songhwa, who she thought were living in the same camp.

"Willow, Songhwa. I'm dying to see you. You're so lucky to be able to see each other every day, and support one another. If only I could be there with you, even if my husband is no good, I'd be fine, seeing you. Here, I have nobody I can talk to freely."

Willow instantly felt guilty that she'd avoided visiting Songhwa. No matter what the excuse, it was not right. As she promised herself that she would go to visit her very soon, Willow's eyes fell on the final passage in the letter.

"And Willow, I'm pregnant. This is the fourth month. My morning sickness is so bad I can't eat anything. Just like when you were seasick, I vomit anything I eat. Maybe because he worries about his child, Jo Doksam's told me to rest, so I'm taking things easy and writing to you. Anyway, I'm fine. I used to think of going back but I can't now that I'm pregnant. At the thought of spending my whole life and growing old as the wife of such a bumpkin as Jo Doksam, I can't breathe, only sigh. Anyway, I'll wheedle my husband into letting me go to visit you one day, so stay well until then."

Willow dropped the letter onto her lap and sat blankly for

a while. Despite her negative tone, it sounded to Willow as though Hongju was happy about being pregnant.

After the visit to her mother-in-law's grave, Willow was the first to change. Keeping an eye on Taewan's reactions, instead of feeling awkward as before, she began to treat him affectionately, talking to him often, sometimes joking. Taewan also began to talk more, even laugh. They would fall asleep in the evening after cracking feeble jokes, making love, then talking some more, like the newlywed couples in her favorite novels. Now there was nothing more for her to be envious of, except having a baby, but there was still no news. Willow blamed herself for having irregular periods.

When she was a child, her mother had told her that if she wished for something when she saw a rainbow, it would be granted. But Willow had never wished properly. It was rare for a rainbow to appear, and then they appeared without warning. In addition, young Willow had so many wishes that the rainbow would disappear again before she could decide on one. After her father and brother died, Willow had wishes for them to be alive again, but it hadn't worked, and she had stopped wishing on rainbows.

After receiving the letter from Hongju, Willow began to wish upon rainbows again. In addition to thoughts of the baby, she also thought about Songhwa. Willow wrote to Hongju congratulating her on her pregnancy and saying that she would soon be visiting Songhwa. Then she asked Julie's mother if she could find any news of Sokbo and his wife.

On Sundays, Taewan ate lunch at home. Willow often bought meaty bones, simmered them, and then add chopped scallions to the broth before serving. She still thought of her mother and brothers at the sight of the tasty food. She was steadily saving the money she earned by doing the laundry, waiting to put aside a hundred dollars to send all at once, and save on postage.

After finishing his bowl of bone soup and reading the newspaper, Taewan took a nap. Willow sat sewing under the papaya tree beside her father-in-law, waiting for Jaesong's family to come back from church. Before the carriage even stopped in front of their house, Willow ran over. Julie's mother got down holding Tony in her arms, while Nancy and Alice followed Jaesong to the horse's stall that was located next to the office. The children liked to feed the horse.

While Julie's mother was changing out of her Sunday best, Willow held the fretful Tony. Even for that brief moment, she kept worrying about how Songhwa might be doing. Julie's mother, once she had changed her clothes, took Tony in her arms and began to feed him.

"Did you hear any news about Songhwa?" asked Willow.

"Sokbo's bride doesn't mingle with the other people in the camp, so it was hard to find anyone who knew her. Luckily, I met the family who live next door, so I was able to learn something, but not about their life as a couple. Apparently, there are more people who dislike Songhwa than Sokbo himself."

"What? Why would they dislike Songhwa?" Willow asked in amazement.

"She doesn't do any housework, they say, just stays indoors, so that Sokbo has to take care of her before he goes to work. And people say that since he's not having any fun in bed he's gambling and drinking again."

Willow recalled how Songhwa had taken over the kitchen work for the Pusan Ajimae. She had seemed to be overwhelmed when surrounded by many people, but had come to life on the way to Kahuku. If she had come straight from the secluded valley of Surijae, that might explain it, but surely her eyes and ears had been opened by being in Pusan and Kobe, so why was she staying in her room like that? Willow blamed herself for not going to see her before, and knew she wouldn't feel right until she made sure she was okay.

Willow returned home, discussed the situation with her father-in-law, and asked for permission to visit.

"Better wake Taewan and go together," he said.

"No, let him rest. I'll quickly go across on my own. I'll be back before dinner."

Willow went into their room to change her clothes. She thought Taewan was sleeping but he asked, "Are you going somewhere?"

"You remember my friend Songhwa who married Sokbo? She might be in trouble. I need to go over there and make sure she's okay."

At that, Taewan stood up. "You don't know the way; you'd best go with me." Taewan was already putting on the shirt he had hung on the wall as he spoke. "Come out once you're ready. I'll go to the stable and bring the horse round."

Taewan was gone before she could try to dissuade him. Willow, given no chance to refuse, simply changed her blouse and followed. Too impatient to wait at the house, she went round to the stable. She thought they were going in the carriage, but Taewan was saddling one of the horses.

"Aren't we going in the carriage?" Willow asked in surprise. She had never ridden a horse.

"This is quicker. Don't worry, you can ride with me." Taewan helped Willow use the stirrup to get onto the horse's back. Her first time on a horse, Willow was scared at how high off the ground it was. Once Taewan had mounted behind her and taken the reins, she snuggled back against him. When the horse first moved off, she gave a little scream, but she soon calmed down in her husband's arms.

The horse carrying them trotted down the path across the sugarcane field; her skirt billowed in the breeze. For a moment, Willow forgot where they were going and felt she was on an adventure with her husband.

The wooden fence around Songhwa's house was broken in several places, and the small yard was overgrown with weeds. It looked abandoned with morning glory vines climbing up the front steps.

Willow dismounted and knocked anxiously on the door. "Is anyone at home? Songhwa, Songhwa!" After a moment, a face appeared at a window. Her gaunt face looked pale as a ghost.

"Songhwa!" Willow threw open the door and rushed in. It was a single-roomed house without a partition between the kitchen and the main room. As she entered the kitchen, a swarm of flies flew up from a small meal table lying on the floor. Willow suppressed a feeling of nausea and turned toward the main room. On the raised floor was a mat woven from the leaves of the hala tree, and Songhwa was standing on it, looking blank. Her expression did not change at the sight of Willow.

"Aigo, Songhwa!" Willow went into the room and hugged her tightly. Songhwa tottered, thin as a twig. "Why are you so thin?" Willow was horrified as she stood back and examined her face. It bore traces of bruises. Holding Songhwa steady, she pulled up the sleeves of her blouse and lifted her skirt. Parts of her skin were stained blue and purple.

"For heaven's sake, what is this? What kind of person is Park Sokbo? I'm so sorry. I didn't know you were living like this." Willow hugged Songhwa and sobbed, heartbroken at the thought that Songhwa had suffered this pain alone. Songhwa also burst into tears. At the sight of Taewan, who came in behind Willow, Songhwa grabbed Willow, eyes wide in fright.

"What's wrong? Don't you know Mr. Taewan? You must have seen him on our wedding day. He's my husband." Willow hugged Songhwa and calmed her down.

Taewan looked at them both for a moment, then asked Songhwa, "Where has Sokbo gone?"

Songhwa shook her head, her face pale.

Willow's feeling of horror collapsed, replaced by a rising anger. "Go find him!" Willow shouted. "I'll tear him to pieces. Someone who can do this isn't human."

Once Taewan left, all the strength ebbed from Songhwa. A sudden shower came pouring down; rain splashed in through the window.

Willow made Songhwa sit on the floor, then embraced her tightly. Songhwa was trembling, and Willow remembered throwing stones at her as a child, recalling her scarred face and scared expression. In those days, whenever Okhwa and her daughter appeared, it was taken for granted that they should throw stones. Even after hitting them, she had never even felt sorry. That had been wrong, she now knew. She and the villagers had been no better than Songhwa's husband.

Willow noticed Songhwa's suitcase on a rack in the kitchen. It was the one she had bought in Kobe. She remembered Songhwa laughing timidly as she strutted about, carrying the suitcase at Hongju's command.

Willow jumped up and said, "Pack your bag. Let's go back to my house." At Willow's words, a look of relief spread across Songhwa's face.

The Kaesong ajumoni had told Willow that they needed more workers, so she could ask her to let her work in the canteen. Songhwa could sleep in Dusun's mother's room, since she slept alone. If that didn't work, she even thought of sending Taewan to sleep in her father-in-law's room until they could get a room ready for her. Willow took the bag down from the rack and opened it. Inside the bag were the clothes Songhwa had worn at the wedding. Tears flowed again. While Willow was crying, Songhwa collected the clothes scattered here and there and put them into the bag.

Once everything was packed, Willow led Songhwa outside. Meanwhile, the rain shower had passed and the sun was shining. Willow supported Songhwa as she staggered along, dazed. Water droplets were falling from the leaves, and a rainbow shone over the mountain.

It was some two months after the new year when Willow realized she was pregnant. Even though her period was irregular and morning sickness started early, she had first thought she might be sick, so she went secretly to the clinic in the Japanese camp without Taewan or his father knowing, afraid that they would be worried. When she saw the word "pregnant" that the doctor had written in Chinese characters, dozens of rainbows spread out before her eyes.

The doctor took out the X-ray plate and told her she was in her third month. At the sight of the image of the fetus in her womb, she saw in her mind the faces of Taewan, her father-in-law, and her mother all mixed together. She wanted to announce the news as soon as possible, and at the same time she wanted to enjoy the happiness alone for a while. Willow walked home slowly along a path lined with dazzling yellow primavera trees, with the child in her womb. It was only after she had cleared away the dinner table that evening that she told Taewan and old Mr. So that she was pregnant.

Tears ran down the old man's wrinkled face. "Thank you, thank you. You are a blessing to our family."

Hearing his hoarse words, Willow also teared up.

At the table, Taewan showed no emotion, but as soon as they were alone in their room he hugged her tightly.

"What are you doing? I can't breathe!" Willow couldn't help laughing as she spoke.

Taewan took Willow's face in his hands and kissed it all over. She could feel with her whole body how fond he was of her. Willow was also utterly happy.

"What are you doing? I'm pregnant like any other . . ." Willow spoke bashfully, pushing Taewan away because she was feeling nauseous.

Songhwa tried hard to keep Willow well fed, making something different for each meal. Once it was porridge boiled with pine nuts. Even the smell was enough to make Willow's stomach churn, but at the thought of the child in her womb she put a spoonful in her mouth, and swallowed it like bitter medicine. Songhwa watched with anxious eyes. Willow had only eaten three spoonfuls before she pushed the bowl away.

Songhwa sighed.

"Truly, I'm only staying alive thanks to you," said Willow with a haggard face. She wondered who would have cared for her if it weren't for Songhwa. To say nothing of Taewan, even Julie's mother would not have been as relaxed as her friend.

Songhwa giggled.

Three days after they had taken her home with them, old Sokbo had come visiting. Instead of Songhwa, Willow and Taewan, Julie's mother and Jaesong met with him. Songhwa hid in Willow's room, trembling like a cornered animal.

"At first I tried to give up my bad habits and live a good life.

But even then, she wouldn't come near me. She gave up doing housework and went out when night fell . . ."

At Sokbo's empty excuses Willow lost her temper and raised her voice. "How can an old man like you expect her to love you right away? You have to try even harder, not beat her. Don't you have any human feelings, or do you just walk around like a soulless corpse?"

"She says that she'd rather die than go back with you. What do you have to say for yourself?" asked Taewan.

Visibly shamed, Sokbo said that if Songhwa wanted to stay here, he would also like to work in this camp. Taewan and Jaesong only accepted him, with Songhwa's approval, after receiving a signed agreement that he would never again beat her, he would quit drinking and gambling, and would work hard on the plantation. They also provided a place for the two to live.

"Songhwa is like a younger sister from my hometown. If you ever so much as lay a finger on her again, you'll be sorry," Julie's mother threatened.

With Willow at her side and the camp's wives taking care of her, Songhwa gradually recovered. When any of the women was ill or had a headache, Songhwa would treat them with acupuncture. They said she was better than the doctor at the clinic. Songhwa also worked well at the canteen under the Kaesong ajumoni and James's mother. During this time, Sokbo kept to his agreement, and Songhwa's attitude toward him changed. Rather than considering Sokbo as her husband, she pitied him as an old man.

9

1919, CAMP SEVEN

In mid-March, agitation grew within the Korean community in Hawai'i as news of the Korean Independence Movement reached them. The Manse movement that had started in the large cities including Gyongsong was spreading all over the country. Men, women, old people, children, students, peasants, workers, even gisaengs, all shouted "Manse! Long live independence!" with a single heart. Now the cry that had spread across all the provinces of Korea was echoing on the far side of the sea, all the way to Hawai'i. Even the American newspapers gave major coverage to the Korean Declaration of Independence.

Whenever the workers from the camp who attended rallies in Honolulu came together, all they talked about was the Manse movement. Although thousands of people had been killed or injured by the Japanese forces, and prisons were filled with protesters, the movement still burned strong. On hearing how a student whose arm had been severed by a Japanese police officer's sword had picked up a Taegukgi flag with her other arm and went on shouting, "Dongnip manse!," all Koreans clenched their fists in solidarity.

Willow's morning sickness passed, but her physical discomfort was replaced by anxiety that her younger brothers might have been among the protesters. Although Gwangsik and Chunsik would likely be safe in remote Ojin Village, she worried about Gyusik in Kimhae. There had surely been a Manse protest there. Gyusik had good reason to hold a deep grudge against Japan. Willow finally understood what her mother had said to Hongju's mother on the night she came back from burying her brother:

"How can they talk of vanquishing the Japanese when even our king couldn't do it? That's how their aboji died, and now they've killed my son, but I won't hate them or blame them. And I'm not going to tell my remaining sons to take revenge on the enemy."

Japan, which had murdered the empress of Korea in 1896, taken over the country, and poisoned its emperor, grew stronger after the Great War. Willow worried, not only about her brothers, but also about Taewan, here in Hawai'i.

On March 3, Yongman Park, who had heard in advance of the plans for the March 1 declaration of independence, held the opening ceremony of the Korean National Independence League with about 350 people gathered from each island of Hawai'i. Taewan, who became the representative of the northern region of O'ahu, was often away, not only on Sundays but also on weekdays when he was supposed to be working. The Provisional Government of the Republic of Korea was established in Shanghai, China, with Syngman Rhee as prime minister and Yongman Park as foreign minister. Now that they were no longer a king's subjects or stateless people, but citizens of the new Republic of Korea, people flocked to make donations to the Provisional Government.

However, the difference of viewpoint between the two leaders remained. Depending on which leader they followed, the Koreans in Hawai'i had long been divided into factions, and the emotional gulf was growing deeper. Taewan was outraged that Syngman Rhee, who had petitioned U.S. president Wilson to grant him the mandate to rule over Korea, had become the head of the Provisional Government. Several workers on the plantation who were supporters of Dr. Rhee left after an argument with Taewan. He had even raised his voice to Jaesong.

Willow, who did not usually meddle in plantation matters, could not help speaking up. "Korea's independence is important, of course, but at the same time earning a living is also important, isn't it? If you abandon the work on the plantation like this, what will become of us?"

"It's not for our children that we're seeking our country's independence, it's for ourselves." Taewan said, eyes blazing. "In that way we become worthy parents for our children."

Willow could not sleep at night for fear that Taewan might suddenly leave for China, where Yongman Park was.

"Isn't it a matter of small fish getting hurt when whales are fighting? Taewan is only supporting Yongman Park's side, but isn't either side wrong on its own? Both hands have to come together in order to clap. Leaders are like parents, they should set a good example for their children, shouldn't they?" Willow asked her father-in-law after three more supporters of Syngman Rhee left the plantation. Even Julie's mother had lost her temper.

"Those so-called leaders are not a patch on you. However, Syngman Rhee was the first to divide our people. Chairman Park is the one who got him a job as editor in a newspaper allowing him to settle in Hawai'i, so it's wrong of Dr. Rhee to act as he does."

Seeing even Mr. So supporting Yongman Park, Willow grew yet more troubled. The women were not to be held back either. Members of the Korean Women's Association, which had existed before the announcement, set up a new Korean Women's Relief Society, designed to help those who had supported the

Independence Movement and suffered injuries or imprisonment in the aftermath.

Willow's eyes widened as she read the names of the members of each region's delegation in the newspaper. Jang Myongok was among the names for Big Island. Unless there was someone else of the same name on Big Island, that must be the same Jang Myongok who had accompanied them after they met at the inn in Kobe. She recalled Myongok crying in despair on seeing her old husband, so unlike his photo, in the hallway of the immigration building. It was hard to imagine her working for her country. In Kahuku, Julie's mother had long been active, unlike her husband, who was not involved in political activities.

"I don't want to go back to Korea," she explained, "I want my daughters to study as much as they want and live freely. Even though Korea has never given me anything, if you ask why I've got involved, it's because Korea is like a married woman's family home. Unless her family is strong, people will take advantage, right? That's why the Japanese workers here so often go on strike. It's because they have a strong country supporting them that they can stand up to the haole."

As Julie's mother said, the Japanese workers often went on strike, demanding higher wages and improved working conditions. Whenever that happened, the white plantation owners tried to break the strike by bringing in Korean or Filipino workers instead of meeting the demands of the Japanese. The pay, although temporary, was high and sentiment toward Japan was poor, so the Korean workers were perfectly willing to participate in crushing the strike.

Her words resonated in Willow's heart. If Hongju was able to live anywhere, as she was and as she wished, that might have been due to her strong family, who had been able to rescue their widowed daughter from her in-laws' home. Her own mother had told her not to think of Korea, and to enjoy life, but once she had left, just as she could never forget her home, the same was true of Korea.

Willow wanted the independence of Korea as much as anyone. If the country became independent, there would be no need to worry about her brothers being injured or what might happen to her husband. On the other hand, she did not wish to sacrifice her family or herself any further for the country. She felt that by joining the Korean Women's Relief Society she would only be encouraging Taewan. Keeping her distance and pretending not to know what her husband was up to was the only way she could think to express her feelings on the matter.

Willow told Julie's mother that even if she didn't join the Relief Society, she would do anything she could to help.

Julie's mother said they were going to embroider the Korean flag on pillowcases and handkerchiefs and send them to Honolulu headquarters. "Then our members there can sell them to raise funds."

The women gathered in Dusun's mother's room once the day's work was over to embroider. Willow completed three while the others made two. Songhwa, who was doing embroidery for the very first time, gradually improved. The sewing also gave them a chance for idle conversation. As stories of hard times on first arriving brought tears to their eyes, and they laughed at embarrassing mistakes, they didn't notice how time was passing.

It was only when Taewan came in asking "What are you doing? Aboji's worried about you" that the women finally realized how late it was and quickly left for home.

"Aigo, how lonely I am without a husband," Dusun's mother

lamented. "Off you all go to your men. I'll just stab my thighs with a needle and sleep alone."

James's mother countered, "There's any number of men, so why stab your thighs? Shall I send one in?"

Willow and Songhwa blushed.

Willow liked to walk along the road at night, listening to the sugarcane leaves swaying in the wind. As she walked holding Taewan's arm, pretending it was so dark that she could not see where she was putting her feet, the thought struck her that she was happy. Still, she looked around, feeling that misfortune might be lurking, on the lookout for an opportunity.

July came, bringing a letter from Hongju saying she had given birth to a son in May. The clinic told Willow that her delivery would be in late September.

"*That man shook at the thought of buying me an orange, but the moment he saw his son he threw a party for everyone in the camp. I was the one who suffered, I don't know why he was so happy. The baby's name is Songgil. Later, when he goes to school, he'll use the American name Donald. He's good-looking, not like his aboji. Fate has twisted and turned to get me here, but I'm really glad my first baby looks like me. I have to say that I treat Jo Doksam well. Although he's just the same now as he was before, now that I call him Songgil's aboji, I feel fonder of him. Now I only have one worry. His aboji has to stay healthy until Songgil is grown up, but he's already a wrinkled old gourd.*"

Hongju's personality was no different after she'd given birth. Willow smiled as she read the letter to Songhwa, then suddenly felt sorry. If she had still not been pregnant, she wouldn't have been able to smile like that. Willow controlled her happiness and asked, "Songhwa, do you want to have a baby soon?"

Songhwa shook her head. "Not at all."

"Why?"

"I'd be no good as an omma."

Willow recalled Okhwa. She had been crazy as far back as Willow remembered, always taking Songhwa about with her. Songhwa must remember how her mother would keep laughing even while people were throwing stones at them. She must remember her mother's life and death. Willow's heart ached.

Songhwa added in a soft voice, "Once the old man is dead, I'll leave here in a flash."

"But where would you go?" asked Willow. "We should go on living as we are. Hongju says that later she'll come to live in O'ahu too. It will be so nice to talk about the old days together. Besides, once your old man dies you might meet someone you like and begin a new life. There are bridegrooms all over Hawai'i. I'll act as matchmaker."

The women in the camp observed Willow's morning sickness or the shape of her stomach and tried to deduce if it would be a son or a daughter. For the same reasons, some said it would be a son, others a daughter. As her due date approached, she didn't care whether it was a son or a daughter, but secretly worried because her father-in-law and Taewan probably wanted a son. But the old man eased her worries when he said, "A son is good because he's a son, a daughter is good because she's a daughter. Don't worry about it, just have a safe delivery." He told her that Taewan felt the same.

Willow kept asking the other women for advice as she prepared for childbirth. She bought cloth in Honolulu, made diapers and blankets, as well as two more sets of baby clothes, copying those her mother had made. When making some handkerchiefs, she was hesitating as to what color she should use for the hems, and Songhwa picked up some blue thread and handed it to her.

"Use this. It's a son." Her eyes sparkled as she spoke.

"Is that true? Can you tell?" Willow asked in amazement. When Willow kept asking if it was true, Songhwa pretended she had never said anything of the kind.

Not only Willow, also Taewan and her father-in-law prepared to welcome the baby. Taewan got hold of a dry koa tree and made a stout crib for the baby, while the old man kept walking round the yard with his cane, saying that he had to have strength to look after his grandchild. He prepared names, Jongho if a grandson and Jonghwa if a granddaughter.

Once they were in bed, Willow said to Taewan, "If we're to go on living here, don't you think the baby should also have an English name? If it's a daughter, I'll choose the name, and if it's a son you can give him a name."

"I haven't thought about it . . . Richard or David sound good."

"I like David."

"And have you thought about your daughter's name?"

"Yes, if we have a daughter I shall call her Pearl."

"Pearl? Pearl?"

"Yes."

"I've never heard a name like that. . . . What's wrong with Mary or Elizabeth? If she's called Pearl what will you do if she's teased and called Pearl Harbor?"

Taewan disapproved. The original name of Pearl Harbor, that lay to the west of Honolulu, in Hawaiian was "Wai Momi," which meant "waters of pearl," since it was a place with many pearls, but now it was more famous as a U.S. naval base and a shipyard.

"It'll be okay if we tell the child the meaning of her name from a young age, don't worry."

After meeting Esther Kim in Kobe, Willow sometimes used to wonder why her own father had given her the name she had. The pussy willow is the first herald of coming spring, and willow trees take root and grow well everywhere. Did he mean that she should bring happiness to those around her and live well wherever she might end up? She wished she could have asked him. She felt that from pregnancy until the children were all grown up, it was the parent's role to stay alive and answer all their children's questions.

"Why do you want to give her that name?" Taewan asked, laying his hand on her bulging stomach.

"Do you remember when you went to Honolulu for work and I went to buy cloth for diapers? I saw a pearl as I was passing a jewelry store. It looked fine and delicate, prettier than gold or diamonds. I want our daughter to grow up like that, so I want to call her Pearl."

Willow laid her hand over Taewan's on her stomach. Actually, if she could have chosen her own name as Esther had done, it was the name she would have chosen as her own. Instead, she wanted to give that name to her first daughter.

"In that case I reckon it's a good name. Let's use it if we have a daughter. Still, judging by how strongly he's kicking it must be a son. David, enjoy your stay in your omma's womb and come out healthy."

They both laughed.

Although he had decided on the baby's names, and wept at the sight of the baby's clothes and diapers hung out after washing, and painfully made his way round the yard, one step after another, old Mr. So did not see the birth of his grandchild. One day Willow went to the kitchen at dawn and was puzzled to not see her father-in-law already up as usual. She went to wake him, carrying his breakfast, and when there was no answer, cautiously opened the door of his room. The old man was still asleep. Willow closed the door again before a thought struck her; her legs gave way and she collapsed. Taewan came rushing to the kitchen on hearing a clatter of dishes, and saw Willow on the floor. Trembling, Willow pointed toward the old man's room.

"Oh, Aboji, Aboji . . ."

Taewan rushed into the room, calling his father; then a sound like a howling beast was heard.

Mr. So passed away a year before his sixtieth birthday, in early August. Julie's mother, who had always regarded the old man as her uncle, cried as she said, "He was tremendously fond of you. He must have thought it would be difficult for you to go on caring for him while you were looking after a baby, and so he let go of life before the baby was born."

Jaesong ignored their past arguments and comforted Taewan, saying, "It was a blessing for him, dying in his sleep after gaining a daughter-in-law and seeing her pregnant with his grandchild. Let's calm our hearts and send him off well."

The old man was buried in the Kahuku Plantation cemetery, it being difficult to get to 'Ewa because of the hot weather, the distance, and the difficulty of transportation. A gravestone was erected with the help of the camp people.

SO GICHUN
1860–1919

"Aboji, later on we'll lay you to rest beside Omoni and your son. Rest in peace here for now." Willow stood crying in front of the old man's gravestone.

Her father-in-law had made her feel a father's affection. If she had not been warmly welcomed and treated so affectionately by him, she might not have been able to face the hard times she had to endure. It was as though someone who had been firmly planted in her heart, like the tree at the entrance of her home village, had been uprooted. Willow was overwhelmed with loss and mourning. Taewan, who had thus lost the entire family with whom he came to Hawai'i, was also deeply saddened. Songhwa stayed as a close as a shadow to Willow, and took care of her.

Willow had only to glimpse the chair under the papaya tree, where the old man used to sit, and she would burst into tears. Whenever she looked at the baby's clothes and the cot in their room, tears blinded her. There were more tears over her father-in-law's now-unused rice bowl, chopsticks, and spoon. Everything that Willow laid her eyes on reminded her of his absence. She was so depressed she couldn't bring herself to go to work.

A couple of days later, Taewan came back from work and sat down opposite Willow at the supper table prepared by Songhwa. After Taewan pressed a spoon into her hand and put some grilled fish on top of the rice, Willow gratefully ate a few spoonfuls. Once he had finished eating, Taewan said, "This Saturday evening, we've been invited to a party at the Puerto Rican camp. Let's go together."

The Puerto Rican camp was the camp closest to Camp Seven, but they had little contact. According to Dusun's mother, who once lived in the same camp as the Puerto Rican workers, they were a lot of fun.

"By 'we,' do you mean everyone in our camp?"

"No, I was thinking that we and Jaesong with his wife,

James's family, and a few younger people. Let's go, it'll be a good change for you."

Whenever she felt the child in her womb kicking actively as if trying to rouse her, Willow would start to think that she should pull herself together and resume her daily life. Still, it wasn't long since her father-in-law had passed, so she was reluctant to go to the party. If this were Korea, she would have to spend at least a year in mourning.

"It might be better if we lived Korea-style," said Taewan, "but here people go back to work the day after burying parents, siblings, or children. Aboji surely wants you to cheer up quickly and have a healthy child."

Willow decided to go.

Everyone working in the communal canteen was glad to see Willow when she arrived to help with the food for the party. The Kaesong ajumoni tapped Willow on the back. "It's good you're here. The dead are dead, and the living have to go on living."

Dusun's mother said, "You've grown so thin. Mr. So was blessed to have such a daughter-in-law. Even if my own aboji passed away, I wouldn't be able to cry as sadly as you. Everyone felt sad, seeing you."

"Thanks to you, I cried a lot thinking of my own aboji. The old man's funeral was like a funeral for my own at the same time," said Julie's mother, who had only learned belatedly that her own father had passed away.

"That's why there's a saying that if you go to someone else's funeral and want to shed a tear, you have to give priority to your own sorrows. I cried thinking of my omma," James's mother agreed.

The Kaesong ajumoni produced the ingredients. "Songhwa

took good care of Willow. That's why friends are important. Now let's cook some food."

Adding noodles and sauce after frying various vegetables and sliced pork, they cut up scallions, leeks, and zucchini and used them to make pancakes with a flour batter in an oiled pan. There was a lot to do, in order to have enough to give to those who were not going to the Puerto Rican camp. It was a treat paid for by Taewan in gratitude for all the help they had given during his father's funeral.

They were seven to go to the Puerto Rican camp: Willow and Taewan, Songhwa, Jaesong and his wife, James's father, and Dusun's mother. The Kaesong ajumoni and James's mother decided to stay and serve the food to the camp workers. Most people preferred eating and drinking comfortably at the camp rather than going to sit down somewhere where they couldn't speak the language.

The ridge of Koʻolau Mountain glowed red. As twilight fell, the heat also eased. The three men walked ahead and the four women followed. Julie's mother taught them what the Puerto Ricans said to greet each other.

"*Hola*! Easy, isn't it? Repeat after me."

Willow and Songhwa shyly imitated her. Then Dusun's mother taught them how Puerto Ricans greet each other, pressing cheek to cheek. At the sight of Dusun's mother standing in the road demonstrating that with exaggerated gestures, Willow could not help bursting into laughter, then covered her mouth with her hand in surprise. There she was laughing out loud only a few days after her father-in-law passed away! She worried that others would find fault, but Taewan was also laughing along with her.

Willow had assumed that people working on a plantation with haole lunas would soon learn English. However, even those who came long before Willow did not know how to speak it. Instead, Pidgin was a language created to enable plantation owners, lunas, and workers to communicate, or workers from different countries. There were no problems working in the fields with people who used English, Japanese, Hawaiian, or European languages. Using Pidgin on the plantation, and living among people from Korea at the camp, there was no inconvenience in not being able to speak English.

When they entered the Puerto Rican camp, they found each house decorated with flowers to mark the festival, and there was a long table set up in the village square. Adults wearing their best clothes were busy preparing the party, while the children were running about and playing. The children were the first to come flocking as they entered the square. Several adults approached and welcomed the visitors. A man who had shaken hands with Taewan put his cheek against Willow's cheek. If she hadn't known in advance, she might have screamed.

Taewan, who could speak English, spoke on their behalf. There seemed to be few people who could speak English on their side, too. The representative of the Puerto Rican camp was a man named José with his wife, Diana. Their ages were hard to estimate, but both looked kindhearted.

"Hola!" Julie's mother said, and handed the food she had brought to Diana. From then on, they talked using a mixture of Pidgin and their native languages, and it seemed to work.

They were led to a table with a vase of flowers in the center. There were only empty plates, glasses, forks, and knives on the long table formed by putting two tables together, but no food. José and Taewan sat side by side at the top, and Willow, Songhwa, Jaesong and his wife, Dusun's mother and James's father sat next to each other, while José's family and friends sat on the other side. The other people sat around small tables. Diana, whose place was directly opposite Willow's, had no time to sit down, as she had to keep coming and going to the kitchen.

Unlike in Korea, where all the food was served at once, in Puerto Rico it was the custom to eat one dish after another. They explained that usually they were busy working hard, so they could not follow custom, but they liked to observe it on holidays and during special events. Several women and men brought wine and baskets of bread, which they placed here and there. Willow's mouth watered at the savory smell of the bread. A man poured wine into every glass on their table.

José said something that Taewan repeated in Korean. "He says that they have heard about the Declaration of Independence and the March First Movement in Korea. In Hawai'i, he saw Korean women with babies on their backs who were selling food and handkerchiefs they had made. He said he was impressed by what they do for their country."

Willow met the other women's eyes and smiled. Among the handicrafts there must have been articles they had embroidered. They hadn't done it to show off to other people, but she was proud to think that he was impressed.

Dusun's mother said, striking her breast proudly, "Tell them that we did some of the embroidery."

Seeing that, the other people from Korea and José's family and friends all laughed. Taewan laughed and continued to translate for José.

"He says that Puerto Rico was a Spanish colony for four hundred years. However, twenty years ago there was a war between Spain and the United States and it became an American colony."

Four hundred years! Everyone's eyes opened wide.

"People in Puerto Rico have an independence movement, but the voices demanding to belong to the United States were louder, so they received citizenship two years ago. But it's a half citizenship, meaning that they can't take part in mainland elections. José says he is envious and respectful of our people who are united in the Manse movement. That's why they've invited us to the feast day of their patron saint."

After translating, Taewan added something in English. He seemed to be saying thank you for inviting them. José offered a toast and everyone raised the glasses standing in front of them. As she was pregnant, Willow merely raised the glass to her lips before putting it down again, then looked at Songhwa in amazement. Her glass was empty! She caught Willow's eye and laughed. Songhwa's face, which had remained dull like a paper flower, even after moving to Camp Seven, blushed red. Away from Sokbo, she seemed to be letting herself go. Willow's heart ached for her.

The food was served. They explained that in Puerto Rico, too, they ate rice. It was cooked with oil, tomato sauce, and meat. Along with that, there was also pork cooked with vegetables and tomato sauce, and fried bananas. The food wasn't served individually but placed in large dishes from which people helped themselves.

Julie's mother helped herself to some rice and told Willow, "Their tomato sauce is like our bean paste and red pepper paste. It seems to go into every dish. Try something. It's not bad."

Willow was reluctant to try food that looked unfamiliar and smelled of unaccustomed spices. Now that morning sickness was over, she fortunately did not have to worry about vomiting in front of people. Songhwa speared a fried banana with her fork. So far, Willow had eaten a banana just once in her life. It had smelled good, and melted away in her mouth, leaving a taste of honey, but she had never dared to buy any. Dusun's mother explained that there were many types of bananas, and that fried bananas were a different kind. Taewan, who was enjoying the food, asked Willow if she didn't like it. Diana also urged her to eat with gestures. Embarrassed at the attention, she quickly picked up a fork.

The Puerto Rican workers on the other side were eating the fried noodles and pancakes Julie's mother had brought, and raised their thumbs in appreciation. If Willow merely picked at the food, it would not be polite toward the people who had invited her, and would injure Taewan's dignity.

Songhwa put a few slices of fried banana on her plate.

"It's good. Try it."

It was sweeter and tastier than raw banana, which gave her the courage to try the other dishes. Since her father-in-law's funeral, Willow had only eaten because of the baby in her womb, and this was the first time she had enjoyed it.

Unlike Koreans, who ate in silence, saying that if people talk when they're eating, the blessings run away, the Puerto Ricans had lively conversation while enjoying the meal. As time passed, a nearly full moon rose over the sugarcane field. The sugarcane, bathed in moonlight, looked like a mysterious forest, not a wearisome field. People grew drunk on moonlight and wine.

Someone began beating a drum as if now the party was really beginning, then another started to sing to the beat. The merriest man in José's group stood up and started to dance as if he had been waiting for the music the whole time. Men, women, and children mingled and danced. Diana took Julie's mother by the hand and led her out. Julie's mother went out with Dusun's mother and had great fun. Willow and the others gaily stamped their feet and clapped their hands.

The closer she came to term, the more often Willow had to

pass water, and now she stood up, needing to use the toilet. Songhwa, who was watching people dancing with her mouth open, hastily stood up too.

"No, it's all right, the lights are bright, I can go alone, you stay here." Willow pressed on Songhwa's shoulders to make her sit back down, and went off to the toilet. She was glad that Songhwa was looking happy.

The moon was visible through a small window in the toilet. It was the same moon that her mother and younger brothers could see back at home. Hongju could also see it on Maui Island. There was no knowing when they might all be able to view the moon sitting together. Would such a day ever come? Willow suddenly thought of her father-in-law, grew sad, and quickly returned to the party. Whistling and cheers seemed to indicate that the dancing had grown even more exciting.

As Willow approached the crowd of dancers, she stopped in surprise. Standing in the middle, and moving her body as if possessed, was Songhwa. The drumbeat was keeping time to Songhwa's violent gestures, while others were reduced to onlookers. Not only the Puerto Ricans but also her companions were clapping in time to Songhwa's dancing. She seemed to be in another world.

Surely that woman is mad just like her omma?

There had been rumors that Okhwa's madness had been a sign that she was becoming a shaman. Willow's heart dropped as she realized that Songhwa looked just like Kumhwa when she was performing a ceremony. At such times she would go into a trance, jumping up and down as Songhwa was doing. Willow had never told the churchgoing people, and not even Taewan, that Songhwa was the granddaughter of a shaman, fearing that they might shun or look down on her. Willow rushed forward and caught hold of Songhwa.

"Hey, what are you doing?" scolded Willow.

Streaming with sweat, Songhwa stared at Willow with gleaming eyes.

Willow crouched down on the kitchen floor, clutching her stomach. Julie's mother had told her, "If it feels as if you need to shit, your lower belly twisting till it hurts, then relaxing, and it keeps on, that means your pains have started."

She had started to feel that kind of pain at first rooster crow. It had been agreed that the Kaesong ajumoni would serve as midwife, since she had helped many young women who had come to the plantation as picture brides give birth, and had gained plenty of experience. She said that the first picture brides were young and had nobody to care for them, so there had been a lot of accidents. Everyone agreed that a Korean woman like her was far better than the doctor at the clinic, who didn't speak their language. At the start of her final month, the Kaesong ajumoni told her, "To start with, the birth canal expands slowly, it doesn't mean that the baby is about to come out."

Sitting beside her, Dusun's mother added, "It's only when the sky turns yellow and your husband starts to swear blue murder that the baby comes out."

"That's right. If your husband is beside you when you're having a baby, he won't have any hair left," said James's mother with a smile.

Willow had put up with the pain as she recalled all the advice she'd been given. She had spent the night swallowing back her groans to avoid waking Taewan, and was now engaged in packing his lunchbox and preparing breakfast. Now she could take no more, and one scream followed another. When Taewan, who had been washing his face, came in and found her crouched on the floor clutching her belly, he was at a loss.

"The baby's on its way. Fetch the Kaesong ajumoni. . . ."

"Oh, right. I'll be back soon." Taewan rushed out with a *bang* and a *crash* of the door. Willow made her way slowly back to their room.

Taewan returned with the Kaesong ajumoni, who quickly shooed him away.

"It's still a long time before it comes out. Go to work, the baby can't come out easily if the aboji is around."

He squeezed Willow's hand tightly, then went off to the plantation. After sending their menfolk away, Songhwa and Julie's mother also came over. Julie's mother helped the Kaesong ajumoni prepare to welcome the child, while Songhwa waited and ran errands.

When Taewan came home from work, the child had still not emerged. After being in labor all day long, Willow felt more dead than alive, unable to even greet her husband. She kept thinking of her mother, who had suffered in the same way when she gave birth to Willow and her siblings, and the children and babies she had lost. Willow wailed, calling for her mother, and fell back.

"Don't give up. Try harder."

At the Kaesong ajumoni's words, Willow cried out, and with a final push, using all her remaining strength, she felt the warm baby sliding out.

"It's a son. Where are the scissors?"

Hearing that, Willow relaxed, thanking Heaven.

"Here are the scissors. Oh, look at all the hair he has!" The Kaesong ajumoni cut the umbilical cord, then held the baby upside down and slapped its bottom. The baby burst into tears.

Willow gazed at the baby as it cried; his hair was black and body red. It was her baby. After her journey through hell, Willow was exhausted.

In a faint voice, she asked, "Does he have all his fingers and toes?"

"Yes, everything's there. He's strong." The Kaesong ajumoni gave the baby wrapped in cotton cloth to Willow to hold. Willow felt as though she carried the entire world in her arms.

"Thank you, thank you." Tears seeped from the corners of her eyes. Just like the baby that had fought its way down the narrow birth passage and entered the world, Willow felt reborn as a mother, feeling an inexpressibly deep fellowship with the new life that had survived the months they had spent together.

Julie's mother opened the door and shouted, "Taewan, it's a son, a son!"

The contract for the plantation ended in December that year.

"Chairman Park is asking me to work for the Independence League. In that case it would be better if we moved to Honolulu."

He said that he could also work for *The Korean National Herald*, the League's publication, allowing him to earn a monthly salary, however small. Willow reckoned it would be much better for baby Jongho if Taewan was working in the city, rather than doing plantation work covered in mud. When Willow was a child, she was immensely proud that her father was a schoolteacher. Also, even in the Independence Movement, it was far better for him to be working behind the scenes, rather than engaging in armed struggle.

Jaesong also decided to move to Honolulu for the children's education.

The plantation was taken over by James's father. The Kaesong ajumoni and her husband left for their daughter's house in Wahiawā, where they ran a laundry. Dusun's mother, who lived alone, as well as the unmarried workers, and Sokbo, who had no savings or skills to do other work, remained. The only worry Willow felt on leaving Kahuku was parting from Songhwa after going to all the trouble of bringing her to the camp. After the brief bout of liveliness she'd shown during the visit to the Puerto Rican camp, Songhwa seemed distracted again.

"Songhwa, once I'm in Honolulu, be sure to contact me if there's anything you need. Look after yourself," said Willow, bidding her friend farewell.

Willow asked James's mother and Dusun's mother to promise to take care of her.

In late December 1919, Willow and Taewan left Kahuku with three-month-old Jongho.

Part Two

10

HONOLULU BREEZE

Willow had thought that Taewan would only be working in the Independence League's office, but instead he rented a shop with a room and small kitchen attached to it on Liliha Street, Honolulu. It was a small place between a Japanese tailor's and a Portuguese bakery. Taewan planned to open a shoe store, using the shoemaking skills acquired while attending boarding school.

"I was highly praised by the teacher for my skill. He said that my shoes were the first to sell at the plantation."

Willow felt relieved. Julie's mother had told her, "You can't afford to live in Honolulu on just a single salary."

She had planned to find some sewing to do, at least, while Taewan was out at work, so this was good news. Taewan said that he would take care of custom-made shoes while she would sell the ready-made. Willow learned how to prepare shoe patterns, and look after the display of shoes that he ordered. Taewan put the price tags on the shoes and taught her how to count in English. Willow also mastered the basic English she needed to greet customers and sell goods.

Working together preparing to open the store made Willow happy. Simply leaving Kahuku, which was nothing but sugarcane fields, and coming to Honolulu, the capital city of Hawai'i, seemed like being halfway to success. When Taewan bought a secondhand bicycle, Willow was as proud of it as if it had been a car, full of hope that they would soon become wealthy. All that remained was to hang up the signboard so's SHOES in Hangul and English in front of a few invited guests the next day. After dinner, Taewan said he would take Willow for a ride on his bike.

"What about Jongho?"

Jongho was lying to one side of the room, looking at his fists, babbling as he played.

"If you get him to sleep it'll be all right. Once asleep, he sleeps for a long time."

As Taewan said, Jongho was docile, ate well and slept well. Still, she was reluctant to leave Jongho alone, but she very much wanted to ride with her husband. Once the store was opened and Taewan was working full-time at the office of the Independence League, they wouldn't have much time together. Willow put off washing the dishes and set about getting Jongho to sleep. Jongho, full of milk, didn't wake up even when she shook him. There was nothing to worry about for a few hours.

Taewan locked the store door from the outside, climbed onto the bicycle saddle and balanced it. Once Willow was sitting on the carrier, Taewan started pedaling. Willow hugged Taewan's waist and put her face against his back. As time passed, Taewan began to pant and his back grew damp.

"Is it difficult?" asked Willow.

"There's nothing hard about it. When Jongho is bigger I'll carry the two of you."

Taewan stood on the pedals and accelerated, though it was obviously hard work. They headed for the sea, left the bike standing by Waikīkī Beach, and rested for a while. Willow was content, no longer envious of the relationships of those around her.

That night, sitting next to the sleeping Taewan, Willow wrote a letter to her mother announcing the birth of Jongho and that her father-in-law had died. She also wrote that they had moved to Honolulu, where Taewan would work in an office, that they had opened a shoe store, and had bought a bicycle. Before leaving Kahuku, Willow had sent home fifty dollars that she had earned in the laundry. Now that her mother was the only parent Willow had left, she had realized that if she delayed any longer they might be parted forever without her having bought so much as a pair of socks for her. The regret and sorrow she would feel would be incomparably more than when she lost her father-in-law. Willow added that she would write and send money more often. Just as Taewan donated to the League a sum from his income every month, Willow decided to set aside a certain amount and send it to her mother.

Willow had been planning to live on the monthly salary Taewan received and to save all the income from the shoe store, except for operating expenses and the money for her mother. If she saved enough money to enlarge the store, their income would also increase. Willow, who had dreamed of everyone in Honolulu wearing shoes from So's shoe shop, soon regretted writing to her mother. Few customers visited the store. It was hard to sell even one or two pairs of ready-made shoes a day, let alone custom-made. Taewan was more interested in the Independence League than the store, and his whole salary went to it as a donation. When he first told her that he had donated his entire salary from the Independence League office, Willow was immensely frustrated and angry.

"Couldn't you wait until the store is up and running before donating all your salary?" she asked over dinner that night.

"How is that any different from saying that I should put off our country's independence for the rest of my life. Don't we have to achieve independence before Jongho is grown up? Remember how you said at 'Ewa that providing food was not a husband's only role? That helped me understand a lot. The same goes for being an aboji. As you said, I want to be an aboji who doesn't just stave off hunger, but an aboji who bequeaths an independent country."

"But surely, don't basic necessities come before independence or anything else?" she asked, more calmly.

"With such an attitude, we'll never get our country back, even after a thousand, ten thousand years. Aren't our kin suffocating under the Japanese's yoke now? Compared to the comrades fighting in China, what I'm doing is nothing. They give their lives, while I only give away all that I own."

Taewan was determined. Many Koreans in Hawai'i had gone to Shanghai or Beijing for the Independence Movement. Taewan's eyes were full of an eagerness to follow in their footsteps. Those eyes also seemed to be saying that Willow and Jongho were holding him back.

Willow said nothing more, thankful to Taewan simply for being there with her. If there had been just the two of them it might have been different, but now she had Jongho to feed, dress, and raise. From an early age, Willow had known what it was to worry about the next meal, and she did not want her son to experience anything like that. Unlike in Kahuku, where the vegetables from the garden and the eggs produced by the chickens were plentiful, everything in Honolulu cost money. Willow burned inwardly. Her life knew greater penury than on the plantation and she felt increasingly deprived.

It was not only a matter of economic difficulties. Taewan never took any days off, and spent his evenings in meetings, only coming home late, leaving Willow to close up the shop alone. Willow missed the days in Kahuku, when Taewan invariably returned home at 5:00 P.M. At that time, she was never lonely, because she had Songhwa and the other women. Jaesong's family lived not far away, but Willow had fallen out with Julie's mother.

A couple of Sundays previously, she had paid a visit to their house in the neighborhood of Nuʻuanu in the evening. Honolulu wasn't that big a city; everything in the city center was within walking distance. Even if it were a long way, she would have walked to save the fare. Taewan also decided to stop by later that evening. After moving to Honolulu, Jaesong went to work on construction sites, while Julie's mother cleaned and washed clothes at a haole mansion at the mouth of Mānoa Valley, above Waikīkī. Compared to Jaesong, who was earning forty-five cents an hour, Julie's mother said that although the amount of money she received was small, there were often parties that enabled her to bring home leftover food.

"Do you take Tony with you?" asked Willow as she helped Julie's mother prepare dinner. She would much rather be doing housework than run a shop that was not doing any business.

"At first I took him, but last week I enrolled him in the same kindergarten as Alice."

"Doesn't that cost a lot?"

"It's better than teaching the children myself. It cost more to send Julie to the boarding school on her own before she moved to the public school. It's good for children to meet others, they seem to go flying ahead. You should send Jongho to kindergarten early. If he's left alone, he'll lag behind."

Willow looked at Jongho with a sorrowful expression. Jongho, who was always alone with his mother, had been hiding his face, but he seemed to like the children and moved away from Willow. At the sight of Jongho, who had started to stand up holding on to the furniture, happily playing with the other children, she felt content, yet at the same time sorry.

"If you're going to live and do business in Honolulu, you need to build personal connections. You should join the Women's Relief Society and come to church."

While she was living in Kahuku, Julie's mother had not really taken sides, but since moving to Honolulu she had become a zealous supporter of Syngman Rhee, even moving from the Methodist Church to the church established by Dr. Rhee.

"But my husband is working for Yongman Park, so how could I ever attend Dr. Rhee's church?"

Until then, Willow had never dreamed that she might have a political quarrel with Julie's mother.

"You should stop and think. How can old men training with wooden guns ever defeat Japan? It's hard enough to join forces, but how can we ever achieve independence if we're divided? Did you hear that Syngman has been made president of the Provisional Government? Who else should we unite around? You should talk to him and make him change his mind. Someone who attended the central academy established by Dr. Rhee shouldn't act like that."

Julie's mother waved the ladle she'd been using in the air as she spoke. A portrait of Syngman Rhee was hanging on the wall. When Syngman Rhee became president of the Provisional Government, portraits were sent out to every Korean family in Hawai'i. Taewan had folded their copy and used it to prop up one corner of a wobbly chest.

"Are you allowed to treat a portrait of the president like that?"

Taewan had laughed at Willow's words. "A guy like that as president . . ."

Yongman Park had resigned as foreign minister in the Provisional Government and gone to Beijing. Anti-Japanese armed struggles were being waged vigorously in China and Russia, which were directly connected with Korea, overland. He had then set up the Military Unification Society, together with Shin Chaeho and other opponents of Syngman Rhee's policy of diplomatic independence. The plan was to unify the scattered independence armies that were fighting against Japan. After Yongman Park went to China, the main task of the Korean National Independence League in Hawai'i was to support the Korean Independence Movement throughout East Asia.

In her heart of hearts, Willow also supported Syngman Rhee's policy, but she couldn't control herself when Julie's mother implied that Taewan was ungrateful.

"Taewan studied there before Dr. Rhee came in as headmaster and changed the name, at a time when it had nothing to do with Dr. Rhee. In any case, it's neither here nor there. If I set aside a handful of rice every time I cook, and donate that to the Relief Society, it's for neither of the two sides, but for Korea. Still, hasn't Dr. Rhee divided our compatriots, and used their precious donations on personal whims? How can a leader be causing trouble with that kind of money problems?"

"Is that what your husband says? How can that Yongman Park slander our wonderful Dr. Rhee like that? I can't abide him."

The quarrel continued, until finally Willow took Jongho on her back and walked out of the house before Taewan arrived. It made her cry to think that she had split with Julie's mother, who had been so close to Taewan and Willow, and cared for her like a sister.

It had rained briefly. Willow, who had just put Jongho to sleep, came out and swept in front of the store.

"It's only when the road in front of the house is clean that blessings come in." Her mother used to tell this to her brothers when she reminded them to brush the yard and the road in front of the house as soon as they got up. Willow recalled her mother's words and kept the store clean inside and out. Since it would be impolite to sweep only in front of her own store, she also brushed the road before the Portuguese bakery and the Japanese tailor's. It wasn't why she did it, but the bakery sometimes gave her unsold bread. The old woman at the Japanese tailor's gave her sweets when she went out with Jongho on her back. Her daughter-in-law always looked dismissively at Willow, but the old woman always greeted her with a gentle smile.

Willow sometimes gazed into the window of the tailor's shop. In addition to Japanese kimonos and yukatas, they also sold handkerchiefs embroidered with Japanese patterns, sandals, and fans. There were a lot of Westerners, apparently tourists, who visited the store, as well as Japanese customers. Willow, who prided herself on her sewing, regretted that they had not set up a tailor's shop rather than a shoe store.

On one of these mornings, as Willow was bent low, sweeping the ground, she stopped at the sight of a woman's shoes. The brown shoes and white socks looked familiar. Since opening the shoe store, whenever she met people, their shoes were the first thing she noticed. Before she could even raise her head, she heard a voice that was even more familiar than the shoes.

"Willow! Is it really you?"

It was Hongju. Hongju, wearing the shoes bought in Kobe, was standing there with her baby on her back, carrying the suitcase from Pusan. It was two years since they parted after the wedding ceremony. Hongju had put on a lot of weight in those years, and had also become a mother. Willow blinked, unable to believe that her friend was there in front of her. After Willow had moved, they had exchanged letters once, but there had been no word that she was coming to Honolulu.

"Hey, I'm not a ghost. It's me, Hongju!" Hongju shouted loud enough to make people passing look back.

"Yes, it really is you. My goodness! What a surprise!" Willow threw aside the broom and jumped up and down, hand in hand with Hongju, who had dropped her case. Each time they jumped, the baby shook on Hongju's back, still asleep.

"Oh, the baby'll wake up. Let's see him. You said he's called Songgil? How big he is. Let's go inside quickly." Willow picked up Hongju's case and the broom and hurried toward the store.

"Put the baby down first."

"Shall we? He's so heavy when he's asleep."

Once Hongju had untied the carrier blanket, Willow took the child into her arms. Songgil, who was four months older than Jongho, felt heavy for a child his age. Although Hongju had boasted that he looked like her, his face was more like his father's. Willow smiled and laid Songgil next to Jongho. Hongju came to her side and looked at the babies.

"Who does Jongho resemble? He's not a bit like you."

"He's the spitting image of Taewan," Willow replied proudly. With the two babies lying on a mat with their arms stretched wide, the room was full.

Hongju sat down on the store's chair and fanned herself, sweaty after walking so far carrying her child. Willow went to the kitchen and poured a cup of water. Hongju, after drinking the water, said that she had come with Doksam, who was on his way to a plantation at Waipahu. Waipahu was near 'Ewa, not far from Honolulu.

"Are you moving there?" Willow asked, delighted.

"Not for good. We've come to help break a Japanese workers' strike."

Willow knew all about such things.

"While it's good to visit Honolulu, I have mixed feelings

too. They're workers just like us, and if they strike we ought to be supporting them. It's not right to help break the strike just because we're offered money, is it?"

In fact, Willow had once asked Taewan the same question. It would be better to strike in support, for breaking the strike, even while temporarily receiving high wages, brought no benefit to the Korean workers in the long run.

Willow gave Hongju the answer she had heard from Taewan.

"It's not about crushing the strike for money. It's a way of positively upsetting the Japanese who took over our country, our hearts being motivated by the Independence Movement."

Hongju nodded as if she agreed. "Even my miserly Jo Doksam makes a small donation when he receives his monthly salary. And by the way, Willow, I've joined the Women's Relief Society."

"Really? What made you do that?"

This was Hongju, who had no interest in how the world was going and had rather preferred things Japanese, as being the new style.

"When I first came here, I didn't care whether Korea went to ruin or not, it had nothing to do with me. But after the baby was born I had a change of heart. If our country remains part of Japan, my child has no hope for a better future, and will never be able to go back home. Even if we eat a spoonful of rice less right now, we have to support independence."

As Hongju said, if any of the Korean workers earned any money at all, they were busily using it for their country rather than for themselves. They worked harder in order to raise money to build schools and support the Independence Movement groups. No matter how well some might live, they couldn't escape the sorrow that was the lot of the nationless Korean people.

"Anyway, I live and let live, and I see all of Japan's virtues.

Songgil's aboji went straight to the plantation. I let him go because I want to see you, and smell the city breeze. Could you give me a place to sleep until he comes to fetch me on Sunday?" Hongju glanced around the room as she spoke.

This was Wednesday, so it was only for four nights.

"Of course. Jongho's aboji can sleep at the office of the Independence League."

"Oh, Jongho's aboji is working for them, is he? Have you met Dr. Rhee personally?"

Willow took one look at Hongju's expectant expression, like she was about to ask for a favor, and grew anxious. While she hesitated, Hongju said, "Last year Dr. Rhee came to Maui. After hearing him lecture, I was so inspired that I started to attend church and joined the Relief Society. I reckon there's no one as smart and special as he is in the whole world. How great that your husband supports someone like that."

Willow, who had never expected to hear such talk from Hongju, felt as if she were facing a snowball growing ever bigger as it rolled down a steep hillside. She was afraid that if she told the truth, a conflict would arise as it had with Julie's mother. Since coming to Honolulu, it was almost as if the supporters of Yongman Park and Syngman Rhee considered each other enemies. She didn't want things to be like that with Hongju.

"You go to church?" Willow asked, avoiding her friend's eyes.

"Well, I'm not a serious believer, but if you go to church, you get to meet people, socialize, to hear the sermons, so it's better than not going. Willow, couldn't you ask Jongho's aboji to introduce Doksam to Dr. Rhee?"

The snowball was gaining speed.

"Heh, uh . . ."

"You see, your husband has studied, he works for an organization, it might be different for you but I'm worried that later on Songgil will be disadvantaged because of his uneducated aboji. I want to meet Dr. Rhee and ask him to give Doksam a job in the Maui local branch executive. He would look so much better with a position like that."

A snowball the size of a house was rushing toward Willow.

". . . But, but Taewan supports Chairman Park, Yongman Park."

Willow closed her eyes tightly as she spoke, while Hongju's eyes widened, and she was about to say something when Jongho began to cry. Willow went running into the other room, relieved, and changed Jongho's diaper, then came back into the shop holding him. Hongju, who had been absorbed in thought, softened her expression and held out her hands to Jongho.

"Jongho, come here. I'm your auntie."

Willow's heart warmed at Hongju's words.

Jongho, who was very shy, murmured and snuggled against Willow's breast. It seemed that her son, who had no blood relatives in Hawai'i but his parents, had gained an aunt. Just as her relationship with Taewan had grown stronger thanks to the baby, he seemed to be bringing her closer to her friend, and Willow did not want to lose Hongju.

"Oh, our Jongho is hungry." Willow untied the top of her dress and gave the baby her breast.

"Aigo, you and I, we're real ajimaes now. We'll feed our babies anywhere. By the way, do you have news of Songhwa?"

Willow's face clouded as she nodded. Songhwa was another aunt for Jongho. She wondered whether or not to tell her about Songhwa dancing at the Puerto Rican camp.

People should always watch their mouths. Words become sparks that kindle fires. Those were words her mother had hammered into her since childhood. Fearing that words once spoken might spread like fire, Willow buried gossip deep in her heart. And that applied to the business with Songhwa.

"Not since we arrived in Honolulu," said Willow, grateful that Hongju acted as though she had never mentioned Syngman Rhee.

They continued to talk about Ojin Village. It was less than three years since they left there, but it felt more like thirty years ago. They exchanged news they had heard through correspondence with their families.

Hongju's younger brother said that their youngest daughter had died of the Spanish flu. "Everyone in Korea caught the Spanish flu. It affected the whole world," Hongju said matter-of-factly.

Willow and Hongju decided to go to Kahuku to meet Songhwa the following weekend. Willow wanted to go in any case. Kahuku was the place where she had first lived with Taewan, as well as being the place where she had become pregnant and given birth to Jongho. And there was her father-in-law's grave with so many memories.

On the Saturday, Willow and Hongju left home after an early lunch and took the train from Honolulu Station. They intended to spend the night before returning. Willow felt as excited as if she were going home.

Willow and Hongju found seats, loosened the carrier blankets, and held their babies on their laps. Songgil, who could not remain still for a second, was given a cookie that Hongju had prepared in advance, and Jongho, once fed, fell asleep. Willow and Hongju talked for the entire ride. Even though they had already been chatting day and night for three days, they still had things to say.

"Once the strike is over, I don't want to return to Maui. I'm going to persuade Doksam to let us live somewhere near you. Every time I see you two living in such harmony, I feel sick, but what can I do?" When Hongju expressed an envy quite devoid of jealousy, Willow revealed the story she had kept hidden.

"It wasn't good to start with. On the first night after the wedding, I heard the camp women saying that Taewan had had a first love, and later learned that she had died. He had not wanted to get married, but his aboji forced him to."

Hongju looked shocked. "Oh, what a thing! You must have felt terrible."

"I was so sad that I couldn't write to you or visit Songhwa. But then Taewan opened his heart to me four months after we got married."

"What made him change? You can't be that good in bed, surely?"

"Really! The things you say!" Willow blushed and looked around in case somebody had heard, then told her what had happened at her mother-in-law's grave, which Hongju found as entertaining as a romance novel. "But more recently I've discovered that I have a rival more powerful than any first love."

Willow sighed.

"Who is that?"

"Korea's independence. Before we married, Taewan vowed to dedicate himself body and soul to the Independence Movement at the military academy."

"Oh, I'd hate that if it were my husband, though it's admirable in someone else's!"

Willow and Hongju laughed and talked as if they were in Hongju's room in Ojin Village. A Japanese woman sitting across the aisle frowned and glanced at them, but the two paid no attention.

Alighting at Kahuku Station, Willow took Hongju to the cemetery near the church. At the thought of her father-in-law, who had passed away without seeing the grandson he had so been waiting for, her nose pricked.

Willow put Jongho down in front of her father-in-law's gravestone, feeling light and cool the moment the carrier blanket was off. "Aboji, this is Jongho, your first grandson. Jongho, you must bow to your haraboji." Jongho stood there holding on to the gravestone, then wobbled his way around it. As he performed a kind of hula, bobbing up and down, he seemed to be playing with his grandfather. If her father-in-law were still alive, how he would have adored Jongho.

Willow wiped away a tear.

They were lucky enough to catch a ride on a carriage that was passing as they came out of the cemetery and headed for the camp where Songhwa had lived at first. Then they walked along the road to Camp Seven. It was around the time when people were returning home from the fields. They met Dusun's mother in the street. She greeted Willow as if she were a long-lost relative, and was amazed to see how much Jongho had grown. After she had exchanged greetings with Dusun's mother, she asked about Songhwa, nervous at what she'd be told.

"Sokbo isn't beating her, is he?"

"Nowadays he has no strength left for that. His new bride is having a hard time nursing the old man and doing the laundry."

Willow had something else she was curious about.

"Who is living in our old house?"

"A certain Mr. Jang lives there with his picture wife. She's really tough and started to work in the fields as soon as they arrived. She doesn't want to work in the canteen or the laundry because it pays so little."

To reach Songhwa's home, they had to pass in front of the

house where Willow lived before. She stopped for a moment and looked over the fence. The house and the papaya tree were just the same. The owners being as she had heard, there was no sign of a weed in the yard and the chickens were shut up in their coop. After Willow arrived, she had maintained it as her father-in-law and Taewan had done. Along the sides of the yard, wildflowers had bloomed, and the chickens had roamed over the yard and the vegetable patch. But now, even under the papaya tree, there was not a blade of grass to be seen. Willow was glad that the house was being so well tended, but sad that all her memories had disappeared so completely.

When they reached Songhwa's home, she was out in the yard, and Sokbo had just finished washing after returning from work. Songhwa stared dumbly at Willow and Hongju, looking no worse than when they last parted.

Hongju hugged her and shed some tears. "Songhwa, it's me. Where's your beautiful face all gone?"

"Songhwa, how are you doing? We want to sleep here with you tonight. Will that be okay?"

At Willow's words, Songhwa brought her friends inside. Songhwa was fascinated by the sight of Jongho crawling about and Songgil roaming around, though she showed no interest in her friends.

"Hey, what about some food?" asked Hongju. "We ate lunch early and we're starving."

At that, Songhwa went to the kitchen and prepared a meal. As they had been about to eat dinner, the rice and the side dishes were ready. Sokbo, who had aged over the last few months, seeing the friends enjoying themselves together, disappeared without eating.

Hongju stretched her legs out after eating a hearty dinner and said, "It's like coming home. Songhwa, you're our big aunt." Songhwa's birthday was the first of the three. Next was Hongju, then Willow.

They made themselves at home, feeling comfortable.

"Later, let's all live in Honolulu together. There's no knowing the order in which people will die, of course, but in terms of age, Songhwa's husband should be the first to go. Then you must find a young bridegroom and have some fun," said Hongju with a sincere expression.

Willow laughed as she asked, "Next should be Songgil's aboji. Will you find a new husband too?"

"Well, they say life comes in threes, so of course I will!" Hongju said heartily, looking at Songgil. "Aigo, Songgil, I'm sorry. Pretend you didn't hear that."

Their laughter filled the house.

On the evening of the day they returned from Kahuku, Hongju went off to the plantation at Waipahu with her husband, who came to pick her up. After seeing her off, Willow felt abandoned and sadder than when they parted after the wedding.

Hongju kept her word. Instead of returning to Maui after the Japanese workers' strike was over, they went to live on the Wahiawā pineapple plantation to the north of Waipahu. It was a mere two-hour train ride from Honolulu.

11

TIME OF CHANGE

A new year had begun, but the situation in the store did not improve. There were no orders for custom-made shoes, and dust was gathering on the shoes in the display that they bought at the start. They ought to be changed for the new styles, but she was in no position to do that. Moreover, since Taewan worked for the Independence League, supporters of Syngman Rhee never came by. At first, supporters of Yongman Park came, but in Hawai'i, where a pair of shoes might last forever, there was rarely any need for new ones.

As their stock of rice began to run low, Willow's anger and frustration slowly burned hotter.

Taewan preferred to go out fundraising rather than sit in the office preparing the League's journal. "Sitting in front of a desk fiddling with a pen and talking doesn't suit my temperament." Spending all of his time traveling around O'ahu as well as neighboring islands, and if ever any came, he wouldn't even have time to make the shoes people ordered. When Willow couldn't stand it any longer and broached the topic, he found money for the rent, but things remained difficult. When she saw Jongho hanging around in hope of sweets in front of the bakery or the Japanese tailor's, her heart cracked like a paddy field in a drought. She had reached a point where she worried about their next meal, just as her mother had done. Willow was most upset of all when Jongho hid behind her when he saw his father, as if he were a stranger.

Julie's mother scolded Willow. "You gave him too much leeway to start with. You should have kept nagging him to be a proper family head."

When Hongju had come to visit, Willow took her to Julie's house, because Taewan knew nothing of the incident with Julie's mother, and she didn't want to tell him. She regretted losing her temper over a few words, reckoning she had been narrow-minded to pick up the baby and walk out like that. After a couple of glances, she sensed that the bad feelings had disappeared. Hongju, who had lived in Masan for a short time after getting married, hit it off with Julie's mother at once, and soon they were chatting like old friends.

Willow decided to nag at Taewan as Julie's mother advised, but when she saw Taewan come home with a darkish beard and weary eyes half closed, words failed her.

He's not busy doing bad things, he's not causing trouble.

The mere fact that he did not talk about leaving for China or Russia left her feeling grateful and fortunate. Instead, she decided to take charge of their lives until Korea became independent. That meant she could not simply rely on the shoe store alone. She decided to put into practice what she had previously only been thinking about, and went to a cloth store to buy a yard of linen and several colors of thread. Then, recalling the Western tourists she had seen visiting the Japanese tailor's, she made handkerchiefs and table mats that she embroidered with traditional Korean patterns such as cranes, plums, peonies, and pine trees.

She sat sewing whenever Jongho was playing alone or sleeping, and would often think back to times sewing with her mother. In those days, sewing until calluses formed on her fingers had been tedious, but now she was eager at the thought of how much she might sell them for. When she focused on embroidering, trivial thoughts disappeared and she was happy. Also, unlike when her mother told her what to do, *she* could decide what to embroider, which colors and patterns, so it was more fun. Five handkerchiefs and four table mats could be made from a yard of cloth. She placed the handkerchiefs, each with different colors and patterns, and the table mats, embroidered with different flower patterns but with the borders the same color, on one side of the shoe display case.

As she stood in front of the store with Jongho on her back, Willow's heart raced as an elderly haole couple showed interest in the handkerchiefs and mats in the showcase. The wife met Willow's gaze and smiled. Willow quickly stepped inside and beckoned them to follow. That alone required great courage. The woman came in, pointed at the handkerchiefs and mats, and said something Willow didn't understand. She handed the woman a handkerchief and a mat and told her the price in poor English.

"Thirty cents each for these. Forty cents each for these. Three dollars for everything."

Actually, the handkerchiefs and mats taken all together should cost $3.10, but she knew there was a need for discounts in doing business. The woman carefully checked the embroidery. Willow kept pointing at the sewing box on the small table and then at herself, miming the act of embroidering.

Hearing the word "Japan" in the conversation between the couple, she waved her hands and said, "No Japan. Korea."

The wife said something to her husband, then asked her to give her all the handkerchiefs and mats.

"All, you mean everything?" Willow was so taken aback that she spoke in Korean. The wife guessed what she meant and nodded. When the old gentleman exclaimed "Wonderful," Willow's heart seemed about to explode. Her hands trembled as she handed them their purchase. It had cost her a little over a dollar for the cloth and thread, so she had more than twice as much pure profit left from her first sale. As soon as the old couple left, she closed the store and ran to buy more cloth.

"Jongho, I've earned a lot of money so I'm going to buy you something delicious, and a toy, too. Just wait a minute."

As Willow went running, Jongho, who was firmly tied to her back, cried out excitedly.

Willow's work sold far better than shoes. Sometimes there were people who came to buy handkerchiefs or mats and ended up buying shoes as well. Others ordered tablecloths or asked to have their name embroidered on something. Willow worked even harder at her embroidery. The number of items also increased to include baby bibs and aprons. The embroidered items took the place of the shoes in the showcase. During the day, because of Jongho, it was difficult for her to sit down and embroider, so she worked through much of the night.

While worrying about Willow's health, Taewan saw the significance of selling embroidered motifs from Korea next door to a Japanese tailor. "It's great. What you're doing humiliates the Japanese."

"Don't say that. Those are nice people who adore Jongho and give him cookies. Their customers also come in to see the things in our store." Willow, who knew almost nobody in Honolulu, valued having a neighbor with whom she could share kindly greetings. However, once Willow's embroidery began to sell, the attitude of the old woman grew noticeably chilled. Even if she greeted her, she did not respond, and if she saw Jongho, she pretended not to know him. Willow felt sorry to be taking away their customers, so she swept the street even more energetically in front of the tailor's shop.

The Japanese shop soon began selling more varied items using the latest sewing machine. As Western people could not distinguish between Japan and Korea, they naturally preferred these items, which were better displayed than in her shabby, unattractive shoe store. The number of people interested in Willow's embroidery grew noticeably less, and whenever Jongho woke up he cried to go outside, so she had no time to embroider. When she tried to work in the evenings, she was so sleepy that she pricked her fingers and had to stop or she would leave blood stains on the embroidery.

One day, when Willow went outside with Jongho, he wandered toward the tailor's shop. Willow was following along behind Jongho when the daughter-in-law came out and suddenly emptied a basinful of water onto the ground in front of him. Jongho, soaked, burst into tears.

"Aigo!" Willow rushed over, picked her son up and hugged him.

The woman went in without a word of apology.

"Poor thing, you must have been so surprised." As she went back indoors carrying Jongho, Willow was so angry that she felt like crying. She wanted to say something, but she and the neighbors didn't speak the same language, and she also didn't want to quarrel with people she had to see every day. As she was changing his clothes, she said under her breath what she wished she could say to their face.

Willow hoisted Jongho onto her back, went out, and locked the door of the store. She wanted to get rid of her frustration and sadness, but she had nowhere to go. Julie's mother would still be working, and Taewan would be in the office, but she couldn't go there for something private. Unsure where to go, Willow started walking aimlessly.

On Liliha Street, where they lived, all kinds of people of various ethnic groups and from different countries earned a living in a variety of ways. There were a good number from Korea, but since Willow did not attend church and was not a member of any women's association, there was no one she was close to. In fact, in the divided community, she felt uncomfortable meeting people from either side. Her relationship with Julie's mother, too, was in a delicate state, even if they were careful on account of their close bond.

Willow was desperate for a friend she could easily visit and confide in. As for Hongju, whom she had thought she would be able to meet more often since she lived nearby, they had exchanged letters only once. Hongju, who had recently had a miscarriage, was working in a pineapple-canning plant. She said that Myongok and Makson were also living in Wahiawā and asked Willow to join them. According to the news she heard from Julie's mother, Songhwa was still childless.

Willow missed all of her fellow picture brides. The time they spent together in the same inn in Kobe, laughing and talking, full of expectations of a new life, was like a dream. She even felt nostalgia for the night when they had all cried together in one room, in despair after seeing their bridegrooms. Willow felt alone in the streets crowded with cars, horses, and wagons and thronged with people.

She walked on, along North King Street, as far as 'Iolani Palace. She remembered the last queen of Hawai'i, who was driven from the throne and lived as a prisoner in the palace for a long time. The emotions that the queen must have felt, trapped in her room, came sweeping over Willow as if they were her

own. Suddenly a squall of rain poured down as if it were the
queen's tears. People accustomed to the rainy-season weather
continued to do what they were doing, unflustered, or sheltered
under the eaves.

Willow, with Jongho on her back, took refuge under a banyan tree that formed a small forest with its downward-reaching
branches. Lush leaves spread like an umbrella, keeping off the
heavy rain. She felt envious of the tree, whose tightly clustered
descending branches leaned against each other. Jongho, who
had no inkling of what his mother was feeling, jerked excitedly
as he tried to catch raindrops falling between the leaves. When
the rain stopped and a rainbow appeared, Willow wished for
something good to happen.

It was nearly time for Julie's mother or the children to be
home, so she headed in the direction of their home. Under the
carrier blanket, Willow's and Jongho's clothes were damp with
rain and sweat. After wandering the city or standing with the
baby on her back for several hours since leaving the house, she
felt as though her legs were weighted down with lumps of iron.

Their house was above a Chinese vegetable shop. She
summoned up her last reserves of strength and climbed the
stairs, but the door was locked, nobody was home. She felt
like crying. Jongho, whom she had fed once along the way,
was hungry and whimpering. Willow sat down in front of the
door, took Jongho from off her back, and nursed him. After
feeding him twice that day without eating anything herself,
Willow was hungry and thirsty. Jongho, who was crying and
still hungry, suddenly turned his head at the sound of children climbing the stairs.

"It's Jongho!" Julie cried, holding Tony's hand. Nancy, Alice,
and Julie's mother appeared behind them. Willow stood up,
putting Jongho down. He was delighted to see the children.

"What are you doing here at this time of day?" Julie's mother asked, looking surprised.

"I just dropped by since I was in the vicinity. Where have you been?"

"Let's get inside. I have something to talk about with you."

As soon as they were inside, the children played with Jongho, giving the mothers some privacy.

Julie's mother gave Willow a cup of water and also drank some herself before she spoke. "I've just been to our son's school and the kindergarten to register a transfer of schools."

"Transfer? Why?"

"We're moving to Wahiawā."

Willow nearly dropped the cup. If Julie's mother left too, she was at a loss to know how she would survive. Honolulu was already feeling quite empty. "Are you going to work at the pineapple plantation as well?"

"No. A cleaner's. The Kaesong ajumoni contacted me saying there was a good spot available close to the military camp. I dragged Julie's father along and since there's a public school nearby, we've decided to go."

Willow envied her for moving to where the people she most wanted to see lived.

After she was born, in Ojin Village, Willow had always lived in the same place until her picture marriage. In Korea, people who moved around were considered vagabonds, and were looked down upon. If someone came in from another part of the country, they were unwelcome and kept at a distance. However, the hard and unstable lives of those who came to Hawai'i as workers did not allow them to put down roots and live in one place. Most people, those without schooling or special skills, spent their lives moving from one island to another, from place to place, in search of better pay and better work. Nowadays

Wahiawā, with the Schofield Barracks holding more than seven thousand soldiers, and with a large-scale pineapple plantation, was popular. Willow wanted to go there, too. She wanted to live with her friends, like the branches of a banyan tree that grew in harmony with each other.

"That sounds great. I want to give up the shop; business is no good. Couldn't we go there too and find work?" Willow asked, frustrated, knowing that Taewan couldn't leave the office of the Independence League.

"But will Taewan be able to go? Or could you live apart from him?"

For a moment Willow thought about him staying in the office, while she went alone with Jongho, but she didn't want to live away from her husband. Even if he couldn't see his father every day, there was a big difference between a father's presence and being apart. Willow knew better than anyone what it meant to grow up without a father.

She sighed heavily instead of answering.

"If it's because of Jongho, why don't you take over the work I've been doing?"

"But what could I do about the baby?" asked Willow, her expression growing sad again. There was nowhere to leave Jongho, and he was too young to send to kindergarten.

"I already told you. You can take Jongho with you. The garden is big, you can leave him playing, while you work. I know you're good at sewing, which will help. Give it a try."

Julie's mother worked from 9 A.M. to 5 P.M. from Monday to Saturday and was paid six dollars a week, twenty-four a month. The monthly wage for a man working on a sugarcane plantation was thirty dollars, so it was no small amount in terms of time and work.

"Thank you, Onni. Thank you very much."

"Since our move is certain, I'll take you over there. The person I'll introduce you to is really kindhearted. The owners have four kids, and they sometimes give me clothes they don't need, or leftover food on the day after a party."

They agreed to go to the house the very next day, and Willow's steps were light as she returned home with Jongho. She felt as if the twenty-four dollars were already as good as hers, so for once she stopped at the butcher's to buy pork. The owner added in a chunk of lard at no extra cost, saying that he had extra.

Her wish for good luck was already coming true.

After they closed down the shoe store and moved to Punchbowl Street, the rent was less and her workplace was closer. Every morning, after Taewan had gone to work, Willow would get ready and leave for work. Jongho, who was twenty months old now, walked well, but slowly, so she carried him on her back.

The mansion in Mānoa had a garden as large as a park. The owner of the mansion, Mr. Robson, was a wealthy man who owned several large fishing boats. Originally, they lived in Portland, on the mainland, but he said that during a business visit the family had so fallen in love with the Hawaiian scenery that they had moved there. The Robsons had daughters in elementary school and five-year-old twin sons. Willow worked some way away from the mansion, so she only watched the children return from school by car from a distance. She almost never met Mr. Robson, nor even Mrs. Robson, who was in charge of the house.

In the mansion, there were close to twenty rooms, and frequent parties were held, so that in addition to chefs, gardeners, and nannies, there were many other live-in staff and daily help-ers. A native Hawaiian woman named Marika was in charge of the workers. It was she whom Julie's mother had called kind-hearted.

Willow was the only Korean among the staff. Even after ar-riving in Hawai'i, she had always lived among her compatriots, so she was nervous about working with people who didn't speak her language. At the same time, she was glad that she could work without worrying about the Yongman Park faction or the Syngman Rhee faction, and she took courage when Marika smiled and treated her kindly, and from the fact that Julie's mother had done the work before her, so it couldn't be that bad.

Willow was only responsible for the laundry. Julie's mother had worked cleaning the mansion and doing the laundry with two Filipino girls. However, since Willow had a child with her, she did all the laundry alone in a room next to the servants' hos-tel, while they did the cleaning. From there, she could watch Jongho playing in the backyard. Since they were six in the family, she had thought that doing the laundry would be easy but she was amazed to discover that the six of them changed clothes several times each day.

In Korea, it was common to spend an entire season in one suit of clothing. Even in hot Hawai'i, although muddy work clothes might get washed every day, people wore their leisure clothes for days on end. Apparently, rich haole changed their clothes every time they ate, had a party, or exercised. In addition to clothes, bedspreads, duvets, and curtains were also changed on a daily basis. Willow had the impression that it would be possible to clothe and cover all the people of Korea with the amount of laundry coming from the Robson household. Willow belatedly realized how insignificant the boiled egg she had given the ha-ole child at Kahuku Station must have seemed.

Willow was washing, ironing, and sewing on missing buttons or mending torn places, while Jongho played in the small courtyard behind the hostel. The white flowers of plumeria gave off a sweet scent. As Willow watched Jongho playing happily alone with shells, dirt, or flowers and fruit fallen from the trees, she felt both happy and sad. She promised herself that before Jongho was much older, she would save enough money to send him to kindergarten.

One day, Marika brought over a rocking horse that the Robson children had been using. One of the handles and a foothold were broken on the wooden horse, but Jongho was thrilled and never wanted to get off it. Willow had a hard time calming him when it was time to go home.

Willow was satisfied with the work. Dealing with the bulky laundry was hard enough work to physically exhaust her, but there was nowhere else she could take Jongho and work so comfortably. As Julie's mother had said, sometimes Willow was given clothes or toys once used by the twins, and leftover food from parties.

It was too good to give up.

Six months had passed since Willow had started working at the Robsons' mansion. The staff cooked and ate in the backyard. They ate poi, a kind of gruel made by pounding boiled taro, then mixing it with water, and fried fish wrapped in broad ti leaves. Although Marika invited Willow to have lunch with them, Willow preferred her home-cooked lunchbox.

Jongho, on the other hand, loved the Hawaiian food. After tasting laulau, steamed pork wrapped in taro leaves, he ate everything they prepared. When lunchtime came and Willow brought out her lunchbox of rice and pickled radish, Jongho would run across to the workers' table. Willow gradually followed him more and more often, to have lunch with the others.

Willow was given new tasks besides washing. Shortly after she began to work there, a stain on the hem of a dress belonging to one of the Robsons' daughters could not be removed, so she asked Marika if she could embroider something to hide it. Mrs. Robson noticed the embroidered flower pattern, and called Willow up to the house. Willow entered the garden around the mansion for the first time, following Marika. The garden seemed to contain all the trees and flowers that you could see in Hawai'i, with beautiful birds flying about. On one side, there was a playground with swings, a slide, bicycles, a small log cabin, and a sandpit. Willow was filled with envy. She longed to bring Jongho here to play, seeing how excited he had been for the broken rocking horse.

Willow entered the living room barefoot, Marika smiled and told her to put her shoes on. Embarrassed at the sweaty footprints she had left on the floor, she blushed. The interior of the mansion was one hundred times larger than she had imagined upon seeing the Western-style houses in Kobe, and it was full of high-class furniture, the likes of which she had never seen. A large fan was spinning on the ceiling, creating a breeze, and through the glass doors of the living room she could see the ocean, with its white waves dancing.

That beautiful seascape was nothing like the sea that she knew.

Willow sat perched on a sofa, waiting for Mrs. Robson, who, after a while, appeared in a trailing dress. Mrs. Robson showed her a paper with a drawing of flowers and asked her to embroider that on some table mats. She explained it was the Robson family crest. While Marika was translating Mrs. Robson's English into Hawaiian, the quick-witted Willow had already understood.

Mrs. Robson was very pleased with her work, and even paid extra. Willow was thrilled with the unexpected income.

After the Korean Provisional Government in Shanghai split on January 26, 1921, Syngman Rhee returned to Hawai'i, sending the Korean community into an uproar, but Willow paid no attention. Since she didn't work with any Koreans, she hadn't heard anything beyond what Taewan told her and what was in the papers, but she preferred it that way. Taewan was as busy as ever. Exhausted after the day's hard work, Willow would fall asleep without waiting for him. He, too, would come in, collapse, and fall asleep without a word of greeting. It saddened her that although they had been living together for only three years, they were like a couple that had been together for thirty, but she had no energy to think about that for long.

She was more grateful than anxious that there was no sign of a second child.

Willow had no great hopes, no expectation of good fortune. Even though her hands were blistered and her joints ached, she was satisfied to make a living by her own efforts. She was happy that she could dream of a future for Jongho, and felt grateful to the Robsons for giving her a stable job.

At least, until the incident happened.

In the moments between her laundry loads, Willow would check on Jongho in the backyard. As he approached his second birthday, Jongho began to wander from the yard. His curiosity had grown beyond his previous shyness, and she worried that Jongho might disturb the garden. The garden, tended by three gardeners, was Mr. Robson's pride.

On the fateful day, Willow glanced into the yard and her heart sank. Jongho was nowhere in sight. She put down the iron and ran out. She could hear Jongho crying somewhere in the direction of the mansion. She frantically made her way toward his cry until she saw the Robson twins standing together, glowering in the play area, while Jongho was on the ground, and a child's bicycle toppled at his feet. Willow was more worried about the bike than about the weeping Jongho. It would be terrible if a bicycle that looked more expensive than a car got damaged.

"Hey!"

Jongho looked back at his mother's voice and cried even harder. Blood was flowing from his temple.

"What happened?"

Willow rushed over and hugged Jongho. There was a cut right next to the corner of one eye. Jongho continued to cry as he pointed at the twins. A spinning top fell from the hand of one of them. Jongho stuttered that the twin had struck him with the top.

At the thought that his eye might easily have been hurt she felt dizzy with anger.

"Did you really hit him? He might have lost an eye!" Willow shouted at the twins without thinking that they could not understand. One twin began to cry, then the other followed.

Mrs. Robson and Marika came out, alerted by all the noise. Willow expected their mother to scold the twins. She assumed that she would apologize at the sight of Jongho crying and bleeding. Instead of apologizing, Mrs. Robson blamed Jongho for coming into the garden. There was no sign of the kind smiles when she'd received her embroidery. Instead, her expression was icy. The twins went to stand next to their mother and stuck their tongues out at Jongho.

When she saw that, Willow was furious. She thrust Jongho at Mrs. Robson. "Can't you see that this child is bleeding? He was wrong to come into the garden, but is the garden more important than a child?"

Jongho cried even louder.

Mrs. Robson looked disdainfully at Willow, said something to Marika, then turned and led the twins away. Marika gave Willow a complicated look. Fuming, Willow picked Jongho up and went back to the laundry.

Washing his face revealed a small but deep cut. She was even more upset than when she had seen the scar on Taewan's back. "What's to be done? It'll leave a scar." She wanted to attend to Jongho, who must have been shocked, but she still had a lot of work left.

"Listen, I'll buy you something nice later, okay? Now I have to work, so go out and play. But you must never go into the garden again. Is that clear?"

It wasn't until she was about to leave for the day that she was given notice of her dismissal, together with the salary due. Without a word, Willow hoisted Jongho onto her back and trudged home. All the way she regretted not having begged to be given a second chance; it would be difficult to get a similar job again. Also, if she had known she was going to be dismissed, she would have shouted at Mrs. Robson more.

Willow found work cleaning the rooms and washing the bedding and towels at the Haesong Inn, where she had stayed her first nights in Hawai'i. The innkeeper's daughter had gotten married and the innkeeper had hurt her back, so she urgently needed someone.

Taewan, who had to pass the Haesong Inn on his way to the office on North Kukui, said he would take her on his bicycle. From the inn to the office, it was only a ten-minute ride.

Willow held Jongho in her arms as she mounted the bicycle behind Taewan. As they sped along, the breeze reminded her of their family outing, when they first came to Honolulu and opened the shoe store, and she had ridden with Taewan to visit Waikīkī Beach.

When they reached the inn, Willow regretted that the ride was so short.

"It must have been hard work with the two of us," she said, apologetically.

"Some people have to suffer all day long, so that's nothing." Taewan's face was bathed in sweat.

"In that case, you can bring us tomorrow, too. That's right, Jongho, isn't it?" She wasn't above using their son as an excuse to spend more time with her husband.

Jongho smiled and nodded, still excitable from the ride.

"Okay, I will. See you this evening," said Taewan before riding off.

After their time spent together as a family, Willow regained her usual happiness.

The owner of the inn and his wife welcomed Willow.

"I've nowhere to leave the baby, so I'll have to bring him with me. If you agree, I'll work hard, and you can pay me less." After working for so long among foreigners, Willow found speaking Korean strangely awkward.

"How could we be so cruel to a compatriot? We've known Jongho's aboji since we came to Hawai'i on the same boat."

Willow was moved by their kind words. The sorrow she had suffered at the Robson mansion was fading. Willow told Jongho to play in the backyard and immediately started to clean rooms where the guests had left. When he started exploring the unfamiliar backyard, she worried about the stream in front of the inn, but the innkeeper told her not to worry, she would look after him.

Haesong Inn was still crowded with picture brides. Just as when Willow first came, it was full of the laments of women in despair on finding that their bridegroom was unlike his photo. Willow, who understood their pain, wept together with them and comforted them. The salary was less than she had been receiving at the Robson mansion, but she was comfortable.

On a day in August, Willow left the inn in the evening, holding Jongho's hand. An ambulance siren could be heard in the distance. Jongho pulled Willow's hand and led her toward North Kukui, not home. He knew that his father's office was in that direction.

"Hey, shall we have dinner with Aboji?"

That day, Willow had received a tip from a haole guest. Since she had some unexpected money, she thought the three of them could eat out for once. With Jongho jumping with excitement, they headed for North Kukui along the side of the stream. As the building housing the Independence League came in sight, Willow stopped, astonished. An ambulance was parked in front, as well as a police car, and people were swarming about.

Willow's heart raced and her legs trembled. Jongho led the way ahead of Willow. They slipped through a gap between bystanders. Several people were being taken away by the police, and the injured were being helped into the ambulance. All were Korean.

"Aigo, what's happened?" Willow screamed at Taewan, who was about to get into the ambulance, a handkerchief pressed to his brow.

He gazed at Willow in surprise.

"What's happened here?"

Taewan, his face hard-set, didn't so much as glance at Jongho.

"Are you badly hurt? Who did this?"

Taewan clutched her hand and said in a low voice, "It's nothing serious, don't worry. Just go home. Once you're home, keep the door locked."

Willow grabbed Jongho, who struggled, saying he didn't want to go, hoisted him onto her back, and walked away. Her legs were trembling, but she clenched her teeth and hurried home. Had Japanese imperialism reached Hawai'i? She found it hard to breathe at the thought that violence had come upon her husband at the office.

It was past 11 P.M. before he came home. Willow had been anxiously waiting, but on seeing him with bandages wrapped around his eyebrows and head, she burst into tears.

Taewan had been injured by supporters of Syngman Rhee. After returning from Shanghai, Dr. Rhee had founded a group called the People's League. As a group designed to support the Provisional Government, they had chosen Syngman Rhee, the president of the Provisional Government, as the president of their league. However, the magazine *Pacific Times,* the organ of the Independence League, had published an article titled, "Syngman Rhee: Whereabouts Unknown," claiming that Syngman Rhee had caused division within the Provisional Government and then run away because he could not cope with the difficulties.

Infuriated by the article, women who supported Syngman Rhee had invaded the office, demanding that the disrespectful article be corrected. The reporters had shown the women a letter received from the staff of the Korean Red Cross in Shanghai, which the article was based on, and sent them away. The scene that unfolded in the evening was after the husbands of the wives who had been driven out of the office attacked. The raiders were taken to the police station, and the injured were treated in a hospital. Taewan, who was not seriously hurt, had returned to clean up the office after having his wounds dressed. But at about eight o'clock, the raiders had returned, beat up anyone they found there, and smashed the printing press.

Through tears, Willow said, "You mean it wasn't the Japanese who attacked and hurt you, but our fellow countrymen? How can that be? Independence and whatever else, I hate it all. For me, you are my priority, not independence. Quit right now. We should leave here, like Jaesong's family, go to Wahiawā and forget everything—Korea, independence, everything—and live peacefully."

Taewan fell silent, as if he were at a loss for words.

The incident, which had been a fight between Koreans, caused a scandal after it was reported in the Hawaiian newspapers. The conflict between Koreans only deepened. For the next few days, Taewan went to work with a grim expression. Willow watched him nervously, feeling as if the worst was yet to come.

A few days later, he came home early, bringing pork and a toy he had bought for Jongho. It was a wooden car with wheels that turned. For Willow the car was more welcome than the pork. Jongho refused to be parted from Taewan that night. Expectation and anxiety were tightly joined in Willow's heart as she hurriedly prepared supper with the meat he had bought for them.

They sat around the table. Jongho was so smitten with his father, who had kept him entertained, playing with the car while

Willow had cooked, that he insisted on eating supper sitting on his lap. Seeing this brought tears to her eyes. The three of them, sitting together eating rice, even without side dishes—that was Willow's daily dream. At the same time, seeing Taewan acting so different than normal weighed on her heart.

After eating, Taewan sipped water mixed with scorched rice. "I've heard from the Kaesong ajumoni's husband. They need someone to work in their laundry. Their daughter is leaving for the mainland, and it's too much work for the two of them alone."

"What did you tell him?"

"I said I would discuss it with you."

"What is there to discuss? Let's go. I don't want to stay here anymore."

Seeing Willow so excited, Taewan paused before continuing. "I want you and Jongho to go to Wahiawā alone. Being with them is much better than living here with strangers. You know how decent they both are, and they were like brother and sister to my parents."

Willow's heart fell. "And what about you?"

Taewan turned his gaze away. "I think I have to go to China. Office work doesn't suit me, and I don't want to fight with the People's League here. It's not my compatriots I should be fighting against, but the Japanese. Chairman Park is forming the Republic of Korea Government. I have to go there."

Any government established by Yongman Park was bound to be a government based on armed struggle. Willow was stunned. What she had dreaded was finally happening.

"Don't go. I won't let you go. You know how my aboji died! Maybe you don't realize how much my omma and we children suffered. Don't go. What if you never return?" Willow's words mingled with tears. The room was filled with the sound of her weeping.

Jongho wiped the tears from her face with his small hands.

Seeing that, Taewan's expression grew even more determined. "I have to fight, in order to ensure that your aboji's death, and brother's death, were not in vain. I want to be a worthy aboji to my child. If later, Jongho asks where I was back then, I have to have an answer, don't I? If I don't go now, I'll regret it for the rest of my life. It can't be otherwise.

"Jongho, your aboji's going to come home after defeating the Japanese bastards and freeing our country, so you look after your omma like a brave boy, okay?"

Jongho nodded vigorously.

Taewan went with them to Wahiawā to help carry the luggage. With Taewan's departure approaching, Willow regretted every passing moment that the words she wanted to say stuck in her throat. Even the fact that Hongju lived in Wahiawā was no comfort.

When they got off the train, they were struck by the number of soldiers in uniform. Some of the Koreans living in the Wahiawā region worked on pineapple farms or in canning plants, but most of them ran shops for the Schofield camp soldiers. Except for the soldiers, there were few haole to be seen. In the street lined with shops such as laundries, barbershops, restaurants, tailor's shops, grocery stores, furniture stores, and shoe-repair shops, there were no big, impressive buildings like in Honolulu and the rhythm of life felt different. Taewan, carrying the luggage, walked in front and found the house, while Willow followed with Jongho on her back, swallowing back her tears.

The laundry run by the Kaesong ajumoni's family was on Palm Street. The elderly couple had been waiting for their arrival and greeted them joyfully. The shop was located on the street side of a building with a blue tin roof, and at the back there were two rooms, with a wooden-floored space that doubled as the kitchen, that was barely large enough for a meal table. The laundry room and a toilet stood on one side of a backyard where the clothes could be dried.

Willow helped the Kaesong ajumoni prepare supper while Taewan talked quietly with her husband. As Willow moved about blankly, the old woman seasoned spinach and said, "It can't be helped. We all have to play a role, without exception. Armed fighting isn't the only kind of independence movement. It's also being patriotic to send your husband off quietly."

Willow reckoned it was easier to talk like that when it was happening to somebody else. Nevertheless, her words became a source of comfort and strength for her.

After Taewan decided to leave, Willow kept thinking of her mother. If she knew what was happening, her mother would say, "My daughter's fate is just like mine." Her mother had feared that what happened to her husband might stir up her remaining children to join a rebellion, and so she never spoke of it.

Had she not known what he was doing beforehand or had she not been able to make him stop, or had she maybe been proud of him? Above all, Willow wanted to know how her mother had gone on when he left home and there was no news. Was it only because of the children? Willow loved Jongho, but would that be enough for her to endure a life without her husband?

Willow filled Taewan's bowl to the brim with rice and pressed it down.

The five of them sat around the table. Whenever Jongho

found himself in an unfamiliar place, his shy side took over and he remained silent. The Kaesong ajumoni explained the situation with the laundry. The elder brother of her son-in-law, who was running a grocery store in Los Angeles, had written to his brother, who was helping run the cleaning business with her, suggesting that they go into business together. The two brothers first came to work on the sugarcane farms, but quite soon the older brother went across to the mainland, while the younger one, who had married the oldest daughter of the Kaesong ajumoni, stayed in Hawai'i. Since the son-in-law wanted to be with his older brother, and her daughter wanted her children to grow up in the United States, they had decided to go.

"They urged us to go with them, but there was no work for us there. What would we do? Besides, I wouldn't feel comfortable leaving my other children behind. Our younger boy keeps telling us to give up the laundry business and move to Honolulu, but we feel an obligation to our regular customers. That's why I asked you to join us."

They made most of their money doing all the washing for their soldier customers, from their uniforms to their towels and socks, for four dollars a month. The competition was fierce, and even regular customers might go elsewhere if someone offered a lower price. The Kaesong couple had earned a reputation for reliability, so they had a good number of regulars.

"My husband goes into the barracks every morning to deliver, and pick up, laundry."

They decided that when the laundry came in, the Kaesong ajumoni and Willow would do the washing together, then Willow would do the ironing and repairs. Lastly, it would be the Kaesong ajumoni's job to sort the laundry by customer.

"I'm going to do the cooking, so you don't have to worry about that."

"What a blessing to sit and eat the food you prepare," said Willow with a smile.

"We'll still be one pair of hands short, so I'm thinking of hiring someone else as well."

She said she would pay her a salary of twenty-five dollars and gradually increase it. Willow, obliged to live apart from Taewan, would have been grateful just for her food and a place to sleep.

"Ajumoni, please look after my wife and child while I'm away," said Taewan.

"Don't worry. The work may be difficult, but I won't make life hard for her. When we were living on the plantation at 'Ewa, your omma took care of me like a younger sister. Even just for her sake, I'll take good care of your family, so you must stay in good shape and come home safely."

Her husband, who had already spoken with Taewan, nodded in agreement.

Taewan spent the night. The room that Willow and Jongho were to use was no smaller than that on Punchbowl Street. Once the three were alone together, Jongho clung to Taewan, babbling happily, and she could not help shedding tears. The couple had no time for themselves until Jongho finally fell asleep, after prolonged petulance.

Shaking his head, Taewan, who had been acting with more vigor since deciding to leave, sighed heavily as he spoke. "I'm ashamed that I haven't been acting as a true family head should, and now I'm leaving like this. Please look after Jongho while I'm away, and keep yourself well. Later, we'll have the rest of our lives to talk about the old days. Don't worry if I don't write often, because no news is good news."

Willow had been biting her lip but now she opened her mouth. Remembering what the Kaesong ajumoni had said, she struggled over each word. "I will send you off peacefully. But still I want you to promise me one thing."

Taewan raised his head and looked at her.

"You must not die. No matter what happens, you must come back alive. Jongho and I will be waiting for you every day." Willow spoke with a trembling voice, but she did not cry.

12

UPPER VILLAGE, LOWER VILLAGE

Very early in the morning, Willow saw Taewan off before the Kaesong couple were up. In Taewan's bag there was a Taegukgi embroidered by Willow, who had prayed for her husband's safety and good luck, stitch by stitch, as she made it. Willow later learned that Taewan was also taking a sum of money donated by their Wahiawā compatriots.

A fog had settled over Wahiawā, so thick that it hid the signboards of the shops on the opposite side of the street. Taewan briefly hugged Willow before vanishing into it. Once he was swallowed up by the fog, she wondered if he would never return. Willow took a couple of steps, calling him, then collapsed. The emotions, which she had held under control all through the night, burst free, leaving her without strength. She could not stand, could not think, trapped in the mist that veiled everything.

The sound of Jongho crying pierced the fog. A voice inside her head said, *Willow, wake up. You are Jongho's omma.* At first she thought it was her mother's, but then realized it was her own. Caring for her child took precedence over anything else.

Willow struggled to her feet, staggering to the room where her son was crying. His cries were full of fear at being alone in a strange room. Willow hugged him, and once he was in his mother's arms, he fell back to sleep with a peaceful expression. The child's breathing began to fill the empty shell that remained of Willow. Until Taewan returned, she was going to have to act as his father too. She had no time to wallow.

Willow went out to the laundry room, lit the lamp, and began looking around her new workplace. Washing, ironing, mending, it would be the same kind of work that she had been doing at the Robson mansion. Willow checked the sewing box and the iron. Lastly, she sat down in front of the sewing machine and imagined herself skillfully using it. She imagined meeting Hongju and Julie's mother, spending time with Myongok and Makson. New hope arose within her, full of the courage her son gave her.

Hongju did not as yet know that Willow had come to Wahiawā. Taewan wanted to come and go quietly, without telling anyone. The previous night, the Kaesong ajumoni's husband had said, "It's a small place, people will soon find out, there's no need for you to tell them."

Willow decided to meet Hongju only after she had properly mastered the work in the laundry. Learning how to use the sewing machine was an urgent priority.

Jongho kept himself entertained playing with the toy car that Taewan had bought and the toys that the Kaesong ajumoni's grandchildren had left behind. Willow learned to use the sewing machine from the Kaesong ajumoni. It was amazingly convenient, because it did in a flash work that had taken her hours by hand. Her backstitching wasn't regular yet, but she felt she would soon master it with practice. The Kaesong ajumoni was happy with her work and progress.

"Since you have good eyes, you'll learn fast. I can't tell you how long it took me just to thread the machine. Now my eyes are so dim, I can't even sew."

Willow showed her Hongju's address and asked where it was. She said it was not in downtown Wahiawā, but nearly an hour's walk away, above the pineapple plantation. It would be difficult for them to meet on weekdays, since both were working, but it would be great to make a surprise visit without warning, as Hongju had done last time. She could already hear Hongju's loud voice in her mind. She also wanted to find out where Myongok and Makson were living. She couldn't meet them before Hongju, but it would be all right to see Julie's mother first.

Willow asked the Kaesong ajumoni, "Is Jaesong's family's laundry far from here? I've not seen her."

"My husband meets Jaesong when they visit the camp, but I haven't seen her for a long time."

Willow soon understood how busy Julie's mother must be. The only time from 9 A.M. to 9 P.M. when Willow could rest for a moment was after lunch. Julie's mother would be even busier, because she had four children and she was doing all the work with just her husband.

On her second Sunday in Wahiawā, Willow had been planning to visit Hongju after the Kaesong ajumoni left for church, but she didn't feel well. Maybe she was overdoing it because she had been working hard to fill the empty space left by Taewan's absence, but she kept feeling weak. She feared she might fall sick if she didn't rest. It would be terrible if she grew ill and caused a disruption in the laundry work.

Willow decided to spend the day resting, telling Jongho, "I'm not feeling well. Why don't you go play in the yard?" As she laid a pillow on the floor and prepared to lie down, Jongho whined that he wanted to go out somewhere. Perhaps because the Kaesong couple spoiled him like grandparents, he had grown more demanding since coming to Wahiawā. "If you go on like this I'll tell Haraboji not to give you a bike ride. And I'll write to your aboji that he's not to buy any toys for you."

At her scolding, Jongho went out into the backyard, pouting. Willow fell into a deep sleep without time to feel sorry for him, but woke with a start upon hearing a voice outside.

"Hey, are you inside? It's Hongju."

Willow jumped up and ran outside without bothering to put her shoes on. Hongju and Julie's mother were standing together by the front door. Flustered, Willow undid the latch, at which Hongju flung the door open and hugged her.

"I've only just heard you were here. Why didn't you tell us you were coming?"

"That's just how it was. I'm sorry. But you've come together?" Willow looked from one to the other. Hongju and Julie's mother glanced at each other and smiled in a friendly manner.

"March and I attend the same church," said Hongju.

"Who's March?" Willow asked, looking confused.

Julie's mother said, "It's me. My name is March." Willow had known Julie's mother for a long time, but she had never known her name. Hearing people's voices, Jongho came running in. Hongju held out her arms to him.

"Jongho, do you remember your aunt? How you've grown!"

Jongho seemed not to recognize Hongju, let alone Julie's mother, and hid behind Willow.

"He was only a baby last time he saw you, how could he remember. And where is Songgil?" Willow asked as she ushered them into the house.

"I left him at Sunday school. Myongok is a teacher in the Korean language school at the church. Makson also attends the same church."

Hongju seemed exhilarated, socializing with other people

like the branches of a banyan tree. It was the life Willow had been longing for.

"Where did Taewan go? Is he in Honolulu?" asked Hongju, looking around the room, filled completely by the table. Willow, who was preparing tea, hesitated for a moment when she remembered what the Kaesong ajumoni's husband had said. But she didn't want to keep it a secret from Hongju, or Julie's mother.

"Jongho's aboji has gone to China. Keep that to yourselves."

After setting tea in front of Julie's mother and Hongju, and sitting across from them, Willow said, "I didn't know you still went to church. If I had known, I would have asked the Kaesong ajumoni if I could go with her."

"There would have been no point. We attend different churches." Julie's mother explained that there were two Korean churches in Wahiawā, the Methodist Church and the Christian Church founded by Syngman Rhee. Dr. Rhee, who had first founded a Korean Christian church in Honolulu due to conflicts with the Methodist Church, had opened a church in Wahiawā, where many Koreans lived. Wahiawā was a place where the unity of members of the People's League and their devotion to Syngman Rhee were stronger than in Honolulu.

The Korean Christian Church, on Palm Street near the laundry, was called the upper village church, and the Methodist Church on Olive Avenue was called the lower village church. The Kaesong ajumoni, who had been a Methodist even before leaving Korea, continued to attend the lower village church. After leaving Kahuku, Julie's mother, who had become a passionate follower of Syngman Rhee, moved to the Korean Christian Church, and now attended the upper village church in Wahiawā. Willow suddenly understood why the Kaesong ajumoni had been so reticent whenever she talked about Jaesong's family.

Since neither she nor her husband attended any church, Willow had been unaware of church politics.

"Are people even divided over attending church?" she asked, clacking her tongue and glancing at Julie's mother. The two of them had fallen out once before and Willow didn't want to be estranged again from someone who had been like a sister to her, on whom she had relied and from whom she had received so much help.

"The Independence League keeps making trouble. Who was it that wrote that lying article saying that Dr. Rhee had caused trouble in the Provisional Government and ran away?" said Hongju in a raised voice.

Before the astonished Willow had time to reply, Julie's mother added, "She's right. How could they slander a man who thinks only of our nation, day and night, and is working so hard for its citizens? It's like I said before. You should make Taewan come to his senses. Was your husband involved in that? If so, he did well to run away. If the Independence League's newspaper staff ever show their faces again, there are plenty of people on the lookout for them."

Willow was trembling.

"No, Taewan didn't leave because of that. He didn't run away, he left because he couldn't stand seeing compatriots fighting each other. It was to fight against the Japanese that he went, leaving his wife and child behind."

Willow, who had been enduring Taewan's absence, burst into tears.

Hongju seemed sorry, stroking Willow's back.

"Don't cry. I was wrong. We should never say anything that would upset the other. We've always been like sisters. I would hate to take sides against you."

At Hongju's words, Willow wept even harder.

"Please don't cry, dear. I spoke as I did because I was worried about Taewan, who's like my brother-in-law. As Hongju said, we belong together. We mustn't let partisan issues separate us." Julie's mother also held Willow's hand as she spoke. Willow calmed down as the resentment she had felt toward the two of them faded.

After Hongju left, Willow went to Makson and her husband's barbershop to have Jongho's hair cut. There was a barbershop next to her home, but she wanted to see her old friend. Myongok's furniture store was even farther away, so she decided to go there next time. Both of them also attended the upper village church, but Willow believed that, like Hongju and Julie's mother, they would give priority to their earlier close relationship.

Willow entered the barbershop with a smile. The small shop held a large mirror and two chairs for customers. Makson's husband was cutting one customer's hair, while Makson was washing another's, carrying a baby on her back. Another child, sitting in a corner chair and sucking on a lollipop, must be the elder daughter. As soon as he had finished, Makson's husband looked back. It seemed that Makson had taken him in hand, as he looked cleaner than before. They had not exchanged a word back then, but she felt glad to see him again after three years.

"How are you? Do you remember me?"

At Willow's greeting, he smiled awkwardly and nodded. After she had finished washing the man's hair and handed him a towel, Makson looked at Willow. Her belly projected between the strings of her carrier blanket. With her heavily freckled face, the age difference between Makson and her husband did not seem so very great.

"Onni, it's me, Willow. How are you?"

"I heard you'd come. What do you want?"

Confronted with an unexpectedly lukewarm welcome, Willow gently pushed Jongho forward. "Umm, to have his hair cut. . . ."

After glancing at Jongho, Makson said nothing, but put a child's cushion on the empty chair. There were none of the greetings that should have been natural after not meeting for such a long time, and she showed no interest in the child. Willow suppressed her embarrassed, sad feelings, and sat Jongho on the cushion. He stared around with a frightened expression, then burst into tears when Makson put a cloth around his neck. Makson, pregnant and carrying a baby on her back, seemed to be breathless whenever she moved.

"It's all right. They're going to make you look pretty. If you behave, Haraboji will take you for a ride on his bicycle."

Although Willow tried to calm him, Jongho kept crying and asking to get down.

"If you keep on like this, I'll write to your aboji not to buy you any toys."

For Jongho, his grandfather's bicycle and his father's toys were stronger than any bogeyman. But still, he did not stop crying. The man who had stood up after having his hair washed remarked:

"His aboji seems to have gone off somewhere."

Willow said nothing, as she remembered Julie's mother saying that the members of the People's League were on the lookout for Taewan. Even if she attended the upper village church and belonged to the People's League, Willow had not expected Makson to treat her like this. She thought about walking out of the barbershop right away, but if she did that, she would become the same kind of person as they were, so she took it patiently and comforted Jongho. In the meantime, as Makson's husband, who had finished cutting the hair of the previous customer, approached with his scissors, Jongho started crying bloody murder. Just when Willow was on the verge of tears, Makson's daughter offered Jongho the lollipop she had been licking. Jongho took it before his mother could prevent him, and instantly stopped crying.

"Thank you, dear, you shouldn't have," she said, reflecting that adults were often less kind than children.

Makson, who was applying shaving foam to the customer who had been having his hair cut, turned her eyes away in embarrassment. Her husband started cutting Jongho's hair. Makson's daughter stayed beside Jongho, keeping him amused. She was only one year older, but acted like a big sister. Thanks to her, Jongho's hair was safely cut. Makson took the money for the haircut and put it in her front pocket, avoiding Willow's gaze. Nobody said a word about coming back another time. As she was about to leave the barbershop holding Jongho's hand, Willow turned and asked Makson's daughter, "What's your name, dear?"

The child said "Betty" in a clear voice.

"Buy yourself another sweet. You are kind and pretty, so this for you is from your auntie." Willow left the barbershop after pressing a penny into the child's hand. Setting aside any thought of visiting Myongok, she went plodding homeward. It seemed several times farther than when they had come.

About a month after Taewan left, Willow realized that she was pregnant again. That was why she had been feeling so weak. There was no news from Taewan yet. The Kaesong ajumoni was worried about her having to raise two children alone, but Willow was overjoyed, feeling that the presence of children would be a talisman protecting Taewan, and that two would have greater power than one. It seemed that the child in her womb was aware of her mother's situation, for she had less morning sickness than with Jongho. Willow tried to eat well and stay healthy for the child.

In Wahiawā, there were more Asians, including Koreans, than haole or natives. The American and Hawaiian authorities excluded and held in check the Chinese and Japanese, who had grown in power. Thanks to the preference for Koreans in the Schofield camp, the Korean community in Wahiawā flourished more than Korean communities in Honolulu or on the mainland, and people arrived in a steady stream. Mostly, they were glad to mingle and live with other Koreans. However, internally they were still divided between churches, organizations, and leaders, and relationships were as complex as a spider's web. Since Honolulu had been large and Willow rarely met people, she had not experienced this situation directly before, but it could be felt vividly in this small, close-knit community.

Most of the people attending the Korean Christian Church were members of the People's League founded by Syngman Rhee. Many of them did not simply support Syngman Rhee, the president of the Provisional Government, but almost worshiped him.

The Kaesong couple were members of the Korean National Association, which had been established in 1910, combining several previous organizations, and meant to encompass all Koreans in America. Many people changed churches or organizations depending on which leaders they supported, but the Kaesong couple did not change their affiliation.

"I know that Dr. Rhee is setting up a school for our compatriots and is working hard for independence. Even so, Dr. Rhee is not Christ."

After that first visit, Willow never saw Julie's mother, who had said she didn't want them to be divided by such issues.

Syngman Rhee often visited Wahiawā, and people competed fiercely to invite him to their homes. Julie's mother, who succeeded in inviting him to dinner, hung a picture of Syngman Rhee and her family conspicuously in her laundry.

Hongju envied Julie's mother. "It's really a good likeness of Dr. Rhee. Even though I want to invite him, our house is so shabby, I'd be ashamed to invite anyone." Hongju came to the laundry every Sunday afternoon, and waited for Songgil's Sunday school class and Doksam's meetings to be over. During that time, she would complain about all kinds of things. Unlike Willow, she interacted with a lot of different people. Doksam had become an executive of the Wahiawā branch of the League, but Hongju wanted her husband to take a higher position. Willow was astonished to hear from Hongju that a member of the People's League would be fined for meeting or interacting with a member of the Independence League.

"How can there be such rules? You'll lose all your salary in fines for coming here every Sunday." Willow spoke half in jest and half worrying, but Hongju snorted.

"You don't attend the lower village church, and you're not a member of the Independence League, so why should I pay a fine?"

Willow felt that even if all the people in Wahiawā shunned her, so long as she had Hongju and the Kaesong couple she would be all right.

Earlier that day, Willow was watching Jongho playing outside as she waited for Hongju. Jongho enjoyed playing with the Filipino child next door. The two of them were the same age, and played well together, while speaking Korean and Filipino respectively. Adults took sides and divided according to nationality, race, or religion, but there were no such boundaries between children. The Kaesong couple returned from church.

"Did you have a good time?" asked Willow.

The husband went inside first, saying he would rest.

The Kaesong ajumoni asked, "Are you waiting for Songgil's omma? She's in the Baekga store."

The Baekga store was a grocery store on the corner of the main street, and the store's daughter-in-law was also a picture bride, the same age as Willow.

"Hongju was alone?" asked Willow, finding it odd that she'd stop there.

"Julie's omma, the wife from the barbershop, the wife from the grocery store, and several other women . . . Ten or more of them, they seemed to be some kind of gye, a savings group."

Hongju and Julie's mother, Makson and Myongok were all there? Willow had no idea that Hongju was part of a gye. That system for mutual aid was a long tradition in Korea, where there were many such groups helping to raise funds for the four great ceremonial occasions in life, but in Hawai'i the wives from Korea had few resources, so they mainly organized a gye to help cover daily living expenses. It was also a means of fellowship. The Kaesong ajumoni, who had a gye with members of the lower village church, said that on days when payments were due they would gather together to eat and also go to the beach once a year. Sometimes the person in charge ran away with the money and caused an uproar, but the system still had a lot to be said for it, and Willow longed to be a member of her own.

"Even if they asked me to join, I wouldn't," Willow lied, feeling sad that she'd not been invited. "Women gathering to look like men, talking and talking, it's no good."

"Right. They're all from the upper village church, so they wouldn't let you in anyway, and if they did, they'd give you the cold shoulder. But I'll have a word with the others next time we have our gye."

Her words were of no comfort. Willow wanted to be with Hongju, Myongok, and Makson. She wanted to get on well with them. Although it was her day off, she went out to the laundry and started working with the sewing machine. She found it hard to control her seething emotions if she sat doing nothing.

Hongju came to the laundry with Songgil in the evening. Willow did not stop sewing and paid no attention to Songgil. Hongju also remained standing, saying that Doksam was waiting and that she had to go right away.

"I was late because I had something to do. I was leaving, but stopped by for a moment because I thought you might be waiting."

Willow's voice grew cold. "I wasn't waiting. I was busy, too."

Hongju glanced at her briefly before speaking. "Aigo, you're upset, that's why you're taking it like that. Maybe you've heard, but I decided to join a gye. I told them that I wanted to do it with you, but they said they wouldn't do it if you joined."

Willow threw aside the military uniform she had been working on and shouted, "You joined a gye with people who say things like that? You have no loyalty. If I were you, I wouldn't have joined."

Hongju's face flushed and she too raised her voice. "Aigo, such ingratitude! Do you know how hard I work every day to protect you, to help you day and night?"

"Who asked you to do that? I don't belong to the same church and I have no wish to associate with such an exclusive lot." Willow picked up the uniform and sat down again in front of the sewing machine.

Hongju stood for a moment watching her, then said, softening her voice, "Don't be like that. Come to the upper village church with me. Or at least join the Women's Rescue League. If you do that, nobody will accuse you of being an outsider."

"Get out, and don't come back with that kind of talk. You can spend a thousand years, ten thousand years with the people from the upper village church if you like," snapped Willow before going back inside.

Nineteen twenty-two had arrived. Jongho was in his fourth year, and the child in her womb was in its fifth month. Jongho could talk properly now, and every morning, upon opening his eyes, he would say "Good morning" to the picture of his father. When Taewan proposed having a family picture taken before he left, Willow hesitated, with a foreboding that it might be their last picture, but now was glad that he had insisted. Thanks to it, she was able to see him every day and reminisce about the times the three of them had spent together. There was no news after Taewan arrived in Beijing and sent a letter stating that he had met Yongman Park. She couldn't even reply, because he said he would be on the move.

After their quarrel, Hongju cut off all contact. Willow grew as lonely as she had been in Honolulu. Her sorrow was all the greater that they had drifted apart while living so close to each other.

One day, Jongho came in after playing outside, looking for his father.

"Look at the picture," said Willow.

At her words, Jongho swatted the picture frame, knocking it to the floor. "That's not my aboji. I want a real aboji." Jongho angrily kicked the frame.

Willow struck Jongho on the back. "What are you doing?

When did I teach you to be so rude? Apologize and return the photo to its proper place."

But Jongho didn't move. Neither did he cry.

I hate the Independence Movement and patriotism. My child doesn't need a country, he needs an aboji. Come back at once.

Longing and resentment collided in Willow's heart.

Another day, the Kaesong ajumoni said, "Jongho, let's go to church together this Sunday. After the service, Mr. Roh of the Independence League is giving a speech. He's just come back from China, so you'll be able to hear news of your aboji."

Willow had met Mr. Roh a couple of times, when he worked with Taewan at the office of the Independence League. On Sunday morning, Willow washed Jongho and dressed him in his best clothes, then put on her pink blouse and skirt. Her face was looking haggard, so she applied some makeup.

The church congregation welcomed Willow and Jongho. Willow, feeling lonely at the loss of her husband and friends, had wanted to regularly attend church with the Kaesong ajumoni. She wanted to socialize within a community, and she wanted to trust in God, praying that Taewan would return safely. However, if she attended the lower village church, she knew that she might be forever separated from Hongju. As Taewan's wife, she could never go to the upper village church, so it seemed she could attend neither.

Willow waited impatiently for the end of the service, to learn news from China. Finally, Mr. Roh mounted the podium. Willow sat up straight, her heart ready to burst out of her body. Mr. Roh announced that Yongman Park had decided to build an Independence Movement military base, using the farmer-soldier, armed-struggle theory in the region of the Hun River, in China. He said that Park was setting up a bank to raise funds to support the construction. In his talk, he mentioned several names that Willow did not know, and Taewan was not one of them.

"We will gather all the Independence Movement troops active in Manchuria to form an army, like the military academy over the mountain. If we are self-sufficient for food, raise money to purchase weapons, and gather recruits for military training, we can become an army with great power. It is a time when we desperately need the support of our compatriots to build an independent military base that will achieve national independence. Chairman Park is also traveling about, day and night, to win support from the Chinese people."

People applauded several times during Mr. Roh's speech, and when it was over, various people made donations. Willow grew dispirited at hearing nothing of Taewan. There were so many people around Mr. Roh, it was hard to get close to him, but she couldn't just go back home without asking. Finally Mr. Roh approached her. Willow hastily stood up and greeted him. She looked around for Jongho, but there was no sign; perhaps he had followed the Kaesong ajumoni outside. After the formalities were over, Mr. Roh finally gave her news of Taewan.

"I saw Comrade So leaving to join the independence base pioneer group just before I left. When construction begins in earnest, Comrade So will be given great tasks. Things will be hard for you, but please endure, it is all for the liberation of our country."

Hearing that he was to take on great tasks, Willow felt more worried than proud. The greater the task, the later he seemed likely to return home. "Do you know the address there?" she asked.

"At the moment, it will be difficult for you to communicate because their place of residence is not fixed. You should wait for Comrade So to contact you. Remember that no news is good news."

After speaking with Mr. Roh, Willow contributed to the Kaesong ajumoni's donation by deducting a dollar each month from her salary. And every night she reminded Jongho and herself, "Jongho, do you realize how wonderful your aboji is? He has gone to perform great tasks. Let's stay firm and live cheerfully until he returns."

The time for her to give birth lay just a month ahead. Willow was uneasy about having the baby without Taewan, and was already worried about not being able to work, even for just a few days. After she gave birth to Jongho, postnatal care had lasted three weeks, but now even seven days seemed like too much.

"Don't say such things," said the Kaesong ajumoni. "I'm going to hire someone for a week, so you don't need to worry."

Willow tried to do as much work as she could before giving birth, but if she stayed sitting for a long time, it was uncomfortable and her back hurt, so she was taking more breaks. Still, she put Jongho to sleep and sat in front of the machine, working on some things that had to be finished.

One day, Willow was so busy sewing that she didn't realize that someone had come into the store until a shadow fell across the workbench. Willow raised her head, startled as if she had seen a ghost. Hongju stood there, holding a big bag, looking like nothing but skin and bones. It was the first time she had seen her since their fight a few months before. She looked around, but Hongju was alone.

Willow's heart sank at the sight of her oldest friend in this condition. "What's happened? What are you doing here at this time of day? Come in, sit down."

Willow hastily stood up and pulled Hongju toward the chair. Hongju let herself be led like a phantom. Willow poured a cup of water with trembling hands. Hongju even seemed to have difficulty taking the cup. Willow eyed her as she cautiously asked, "Have you run away?"

"It's not me who ran away, it's Jo Doksam." Hongju laughed as if she were deranged.

"What? Where? What about Songgil?"

Hongju sighed. "He's gone off to Korea, taking Songgil. He asked me to go too, but I didn't go."

"On a visit? It would've been nice to see your family, why didn't you go?" Going back to her family home and presenting her husband and children was a dream of Willow's from the moment she decided to get married as a picture bride.

"Not a visit, he's gone for good. And if I went back to Korea I'd have to live as a concubine."

Willow abruptly sat down in front of the sewing machine. Hongju talked on, about how Doksam had not been a widower, after all. His wife was alive in Korea, raising their children and taking care of his parents. Doksam, who only had five daughters, had decided to arrange a picture marriage in order to have a son before he was any older. And now that he had a son, he had decided to go back, and buy land with the money he had saved, while pretending to be a miser. "The wily man made a lot of money lending it out with interest, here and there, without my knowledge."

Hongju did not want to return home as a concubine when she had left as a widow. Doksam had said that Hongju, who had given him a son, was his favorite spouse, and that once back home he would divorce his wife, but she didn't believe him. Above all, Hongju had never loved Doksam very much, if at all.

"What wicked people there are in the world. You did well not to go. But how will you live without Songgil?" Willow's voice, which had been strong, dropped at the mention of the child.

Even without listening to her reply, Hongju was looking half dead. "It's been five days since I last saw him, and I'm not dead yet," Hongju muttered, barely moving her dry lips. "Willow, I'm sorry. I had nowhere else I could go."

"Don't be so silly, dear. Of course you had to come to me. You did well to come." Willow kept talking as she led Hongju inside.

The Kaesong ajumoni, once she understood Hongju's situation, welcomed her warmly. "How terrible you must feel, separated from your child. Stay with your friend until you feel better."

That night, Willow shifted Jongho to one side and lay down beside Hongju. Instead of the usual talking late into the night, the room rang with nothing but their sighs, occasionally mingled with Jongho's breathing. Willow wondered what she'd do without her son. Having a child was different from having a husband. Even without Taewan, she had managed to go on living, but without Jongho, she would have neither the strength nor any reason to go on living. Hongju, separated from her child, must be suffering as if she were separated from her heart. Finding Hongju's hand in the dark, Willow squeezed it tightly.

13

RAINBOW OVER WAHIAWĀ

Hongju stayed shut inside the small room as if it were a cave. Willow had to make a scene at each meal before she would eat enough to stay alive. After merely looking on for three days, the Kaesong ajumoni finally went and spoke to Hongju, who was sitting crouched in one corner of the room.

"Can the bonds of blood be broken? The child born from your womb is yours, even if it dies. A child is bound to go looking for its omma."

At that, Hongju started to cry. She beat her breast, writhing and weeping. "I am the one who abandoned our Songgil. Will he still come seeking me?" asked Hongju, as if pleading with her.

"Even if the child is not beside you, you are still their omma. A child lives by their omma's energy even when it is far away. Songgil will think of you and be strengthened."

After being heartsick for five days, Hongju said, "I'll overcome this and earn some money. I'll do anything. Please let me stay here for a while."

"Stay as long as you like. And how about working in the laundry? When Willow gives birth, I'll have to hire someone anyway, so it may as well be you."

Hongju thanked her and started working right away. Her hands were soon swollen from washing clothes, and then she burned them doing the ironing. She even did sewing, which she hated and was no good at, constantly pricking her fingers. It was clear that she was trying her best to forget the emptiness of letting her child go.

Outwardly, she regained her former vitality, but at night, Hongju would cry softly into her elbow. Willow silently shared her friend's pain.

"Willow, once you've had your baby, what about setting up a shop with me?" Hongju suggested one night. "How great would it be if you used your skills and opened a sewing shop, and I run the business end."

When she first heard Hongju's suggestion, Willow thought it was impossible. Above all, she felt an obligation toward the Kaesong ajumoni, who had taken in Hongju as well as herself.

"Next month, I'll be receiving money from our gye, and there's the money that Jo Doksam gave me. All we need is a small shop and a sewing machine, to start."

Willow also had close to a hundred and fifty dollars. It was money that she had laboriously saved from a monthly salary of twenty-five dollars, less one dollar as a donation. Willow wanted to open a store when Taewan came back. Every night, she used to think about what kind of store it should be, and imagine spending the whole day with Taewan as a way of comforting herself. "It's a good idea, but how can we tell Ajimae? We owe her so much."

Compared to working at the cleaner's, it was true that running any kind of store for herself would bring in a better income.

"If it's okay with you, I'll talk to Ajimae about it and ask her advice," said Hongju.

Hongju told the Kaesong ajumoni about her idea. Willow, sitting beside her, worried she might think they were ungrateful. But unexpectedly, she was delighted.

"Instead of going and starting a new sewing shop, why not take this place over? It would be better than starting a new one because it already has regular customers. It'll be easier to attract sewing shop customers if you combine that with the laundry. My husband has been wanting to stop working for a while now, and I can't go on because I have so many aches and pains. We'll go to our son's place in Honolulu and care for our grandchildren."

She said she would arrange with the landlord for them to sign a new contract. As for the equipment, they only needed to pay for the sewing machine, the steam iron, and the bicycle. They would leave behind most of the household items. There could be no better conditions. Above all, there were more than fifty regular customers, each paying four dollars a month. Willow and Hongju put their heads together to plan. The monthly rent was seventy dollars, and they would have to set aside fifty dollars for the laundry and living expenses. Even if they hired another worker, they would be able to cover everything with just their regular customers. Every night, Willow stayed up late planning the future with Hongju. Unlike when she opened the shoe store, this time they already had customers and she was working with a very resourceful friend, who would actually be there with her.

The Kaesong ajumoni decided to leave after Willow had given birth and finished postnatal care. Meanwhile, Hongju, who had learned to ride the bicycle, followed the man from Kaesong and learned how to collect, deliver, and run the business side. She also gave up participating in her organized activities, including the church.

"When I first came back to Ojin Village after becoming a widow, the thing I most disliked was being the object of people's pity. Now I don't want people abusing my husband, clacking their tongues and talking in whispers. And besides, if I'm doing business, it will be better to have a free hand, not belonging to any one group. Willow, let's work hard, make money, and get rich."

Willow's pains began. This time, too, the Kaesong ajumoni acted as midwife. Soon, the sound of a baby crying rang through the house. It was a daughter. Her name was, of course, Pearl, and she also gave her the same name in Korean, Jinju.

The Kaesong ajumoni wrapped the baby in a blanket and gave her to Willow to hold, saying, "She resembles the best-looking parts of both her parents' faces." The newborn made chewing motions with her mouth, as if looking for her breast, then sucked eagerly. Willow looked stunned at the sight of her daughter, born when her father was not with them. Her feelings were different from when Jongho was born. She recalled the words of her mother, *a daughter's destiny resembles that of her mother*, and made up her mind that her daughter should live a better life, in a better world, than she had.

Hongju and Jongho came in and met the baby. Hongju's expression showed signs of longing and pain. Jongho looked confused, a mixture of amazement at the baby and jealousy that his mother had been stolen from him. As Willow fed Pearl, Jongho stuck close to Hongju.

Willow went back to work after a week. Hongju tried to stop her but she wouldn't listen. "My omma took up her needle three days after giving birth. I've been lying here for a whole week, I've rested enough."

The Kaesong couple, who had supported her so kindly, left. Willow felt uneasy, as if she and Hongju were alone on a wind-swept plain, but on the other hand, they were excited to be running the laundry for themselves.

They quickly hired a woman to come in the afternoons and do the washing, as planned. She was a Hawaiian woman named Kalea. Kalea, who was married to a Japanese worker, spoke a little Japanese, and Willow still remembered the few simple Hawaiian words she had used while working for the Robsons. She was able to communicate with Hongju in Japanese and with Willow in Hawaiian. Hongju went to deliver in the mornings and brought back the dirty laundry, which Kalea washed after lunch. When the amount was excessive, Hongju also helped. At first, it was just the regulars inherited from the Kaesong couple, but the work quickly increased as their customer base grew.

"It's all because of me," Hongju liked to say. "The minute I ride in on my bicycle the soldiers whistle and go crazy. I only have to smile once and they become regular customers on the spot." Hongju gave up wearing Korean clothes and put on a dress. Then she had her hair cut instead of wearing it in a bun, and had it permed and let it hang down. From behind, she looked like a young haole girl.

Willow was worried that Hongju would earn a bad reputation in such a small town. If her reputation deteriorated, that might cause problems in the future.

Hongju, who had once said jokingly that she was going to marry three times, waved her hands. "Don't worry. I'm fed up with men."

Willow, who was now fully proficient with the sewing machine, looked at magazines and copied Western women's clothes. Hongju wore those clothes when she went out for deliveries. Then she returned shouting excitedly that she had received an order from an officer's wife. She never forgot to mention how great they looked on her. In some cases, officers' wives visited the store for themselves.

Willow began to wear her Korean dress with buttons on the blouse instead of ribbons, and with the skirt shortened. It was more convenient, and it was cooler in the hot weather. Many Korean wives came asking for similar alterations to their own clothes. Still, there were also customers asking for traditional Korean dress. They were usually the first wave of immigrants who were celebrating their sixtieth birthday, or having their children married.

As Hongju said, it was helpful that neither of them belonged anywhere.

Willow had never spared herself, even when working for a salary, but once it had become her shop, she was reluctant even to take time off to sleep. She was excited to work for herself, and keep her portion of the money the business earned, and even grew impatient with the time it took to breastfeed Pearl.

November came, and the Hawaiian winter was beginning. When she first arrived it always seemed to be summer, and she couldn't detect any real change in the seasons except for a little more rain. But now, after four years in Hawai'i, the slightest variation was distinct.

She hadn't heard from Taewan for several months. According to what members of the People's League were saying, the construction of the Independence Movement's military base had been delayed owing to financial difficulties. Willow didn't just want good news or no news. She resented Taewan, feeling that it was his duty to write to his family, even when things were difficult or hard.

Then news came that Mr. Roh was in Honolulu to raise money. That Sunday, Willow left Jongho with Hongju and went to Honolulu, carrying Pearl. Fortunately, Mr. Roh was in the office of the Independence League. After an initial exchange of greetings, Willow asked for news of Taewan and Mr. Roh told her that he had left Yongman Park and gone to join a unit forming part of the Daehan Tonguibu volunteer army.

Shocked, Willow hugged her daughter tightly. "Where is that? Did something go wrong with Chairman Park?" Why had Taewan left Yongman Park, whom he had deeply respected and followed?

"No, not at all. Comrade So was simply impatient to join the armed struggle against Japan. Chairman Park fully understood and accepted his request."

He explained that the Daehan Tonguibu was a military organization formed by combining independence forces scattered across South Manchuria.

"Even though Comrade So left Chairman Park, everyone is encouraged by the news that their troops are making a great contribution on the field of battle."

"Field of battle?"

When the word "battle," which she had so dreaded, emerged from Mr. Roh's mouth, Willow's face turned pale, and she wondered if next she would hear that Taewan had been shot dead.

"Not so long ago, I heard that Comrade So's military unit raided a police station, killed five of the enemy, and acquired weapons."

That meant that, just as he had killed the enemy, Taewan might also die at any time.

"But is he safe and sound?" Willow ventured to ask.

"We are always praying that Comrade So will be unscathed," Mr. Roh replied with eyes closed. Willow begged him to find out Taewan's address and handed him the ten dollars she had brought with her.

After meeting Mr. Roh, Willow couldn't focus on her work.

Hongju shouted when she put the wrong name tag on a military uniform and made mistakes when sorting the laundry. "Hey, wake up! If you're so absentminded you might get hurt, and then what?"

Hongju was right. An anxious mind can lead to accidents. Willow resolved to be stronger and more determined. When Taewan sent news, she should be able to reply saying that she was doing well. That was the only thing she could do.

A few days later, while sorting laundry next to Willow, Hongju asked, "Willow, do you want to join a gye?"

At the thought of the gye, Willow felt sad. She knew that Hongju was still going to the meetings, but pretended not to know.

"Didn't you tell me that if I went the others wouldn't join?"

"That gye is finished. We're starting a new one. I already spoke to the others."

"What?"

Hongju laid down the military uniform she was holding, put her hand on her waist, and repeated that she had told the others. "Nowadays, I don't belong to any group, and I don't belong to the Syngman Rhee party, too bad if they don't like it. And even if your husband was in the Independence League, you don't belong to any group. It's clear since you don't attend the lower village church. I'm going to form a gye with you, then the others can follow me."

"Aigo!" In order to hide a nascent smile, Willow scowled.

Although Julie's mother was missing, Myongok and Makson had decided to join them. Myongok, who had quit teaching at the Korean language school due to internal conflicts in the church, agreed to join the new gye without hesitation, while Makson, after holding out until the last minute, finally decided to participate, saying that if she fell out with her old friends, she would always regret it. With Yongsun from the Baekga store, and two friends Hongju had met when she was working at the pineapple-canning factory, they were seven in all. They were of the same age, and all were picture brides.

The first meeting was held at the laundry. They agreed to meet on the first Sunday afternoon of each month, and the person whose turn it was to receive payment from the gye would pay for the meal. The basic deposit was ten dollars, and each total monthly payment would be one hundred. Although there were only seven members, Willow, Hongju, and Yongsun each took two shares, which made the ten. As payments were made, the monthly sum would increase, and those paid later would benefit from a higher interest rate than in the bank.

The backyard of the laundry was filled with the loud shouting of children, but even if the children quarreled over the toys or fell down while playing, they didn't go running to their mothers. The women left the children alone while they boiled and ate noodles, talking among themselves. Though they prepared just one kind of kimchi, they enjoyed themselves as if it were a picnic. In moments like this, Willow was sad that among the picture brides who had come to Hawai'i together, only Songhwa was missing. Most of the time, Willow didn't think about Songhwa. In fact, she was so busy that she was even beginning to forget to think about Taewan.

Hongju seemed to be having the same thoughts. "Now that we're all here together it makes me think of Songhwa."

"Yes. It would be great if Songhwa also moved closer," Makson agreed. Kahuku was farther from Honolulu and more inconvenient because there was no direct access. For some time now, Willow and Hongju had been meaning to visit, but they could never find the time.

"Willow, once we've made some money let's go into the rental business. The income is regular, and it's less physically demanding," Hongju said on the day after the first gye meeting. The next most common thing Koreans did after the laundry business was the rental business, buying or renting a house with multiple rooms. It wasn't as hard as doing laundry and the income was more stable.

"Let's call Songhwa and her husband when we start the rental business. We can send Park Sokbo to work on the pineapple plantation and the three of us can do it together."

It upset Willow when Hongju's plans treated Taewan as if he didn't exist, but she wasn't wrong. The activities of the Tonguibu were published in the newspaper, but Taewan's presence at home gradually disappeared. Jongho no longer looked for his father, and the threat of writing a letter telling him not to buy toys did not work any longer, either. Pearl began to shy away and cry at the sight of any man. Willow cut out and kept newspaper articles about Taewan's troop's military engagements with the Japanese army. There was no sign of Taewan's face or name, but once Jongho and Pearl were older, she wanted to tell them the reason why their father had not been there. Her fervent wish was that Taewan would return safely to his family.

On the day of the third gye meeting at Myongok's house, Willow began to write a letter to Taewan, although there was no knowing when it might be delivered. She talked about everyday life as if he were always by her side.

Today was our third gye meeting. There are seven members. Among them, Myongok, Makson, and Yongsun from the Baekga store attend the upper village church. We belong to different groups. Myongok and Makson support the People's League, while Yongsun is in the National Association. Bongsun, who is the same age as us, is also a member of the People's League, while attending the lower village church. Gihwa, who is the youngest, goes to the Buddhist temple. Hongju has stopped attending both the church and the People's League.

Today, it was Myongok's turn to receive the money, so we met at her house to eat, and after a squall a rainbow appeared. Hongju said we should call our gye the Rainbow Group. There are seven members, just as the rainbow has seven colors, so I thought it was because of that, but it seems that the Bible says that the rainbow is a sign that God is with us. Hongju said that we are as different as the colors in a rainbow. In any case, like a rainbow that shines out brightly after rain, we all have the same hopes for only good things to come in the future. By the way, Myongok is going to start a nursery school. We are all hoping she will open it quickly. Because we are all working people, we are desperate for someone to look after the children. When she opens it, I am thinking of sending Jongho. Since she was a Korean language schoolteacher before, she will take good care of the . . .

Willow fell asleep without being able to finish the letter.

Willow and Hongju were arranging the laundry to be delivered the next day. Whenever Willow, who spent the whole day sitting in front of the sewing machine, or Hongju, who after the journey to the base did the laundry with Kalea, moved, they both groaned from all of their aches.

"Having a lot of work is fine, but we'll both fall ill if we go on like this," said Hongju. "In other laundries, six or seven family members all join forces to work. Shall we hire one more person to do the washing and ironing?"

It had already been a long time since Kalea, who at first only came in the afternoon to do the washing, had begun to work all day.

"If we spend everything on wages, what will be left? Pearl isn't much trouble as yet, so let's keep doing as now."

After Willow fixed on a tag, Hongju added the number. Just as they were finishing, the door opened and Makson came in with a baby on her back. After she gave birth to a son, her husband threw a big party. Kalea said that in Hawai'i too, since children often died in their first year, the first luau was important. "Luau" was the Hawaiian word for a party.

"Look who's here!"

When Willow and Hongju saw who was coming along behind her, they both stood up.

"Aigo, who's this? Songhwa!"

"I came outside to try to get the baby to sleep, and saw someone hanging around. She looked familiar, and when I looked closely, it was Songhwa."

Willow and Hongju screamed and embraced her. She was so thin, like a sheet of paper. Willow made her sit down on a chair.

As soon as Makson left the laundry, Hongju asked, "How did you get here? Have you come to visit? How's the old man?"

"Hey, you sound as though you're interrogating her! She'll be too scared to reply," Willow scolded, though she too was intensely curious.

"He's dead," Songhwa said calmly.

"What? How?" asked Willow.

"He went to bed in the evening and died in his sleep."

There was a moment of silence, but no one was shocked. He had passed his sixtieth and sixty-first birthdays, so he had completed his natural span of life.

"He was kind to me these latter years. I don't have any bitterness toward the old man." Songhwa looked sincere.

"My God. How surprised you must have been. What about the funeral?" asked Willow, regretting that she had not been there. When she suffered morning sickness with her first child, and when her father-in-law died, she had received so much support from Songhwa, and now she hadn't been there to return her goodwill.

"The camp people helped, and he was properly buried in the cemetery." Songhwa looked carefree, as if she had finished her housework.

"It's good you've come," said Hongju. "It's good the old man died. What use is a long life? Songhwa, let's live together. Do you know how well our laundry is doing? We'll pay you a generous salary, then you can meet a good man while you're working and get married again."

"Aigo, the ground hasn't even dried on her husband's grave, how can you be talking about that already? Songhwa, first act as a widow should. Let any new bridegroom find you."

Songhwa laughed and said, "Thanks. I'll accept your offer until the child is born, at least." Willow and Hongju were so surprised they were at a loss for words. Her belly was not in the least swollen, so they hadn't even dreamed that she was pregnant.

"Oh, you're pregnant? Is it Sokbo's?" Willow asked without thinking. Embarrassed at Songhwa's expression, which seemed to ask whose child it might be otherwise, Willow quickly added, "Jangsu's aboji was well over sixty when he was born, wasn't he?"

After a brief discussion, Willow and Hongju estimated that she must be about four months pregnant, after counting from the date of her last period.

"The baby should be due around the anniversary of Pearl's birth." Willow worried for Songhwa, who would give birth to a fatherless child. Pearl had also been born without a father, but at least Taewan was still alive.

"Don't worry about anything. What does it matter if there's no aboji around? We can raise it together. We'll even put it through school," Hongju generously offered.

Starting the next day, Songhwa started helping with the work. From housework and caring for the children to ironing, she did whatever was needed. Thanks to this, Willow and Hongju were able to concentrate more on the laundry.

Another year began. They'd renamed the business Sisters Laundry, and it was flourishing. Willow and Hongju more or less forced Songhwa to attend the gye meeting.

"You're going to have a baby, you need to save some money."

Songhwa said she only needed food and board, but Willow and Hongju paid her share instead of a salary.

Among the members, the most sensitive to news related to Korea was Willow, whose husband was now in Manchuria. Willow looked at the newspaper from time to time. She also read the publications of various organizations that she received from other Rainbow Group members. Her heart sank on reading that members of the Tonguibu had entered Korea and blown up a police station in Sinuiju. If he was caught, he was sure to be imprisoned or killed.

The news about politicians was uniformly grim. The Provisional Government was divided into two groups: a reconstructive faction that wanted to fix the problems and move ahead, and a creative faction that wanted to form a completely new government. The split had begun when Syngman Rhee had submitted a petition to the League of Nations requesting a mandate to govern Korea. Now there were rumors that Syngman Rhee would soon be kicked out. Nevertheless, compatriots in America, including Hawai'i, were unsparing in raising funds for the independence of their country. When a support-Korea-products movement was launched back home, the women in Hawai'i launched a buy-nothing-Japanese campaign.

Apart from the news about Taewan or their country, the lives of the members of the Rainbow Group, including Willow, were smoother than ever. The laundry went without saying, and Makson's husband expanded the barbershop. Myongok set up a nursery and kindergarten called Rainbow's Home. There were so many children that Gihwa quit working at the factory and joined her. Bongsun opened a grocery store with her husband, using the money she had saved in the meantime.

Songhwa was their main worry. As the time for her delivery approached, Songhwa's face lost all expression and she spoke less and less, until it was only a few words a day. Jongho slept with Hongju in one small room, while Willow, Pearl, and Songhwa slept in the main bedroom. Willow, who worked tirelessly during the day, would breastfeed Pearl half asleep if she woke up and cried. In her exhaustion, she barely noticed if Songhwa was shivering or talking in her sleep. Hongju also slept deeply. Neither knew that Songhwa went out into the yard in the middle of the night and walked about.

"Songhwa, you have nothing to worry about. Don't worry, just eat well. You're nothing but skin and bones." Hongju worried that Songhwa's body showed no signs even though she was eight months pregnant. The anxious Willow and Hongju forced her to visit the hospital, but nothing was wrong.

Around that time, the biggest event was that Hongju became the owner of a car.

It had belonged to Charlie, a soldier, who was a longtime regular customer of the laundry, but who was being reassigned to a base on the mainland. Charlie, whose wife had died in her early forties, liked Hongju. Hongju also liked Charlie.

Willow had worried that Hongju might end up getting hurt if she dated Charlie.

"What can hurt someone who's already been a widow, and abandoned? I just follow my heart," Hongju had said, waving her worries away.

"You don't realize how cruel a haole can be." Willow cited the scars on Taewan's shoulder, the woman who threw down the egg she gave the child at Kahuku Station, and Mrs. Robson, for whom the only problem had been that Jongho had entered their garden, even though he was injured, in her efforts to dissuade Hongju.

Hongju laughed.

"Charlie's a gentleman. Of all the men I've met so far, Charlie is the most kind and friendly. He's a hundred times better than those Korean men who have no respect for women, and don't know how to take care of their families." She wasn't wrong. As of now, Taewan had been away from his family for several years.

"But why date someone whose language you can't speak?" asked Willow as a final argument against it.

Hongju, who dealt with American soldiers every day, spoke simple English, but she was still at the level of a child. She replied with a smile, "If you want to learn a language, dating is the best method. Once I can speak English well, it will help in the laundry."

Her words turned out to be true. Hongju's proficiency improved quickly while she was dating Charlie, so that soon she could respond quite well to the occasional haole customers. Some even came in because they had heard that she could speak English.

Every Sunday, Charlie stopped the car in front of the laundry and waited for Hongju. Even after Hongju was ready to go out, looking her best, she would make Charlie wait for ten or twenty minutes.

Seeing Hongju deeply in love, and worried for her, Willow asked, "What will you do if you don't get married after starting up rumors all over the neighborhood?"

"Don't worry. She's getting married," said Songhwa suddenly from beside her.

Willow looked at her in amazement. "Is that true? What else do you see?"

After the fever that had briefly shone in her eyes disappeared, Songhwa quickly changed the subject, as if she didn't know what she had said. Songhwa was saying strange things with increasing frequency. And very often, what she said proved to be true. Willow mentally prepared herself to deal with the situation if Hongju married Charlie. Nevertheless, when she learned that Charlie had proposed to Hongju, she felt desperate. Without Hongju, the laundry would have to close. It was impossible for just the two of them to run it, with Songhwa about to give birth and often lost in a trance. Still, she couldn't stand in the way of her friend's happiness, just for her own benefit.

"Great! Get married! Songhwa and I can run the shop. We'll earn less but don't worry, we'll have the money we've saved. Just think about yourself and decide." She was already depressed at the thought of parting from Hongju, but she spoke calmly. She hoped that this time Hongju would have a happy marriage.

Hongju looked perplexed. "What are you talking about? I'm not getting married. If I marry Charlie, I'd become an American. Then I'd be separated from Korea forever. I'm staying here with you." Hongju's eyes reddened. For Hongju, Korea meant Songgil.

Hongju turned down Charlie's proposal and asked him to

sell her the car before he left. When Songhwa seemed about to make another prophecy, Willow said, "You see, Hongju didn't get married, did she?" And laughed.

"She will," Songhwa whispered.

Charlie left the car behind, and left Hawai'i.

With Ford's mass production, cars could now be bought for a worker's annual salary. It was still a costly item, quite out of reach of the hardworking common people. Once Hongju had the car, she got her license right away. The Ford, a refurbished model from 1915, kept stalling, but it was still a great resource, allowing her to deliver faster and in larger quantities than the bicycle.

"I was on the way back when the engine stalled and I had such a hard time. To think of him driving about in such an old car, Charlie must have been a miser, too. All the men it's been my fortune to meet have been full of hot air."

Hongju consoled herself for refusing Charlie with pointless complaining. From the time she first came to Hawai'i, it had been Hongju's dream to drive around in a car. She finally had a car, but she was so busy going back and forth between the laundry and the base that there was no time to enjoy it.

Their first outing was on Easter Day, a Sunday, when most of the shops in Wahiawā were closed. On that day, a great festival for churchgoers, Willow and Hongju also made plans to go to Sunset Beach, in the north, before Songhwa gave birth. Willow and Hongju were looking forward to their first excursion, and Songhwa also looked quite excited, as did the children.

In the morning, Hongju set off in her Ford with Songhwa sitting in the passenger seat, holding the picnic basket, while Jongho, and Willow holding Pearl, sat in the back. Hongju's driving skills were clumsy and jerky. With repeated sudden stops, Willow began to feel sick. Jongho, who had been excitable from the moment they got into the car, hung his head out the window, screaming joyfully.

Aside from her motion sickness, an intense pride also came rising up. Only two Koreans in Wahiawā owned cars, and there were only a few women drivers among the immigrant communities, and Hongju was the first among the Koreans. Willow wanted the people of Wahiawā to see them enjoying an outing in the car, and wished her family back home could be there too. If *she* had stayed in Korea, she could never have imagined such a thing.

When they reached the beach, they unpacked and set up their mats onto the sand. Willow put Pearl down on a mat that Songhwa spread out. Jongho froze, staring at the sea. Waves rising as high as a two- or three-story building raged like dragons. They enjoyed their picnic, eating sandwiches, oranges, and bananas, as they watched waves surging toward the shore, and young men and women rushing into the sea to surf.

Willow had once seen people surfing on Waikīkī Beach in Honolulu. At that time, it had looked like mere exercise or play, but now the waves were so rough and high that it was more like life-threatening acrobatics. The waves seemed intent on engulfing the young people. They watched with bated breath. Willow gasped when one woman disappeared into the waves, and barely dared exhale until the moment the woman came soaring up again. Onlookers cheered and clapped, so little Jongho clapped too.

Following Jongho, Pearl tottered off the mat. Songhwa was up before Willow could move and went after the children. Hongju was quietly looking at the sea, seemingly exhausted from driving. For Willow, this peaceful moment, just sitting there, doing nothing, was so good it made her want to cry.

"Those guys are just like us. Our life is also a kind of surfing," said Hongju.

Willow immediately understood what Hongju meant. As Hongju said, for her, too, life's crises had come raging, innumerable like the waves of the sea. The deaths of her father and brother, the life that had followed, life in Hawai'i as a picture bride . . . Nothing was ever easy. The same was true for Hongju and Songhwa.

Willow put her arm round Hongju's shoulder and watched Songhwa as she followed the children. They, having left Korea together, would go on living together, rising above the waves, painfully, joyfully, passionately.

Every time spray rose from a crashing wave, a rainbow could be seen.

Part Three

PEARL'S STORY

EIGHTEEN YEARS LATER

Auntie Rose poured herself another glass of Scotch. Cigarette smoke rose between her red-nailed, manicured fingers. I was thinking of my boyfriend and only half listening to her. Peter had gone with his family to his grandfather's home in California for the Christmas holiday, and we were spending the first Christmas since we started dating apart.

At dawn on Sunday, December 7, Japanese bombers had attacked the naval base in Pearl Harbor. At first, our soldiers thought it was a training exercise. More than twenty-four hundred people were killed, and a huge number of fighters, aircraft carriers, and battleships sank beneath the Pacific Ocean. Even from Honolulu, I saw black smoke rising from the direction of the base. America suffered the attack helplessly. Not only Hawai'i but the whole country was in shock. Following President Roosevelt's speech the next day, Congress declared war on Japan and young men enlisted in droves.

Wherever I went, people were talking about Pearl Harbor. The mathematics teacher condemned Japan, which had attacked without declaring war, and said that if he were younger, he would join the military. Perhaps belatedly remembering the children of Japanese descent present in the classroom, he stressed that it had been a bad decision made by the Japanese military and government, and that the law-abiding majority of Japanese people were not at fault.

Looking at the percentages of the population of Hawai'i,

those of Asian descent were the majority, and those of Japanese descent were the most numerous among them. Once the war between the United States and Japan began, Korean adults hoped that Japan, which had been trampling on their motherland for more than thirty years, would be destroyed. At the time, I was annoyed that I was being teased about my name. The boys sniggered, needling me, saying Pearl has been attacked.

Even from the beginning, I never liked my name. It was fortunate that my mother had not liked some other jewel and named me Sapphire, Ruby, Gold, or Diamond, but Pearl was bad enough.

Until I entered sixth grade, I never encountered a child with the same name. The first time I did, it was in a novel called *The Scarlet Letter* by Nathaniel Hawthorne, which I read in literature class. She was the daughter born as a result of a pastor's adultery with the female protagonist, not a happy situation to be in. It was a name that Mom would never have given me if she had read the novel.

The second Pearl I came across was the first American woman writer to receive the Nobel Prize in Literature, three years ago. Her book, *The Good Earth*, was required reading at school, as a work that already won the Pulitzer Prize before its author won the Nobel Prize. I started reading it, full of pride that I had the same name as a world-famous writer, but I soon closed the book. The characters were ignorant farmers in rural China, yet all of them spoke elegantly and were brimming with refinement. None of the Chinese around me spoke in that way. Above all, the heroine was so stuffy that she annoyed me.

But this time, Pearl Harbor had been destroyed by an enemy's attack. I would have made a scene if Peter hadn't stepped in and stopped the boys from teasing me with nasty remarks.

That was the start of a special relationship between us. It

turned out that Peter had been in love with me since the year before, back before I even knew that he existed. Peter's Portuguese grandfather, like my grandfather, had come to Hawai'i as a sugarcane worker. Like many first-generation immigrants, his grandpa later moved to California, where Peter was born and raised. His mother was Japanese. Peter said he came to Hawai'i because of his father's business, but he seemed to have come so that we could meet. I also used to say that it seemed that the Japanese troops had attacked Pearl Harbor in order to bring us together. As fate led the way, we kissed at the end of two weeks and soon began to plan a future together.

Our first plan was to attend the same university. I had already made up my mind to go to the University of Wisconsin in the central part of the mainland. Peter, who had been intending to head back to California, said he would apply for the same college as me. If we were to go to Wisconsin together, I had to solve a problem first. My mother wanted me to finish college in Hawai'i and become a teacher, and she was quite forceful about it. Before I began to date Peter, I had already had a big fight with her over the matter. When I went home and we talked during the Thanksgiving vacation, Mom said that if I went to that college, she would no longer consider me as her child.

"David went to UCLA, so why can't I go to school on the mainland? It's my life. It's none of your business! I'm going to Wisconsin."

Mom can hardly speak English. Since she has always lived in the Korean-American community, it was inevitable. My native language was English, but I also spoke Korean to some extent. My speaking skills just did not match my listening skills. Sometimes I would pretend I couldn't understand anything that was unfavorable to me, but everyday communication was fine. I am not particularly bothered by the fact that my mother and my mother tongue are different. Even if they use the same language, parents and children don't communicate well anyway. But when I was fighting with her it was too frustrating. When I switched from stuttering Korean and spoke in English, my mother looked hurt, as if I were wielding a weapon against her. On that day, each of us screamed and quarreled in her own language until I gave up and ran out of the house.

I went back to Auntie Rose's house. I was fortunate to be living with her, because my school was far away. After that, I didn't go home for the next four weeks and decided not to go during the Christmas break. It was a silent demonstration that I would apply for college as I saw fit.

Before the Christmas break, the first person I called was my mother. I hoped she might have changed her mind. However, she said nothing about college and simply told me to take good care of Auntie Rose during the vacation. "It would be nice if you both came together, but since she says she's not coming, forget about coming home and stay with your auntie."

The plan I had prepared as a secret weapon proved to be useless; I was sad to hear Mom tell me not to come home for Christmas. The difference between me saying I wouldn't go and Mother saying don't come was the difference between heaven and earth.

Auntie had belatedly learned of her mother's death in a letter from her hometown. Auntie, who had closed the restaurant on Christmas Eve, was now drunk for the sixth day in a row. Wallowing in sadness, she started to tell stories about my childhood. It was useless to pretend not to understand. Even if there was only an audience of one, she was absorbed in her role as an actor performing a passionate role onstage. Thanks to her, I was spending the worst Christmas season of my life, and now I was growing so irritated that it was hard to control myself.

"Pearl, have I ever told you how we sisters from the laundry took you and Jongho to Sunset Beach?" Auntie said, looking at me with blurry eyes.

"Yes, Auntie. Three times. You also talked about surfers, and about how life was like riding a wave."

I responded quickly, in case she started telling me again, and looked for an opportunity to stand up. I was more concerned with Peter's phone call, which might be coming, than the old stories of my drunken aunt.

Not that Auntie Rose's stories were just boring and irritating. Thanks to them, I was able to learn more about my mother's life, and through that my own. Mom almost never talked about the past. When I asked, she would say that she was too busy living today and could not even remember what happened yesterday. After listening to my auntie for a few days, I reckoned that Mother's lack of memory was a great advantage. According to her stories, Mother's life had been difficult and frustrating. The same was still true of the mother I knew. The biggest reason I quit reading *The Good Earth* was because I kept seeing my mother superimposed on the protagonist O-Lan. It would be too depressing if my mother were to repeat such tales every day.

"Looking back, just after I came to Hawai'i was the time when I was most excited and happy."

I found that absurd. "A woman whose husband was absent, a woman whose husband had died, and a woman abandoned by her husband, those three living together, what was so good about that?" She had been twenty-three years old then, some four years older than I was now. If that's the kind of life waiting for me in four years' time, I swear I'd rather stop living here and now.

"When you say 'a woman abandoned by her husband,' are you talking about me?" Auntie looked at me.

I faced her with an expression suggesting "Who else?"

"If that's what you think, you're making a big mistake. He didn't abandon me, I abandoned him." She drained what remained in the glass. It didn't matter to me one way or another.

"Yes, yes. As you say. Now it's time for you to go to sleep."

I quickly picked up the empty glass from in front of her and stood up. It was my job to do the dishes, the cleaning, and the laundry in the house. From the time she first entrusted my brother to her, Mother made it clear that Auntie should assign as much work to us as would cover the boarding costs. First, just as my brother used to do, I would sit down with her every evening, read out the slips from the restaurant, balance the books, and calculate the earnings. It was not as though she spent the money, but if the calculations were not correct, I had to do them all over again, several times, and if business was bad, I had to listen to her complaints, it was all so boring. I begged to be allowed to do housework.

I was at the sink when my aunt said, "Bring that glass back. Father's dead, Mother's dead, which makes me an orphan."

How could she make such a fuss about being an orphan when she was already over forty? I shook my head as I brought the glass back and put it down in front of her. I reckoned that at such times it wouldn't be such a bad idea to humor her. Auntie Rose would be the only person I could turn to if Mother continued to oppose my going to Wisconsin, and cut off financial support. My auntie, who was renowned for donating generously to Korean-American organizations, could hardly pretend not to know my situation. Besides, college was not the only problem. My mother would never allow me to date Peter, with his different skin color and Japanese blood, let alone marry him. (Getting married as soon as we graduated from college was our second plan.) Then too, Auntie was the only person who might back us up, though I didn't know if my stubborn mother would listen to her.

"Why don't you get yourself something to drink?"

I took a cola out of the icebox, removed the cap, and sat down opposite her.

"Only a cola? You're so uptight, just like your mother. There's only the two of us here, have a proper drink for once. When I was nineteen, I was already a widow, remarried, and had a son." Auntie Rose laughed. It was true that my mother was uptight, but I could never agree to see myself like that. Auntie had no idea what passion lay inside of me.

"No. I'm eighteen years and six months old."

When I entered elementary school, counting my age was the most confusing thing. Wahiawā Elementary School had all kinds of children, not only Korean, but also Chinese, Japanese, Filipino, Portuguese. They were all six to seven years old. I bragged and said that I was eight, but at once I was accused of being a liar. I learned it was only Koreans who said they were one year old as soon as they were born.

Auntie Rose laughed again. "For me, there's nothing good about Korea except for the Korean way of counting ages. If you do it the American way, the time spent in your mother's womb doesn't count, but you're already growing when you're in the womb, aren't you?"

"We're not Korea, we're in America." I had not expected to have to tell her something that I had repeated ad nauseam to my mother. Although she had left Korea more than twenty years before, Mother had never abandoned, not only its language but also Korea-style ways of thinking and living. I couldn't understand how such a person had come to give her child an English name. (Of course, my mother called us both by our Korean names.)

"Yes, this is Hawai'i. Hoping for better luck, I came to a foreign land, stepped in shit trying to avoid something worse, and lived here all this time, enduring whatever life brought." She drained the glass in one shot, all the time whining like an old woman. Then she picked up the bottle of Scotch and refilled her glass, spilling some. I controlled my desire leave the room. If I didn't want to make it the worst Christmas ever, I needed to indulge my loyal but whimsical auntie's fancies. To do that, I had to pretend to listen and ask questions, but there was nothing left for me to be curious about in her life.

I decided to ask about Songhwa. According to Auntie Rose, she, Mom, and Songhwa had been a threesome. But I had never seen Songhwa or heard anything about her from Mother. Maybe that was why I didn't even think of her as an auntie. (Another characteristic of Koreans is that people are called not by name, but by relationship. When I was young, I was often scolded for calling my aunties by their given names.)

"Where does Songhwa live now? Did she marry again?"

Auntie Rose stared at me. I replied silently, *I'm tired of hearing about you or Mother, that's why I asked.*

"Songhwa . . . she went back to Korea." She took another draught of Scotch.

I felt it would have been more interesting if she had remarried. Now, tired of even pretending to be curious, I refilled her glass. I thought it would be better to make her drunk as quickly as I could and put her to bed.

"Do you know why Songhwa went back to Korea? It was because she was suffering from mubyong sickness."

"Mubyong? What's that?" I asked absently as I poured her another drink.

"The sickness when you're becoming a mudang."

"But what's a mudang?"

Auntie Rose muttered something, as if groping for an English word. "Let me see, sha, a shaman. That's what it is."

Auntie Rose's speech was increasingly unclear.

"Ah, a shaman. Songhwa became a shaman?" I leaned forward. A shaman. That was more interesting.

"Yes, originally her grandmother was a shaman. In Korea being a shaman is a very low-class thing. Songhwa's grandmother sent her granddaughter here to get married rather than be despised if she remained."

She was losing the track and might go on for a long time, so I interrupted with another question. "Did she ever do fortune-telling?"

"It can't be called real fortune-telling, but sometimes she would go into a kind of trance and spit out a few words that proved to be true. Hearing that, people sometimes came to Songhwa secretly, even though they believed in Jesus. Still, Songhwa tried hard to overcome her mubyong."

Auntie had reached the bottom of the bottle. If Songhwa were around, I would have wanted to ask her about my fate. Will I be able to go to the college of my choice? Will I be able to marry Peter? She would also be an auntie, so I would have been able to have my fortune told for free.

"But why did she go back? You said that in Korea, being a shaman is a low-class occupation."

". . . For the sake of her child. She left because she was thinking about her child. . . . You don't need to know . . ." Auntie Rose couldn't finish the phrase and slumped across the table. After grabbing hold of the glass that was about to roll off the table, I half carried her to her room. Limp like a sack of flour, she didn't really know where she was as I dragged her along and flopped her onto the bed. Just as I was removing her cardigan, which I thought she would find stuffy, she opened her eyes blearily.

"Pearl, you mustn't hold it against your mother. It was all for your sake . . ."

Was opposing my dreams done for my sake? It would be wonderful if parents could justify everything as being for their children's sake. If she had said it when she was sober, I might have quibbled, but arguing with someone in her condition would be a waste of time.

"Yes, okay. I know. Now go to sleep."

I propped her head up with a pillow and covered her with a blanket. Soon she was snoring. As I was about to go out, the scene inside the room caught my eyes. I hadn't cleaned for a while and it was a mess. Normally, I cleaned it every day, but during the days when the restaurant was closed, my auntie spent a lot of time in her room. When she woke up, I reckoned she would complain that I hadn't done my job properly. Thinking that I should at least tidy up a bit, I picked up the clothes that lay scattered on the floor. A kind of wooden box appeared under the dirty clothes. The lid was open and inside it there were pictures and letters. A letter that had fallen onto the floor was from Charlie.

It was already the wrong time for a call to come from Peter, and I had taken a long daytime nap, so I didn't think I would get to sleep easily. I was intrigued by what my auntie had said about the past, and photos or love letters would serve to kill time.

I picked up the box and left the room. If I put the box back before I went to bed, she wouldn't notice, and even if I did get caught, she would only laugh.

I sat leaning against the head of my bed and opened the lid off the box. From among the confused mixture of photos and letters, I took out the photos first. A photo of my aunt and Charlie's wedding emerged after I put aside some photos taken with the staff of the restaurant, or recent events.

Charlie, who had continued to write to Auntie after leaving for the mainland, returned to Hawai'i several years later. Then he proposed again, offering her a red rose and a ring. From that moment, my auntie was called Rose, though my mom often still calls her Hongju. Her wedding is the first memory of my life. I put on a pretty dress and sprinkled flowers before the bride and groom as they came in. I was embarrassed, thinking that the people were applauding me. I also remember that I was so fond of the dress my mom made that I insisted that I would not take it off even when I went to bed. That's my only memory of when I was five.

There was also a photo of Auntie Rose and Charlie with my family on the wedding day. Auntie wrote down the date on the back of each. In the photo taken on May 14, 1927, there are only Auntie Rose in her wedding dress and Charlie, Mother holding me, and my brother, but no father. The first time I saw my father was the following fall. It's not so much that I saw him for the first time as that I can't remember anything that happened before that. My father said that he came back once before, when I was still a baby. My mom said that my dad sat me on his lap and fed me and sang a lullaby when I was going to sleep, but I can't recall anything.

"David, did that really happen? Did Daddy do that for me?" I had asked my brother, but I couldn't get an answer. My brother grew angry whenever his father was mentioned.

My first memory of my father is seeing him plunged into grief over someone's death. It was difficult even for Mother to get close to him. I later found out that the person who died was Yongman Park, a leader of the Korean community, and that it was because of his influence that my father left home to fight against Japan. Yongman Park was wrongly reported to have collaborated with Japan while in China, and he was assassinated by another Korean.

Father left home again after Yongman Park's funeral. Honestly, I wasn't sorry when he left, he made the atmosphere in the house so dark and heavy. (For a while, my mom made the house as dark as my father.) I liked Charlie much better than my father. After Auntie Rose got married, she lived near our house and ran a new laundry with Mother. Charlie, who worked at Schofield Barracks, often brought something delicious when he visited.

Charlie loved my brother and me a lot. The first time my brother played catch was with Charlie, not his father. It was Charlie who took us to the beach and took pictures of us at every event. He died of cancer three years ago. Even if my father leaves us one day, we won't be as sad as we were then.

When my father left again, Mom was pregnant and gave birth to Michael. That was the time when I learned for certain that children were not picked up from under a bridge or delivered by storks. Most of the Korean children in our neighborhood had five or six brothers and sisters, only one or two years apart, so they mostly played together like friends. My brother was four years older than I was, so he treated me as a child and did not play with me. I was seven when Michael was born, so it was mainly my job to take care of him. Even after starting elementary school, I used to carry him on my back and play with him until it was dark. Of course, this made it difficult to do my homework.

It was in December 1931 that Father came back for good. I was in second grade, and I shared a room with my mom and Michael, and the small room was used by my brother, who was in the top grade of elementary school. My brother was studying hard to enter Leilehua High School. (I wasn't envious of my mother's special treatment of David. According to my mother, the eldest son had to study well, obey his parents, and enhance the standing of the family when he grew up.)

Mother hadn't finished at the laundry that day, and as usual I was caring for Michael, when suddenly there was a noise outside. When I went to see what was happening, my brother was also coming out of his room. We stared at a man with white hair and a shaggy beard standing on the porch with Mother.

"Children, your aboji is back. Come and greet him."

I already knew who it was before she spoke. However, I did not want to admit that this shabby man who seemed about to collapse was my father. He looked old, as if it was not three years, but thirty years since he had left. Also, he was coughing as if he was sick.

"Taewan, go inside. Pearl, you come in too."

Mother embraced him, as if he was a treasure, and went into their bedroom. My father was limping strongly with one leg. I worried that I would be teased by the other children. It was better to be teased for having no father. My brother looked angry, and I went into the room without hiding my disappointment. As Father sat there next to Michael, who was asleep, Mother told us to bow in greeting, Korean-style, on our knees.

That night I had to go to sleep in David's room. He threw a tantrum if I even talked to him, and kicked me when my feet touched him. When I cried and went to the door of the main bedroom, Father told me to come in and sleep there. Michael's place was between my mother and father, and I slept beside Mother. However, I couldn't sleep well with my father coughing all night long, so I went back to my brother's room the next day.

Mom said that Father had injured his leg and fallen sick while fighting the Japanese, and he was a hero. But none of that mattered to me. It didn't make sense for my mother, who had suffered for so long, to say only good things about Father. Auntie Rose seemed to feel the same way. In fact, sometimes, in Mother's absence, she used to criticize Father. But that day she did it openly. I overheard the conversation between her and my mom, while I pretended to be putting Michael to bed.

"Did he make the country independent or did he just make a name for himself? All he's brought back is his broken body. What have you gained by raising your children all by yourself for ten years? You're the one who's worn down, but you're giving him the tonics and bone soup. Why don't you hate your husband?" Auntie Rose waved scissors about as she spoke. I felt relieved that she had pointed out the thoughts and feelings I was too young to deal with.

"Am I some kind of Buddha? Of course I feel hate and resentment. But is there any point in putting that into words? As you said, he's failed to gain independence, he's come home with nothing but his body, and he feels so bad that I feel sorry for him. If we become independent someday, the hardships that we have suffered will have contributed. It will not be a total waste. Anyway, for now, my priority is to nurse him back to health. At present he's not fit to be an aboji to his children." Her voice was dark and feeble, unlike when she told us good things about Father. It wasn't all that nice to know my mom's real feelings. What I needed was a great father, not a pitiful one.

Several weeks later, the churches invited Father to attend. There were two Korean churches in Wahiawā. The children played together at school, but on Sundays they were divided, attending the upper village church and the lower village church with their parents. The churches were usually called the Upchurch and the Downchurch. It seemed that we and Auntie Rose were the only people in the neighborhood that did not attend either. I went to the Upchurch with a friend at Easter and to the Downchurch with another friend at Christmas. I envied the children who went to church with their parents, because when I just went for special events people looked askance at me.

The one that invited Father first was the lower village church. The whole family dressed neatly and went together. Auntie Rose went with us. When I went with my parents, I felt confident. We sat in the front seat and waited for Father to speak. The Independence Movement groups in Manchuria were divided into several factions, just like the Koreans in Wahiawā. Father talked for a time about the Tonguibu, whatever that was, and the Chamuibu, whatever that was. The last group he worked with was the Korean Revolutionary Army. He went on to explain about how that group was formed. Bored, I looked around. The other children were yawning or fidgeting. I was impatiently waiting for him to tell how he had injured his leg while defeating the Japanese army.

The ten-thousand-strong Korea Revolutionary Army not only fought against the Japanese army, but also blew up Japanese government offices and railroads, and punished pro-Japanese factions. The revolutionary forces fought alone or in association with the Chinese army. The battle that took place in 1929 at Liuhe Xi'an was a great success. It was during that battle that Father was shot in the leg. This was the part I had been eagerly waiting for. I looked forward to more tales of military exploits, but that was all. My father was only one of numerous independence fighters, and he was not a leading figure. Still, people clapped when he told how he had extracted the bullet and treated the wound himself. He had returned because of the leg injury, and also because of severe asthma, the result of living in a cold, harsh climate.

When Father said he felt ashamed and guilty for coming back without seeing his country become independent, people shouted "No!" and gave a standing ovation. Some cried "Amen!" and others wiped away tears. I was proud of my father that day.

The situation was different in the upper village church. Someone shouted that Yongman Park was a renegade, and that Father had criticized Syngman Rhee. The church was in such an uproar that Mother, holding Michael, and Auntie Rose led Father out of the church. My brother dragged me along behind them as I cried.

After that, my father stopped attending outside activities and helped in the laundry. I was always confused about whether to be ashamed, or proud, or feel sorry for him.

It was seven months after Father came back that we left Wahiawā. Wahiawā is where I was born and raised. I hated leaving the place I had grown fond of and parting from my friends. We also parted with Auntie Rose, who was moving to Honolulu. I was sad that I would no longer see her pretty clothes, her accessories, or her dressing table covered with all kinds of cosmetics.

Mother made nice clothes for others, but she herself wore only a white skirt and jacket or a white jacket with a black skirt all the year round, like a student wearing a school uniform. Her only accessory was a worn silver ring she called her wedding ring. I hoped that if we had to move, like Auntie Rose we would go to Honolulu, where Mom could open a dressmaking shop and make pretty clothes. Instead, we were going to a rural place called Koko Head, at the southern tip of O'ahu, to run a carnation plantation. (We children had no decision-making powers.)

Mother wanted to leave Wahiawā, where many members of Syngman Rhee's Comrade Society lived, and go to a place where Father could find healing for his mind and body. She said the weather at Koko Head was also better than in Wahiawā.

Our family rode in a truck behind the luggage. I hated farming and the countryside, so I cried all the way, saying I wanted to go back to Wahiawā. I pinched Michael to make him cry too, but he was too excited about riding in a truck for the first time. David sat apart as if he belonged to another family, looking glum. He would soon be going to live with Auntie Rose because of school, anyway, so moving to Koko Head did not really affect him.

"Won't you stop? Why are you so stubborn? Get ahold of yourself!" Mother, holding Michael, was angry.

I pouted and refused to hold on to anything. If it stopped us moving, I would gladly have fallen off the truck and broken something.

"She's just as stubborn as you are," Father said, "but you shouldn't scold her. Jinju, you can make new friends in Koko Head, so do stop crying."

I replied in English, "Don't call me that, my name is Pearl."

I also wanted to live with Auntie Rose. She and Charlie were going into the rental business on Punchbowl Street, buying a building with several rooms, redecorating, then renting them out. (Because the business went well, Auntie bought the building next door and set up a restaurant. The restaurant is on the lower floor of the house I am now living in.) There was only one public secondary school in Honolulu, McKinley High School, but it was difficult to commute from Koko Head. I was envious of my brother, and I looked forward to growing up quickly and becoming a sixth-grade student.

Koko Crater came in sight. It looked like a coconut cut in half. Unlike Wahiawā, where the mountains could be seen in the distance, here the nearby mountains surrounded us like a wall. The truck entered a narrow, uneven road overshadowed with ki-awe trees. A place with no shops or houses seemed like a place where only animals should live. I wept even louder, but just as we arrived in front of our house after crossing wide fields, I suddenly saw the sea and my crying stopped abruptly.

The two-story house, located in the middle of a wide-open

space, had a large living room, a kitchen, and a dining room on the lower floor, and four bedrooms and two bathrooms on the upper floor. I couldn't take my eyes off the sea when I watched it, with its white waves, through the large living room windows. That alone was already fantastic, but then Mom told me that I had my own room. I was so excited I nearly fainted. From my room on the second floor, I could see the fields and Koko Crater. I suddenly felt ashamed at having cried all the way there. What was even more amazing was that the house belonged to us. My mother had bought two acres of land and the house by taking a loan from the bank with Charlie's guarantee. Living in the heart of Honolulu as I do now, I realize that the house was not really so special, but to the eyes of a child who had so far only lived in a rented two-room shack attached to a laundry in Wahiawā, it looked as big and fine as a palace.

There was also a picture of the housewarming party in the box. Back home we also have a family picture that Charlie took in front of the house that day. All the aunties who were members of the Rainbow Group came to the party with their families. The husbands, much older than the aunties, were like grandfathers. My father, nine years older than my mother, said he had been a much younger bridegroom compared to others. Sadly, my father didn't look that much younger than them anymore.

Adults enjoyed themselves with adults, children with children. My older brother and the older girls of his age, who were entering puberty, acted coyly, but I and the other children, who were elementary school students, ran around the house playing. There was no one scolding us for running, nor was there any dangerous equipment for us to hurt ourselves on. It was nice not having to speak Korean, unlike usual days. My father had taken it on himself to teach us to speak and write the Korean language. It wasn't easy to speak, but reading and writing were especially difficult, and boring. Father made us use Korean at home and would not accept demands or requests made in English. But that day was an exception, because there were some children who could not speak Korean at all.

One memory came to mind when I saw the picture of my aunties sitting around the table. We were playing hide-and-seek. I hid in a storeroom next to the kitchen that the other children didn't know about. As I was sitting there quietly, I heard my aunties talking in the dining room.

"At last Taewan has become a real jiju."

"Yes. At the start I fell for him because I had been told he was a jiju."

At first, I didn't know what the word they were using meant. Besides, it was difficult to understand them, not only because of the words but also because when they were together they all talked so quickly.

"It would have been even better if he'd become a jiju thanks to his own efforts, rather than yours."

Finally realizing that the word meant "landowner," I felt a bit disappointed, because Mother, who had always taught us that there are things more precious than money, had liked Father thinking he was a landowner.

"It would have been easier for you to run a rental business with Hongju, I don't know why you've chosen such hard work."

"Although your husband worked on the sugarcane plantation, this is the first time with carnations. Can he do it?"

After the others went on talking for a while, I heard my mother's voice again.

"We have to learn as we go. If I came here, it was in part for my husband, but it was also in part for myself. When I first arrived, I felt really envious seeing people hanging leis around people's necks at the port. I longed for someone to hang a pretty, scented flower necklace around mine. Later, when we arrived at Kahuku and the children welcomed us with leis, they seemed to be saying that I had done well to come. I'm already happy to think that our flowers will be used to welcome, congratulate, and comfort people."

Just then, the door of the storeroom opened and the tagger found me. My mother's face as I went out into the dining room is still vivid. My mother, smiling brightly, seemed to have achieved all her dreams.

However, carnation farming was not easy. There were rich people's villas in Koko Head, but there were also many Koreans and Japanese who grew flowers. The Japanese mainly grew roses, chrysanthemums, and flowers for ikebana, and most Koreans cultivated carnations used in leis, like us. Mother and Father, being inexperienced, went to a neighboring carnation plantation to learn how to grow them. They had to obtain overblown carnation stems, let them put down roots, blossom, and collect the seeds, which were then sown and grown.

Even after Father's return, Mother's hardships did not diminish. Father couldn't do hard work because of his cough, which got no better, and his leg, which remained painful, so he couldn't even do easy things for long. My mother only hired outside workers when she needed a lot of hands, and most of the time ran the plantation with the help of the family. Watering the open ground in the morning and evening was not easy. And since the land where flowers had been harvested had to stay fallow for several months, two acres were not enough. Mom rented some surrounding land and hired more workers. David also came back every weekend to help with plantation work, and when things were really busy, I had to cook while taking care of Michael.

Mother was not only passionate about growing flowers, but

also about caring for the house. She planted fruit trees such as grapefruit and lychee around the house, and as if carnations alone were insufficient, she planted other flowers too. And also raised chickens.

Mother and Father did not seem very close. To me, Auntie Rose and Charlie were a model loving couple. They lived with "darling" and "honey" constantly on their lips, touching and kissing each other, whether or not other people were around. Mother and Father said almost nothing to each other, even though they were together all day. Yet Auntie said that they loved each other a lot. I remembered clearly what Mother said to Auntie when Father returned. But when I asked if she hated him, and was only living with him out of pity, she said I was too young to understand and that what adults say is often different from what they think. (That seems to be right. Mother doesn't express bad feelings well.)

Mother went on to have two more children, Paul and Harry. They are two years apart and sometimes seem like they are from a different family. Of course, it isn't a bad thing for parents to get along well. Except for the fact that Mother almost died giving birth at such a late age, and I had younger siblings I had to take care of, once again.

After the youngest, Harry, was born, I got angry and told her to stop having children. She told me that, like me, she had been the only daughter between one older brother and three younger brothers. She had wanted to have a sister for me, but it didn't work out as she wished. I felt so bad that she'd had more children just for my sake.

Like an old man, Father would take frequent breaks while working in the field, or sit in the living room and watch the sea. Father, who struggled to teach us Korean, seemed to be suffering not only in his body but also deep in his heart.

When I approached him as he sat alone, he would pat my head. Then, even if we didn't say anything, I felt like we were having a conversation.

Since entering McKinley High School and living at Auntie Rose's house, I have come to love our home at Koko Head, which has fresh air, bright sunlight, flower beds, and the sea. The next picture was of me standing backstage with Auntie Rose, wearing thick makeup and Korean-style clothes. Looking at the date, I saw that it was taken after the March First commemorative performance when I was in ninth grade. The annual March First celebration was the most important event of the Korean-American community. On that day, the Fraternity Club members were kept very busy.

Mom made David and me join the Fraternity Club, a group for second- and third-generation Korean children. We used to meet once or twice a month to learn about Korea. Parents sent their children to the Fraternity Club because they wanted their children born in Hawai'i to learn about the history and traditional culture of Korea, but most of us thought of it as a social gathering. It was at the Fraternity Club that my brother met his first love. Although the groups were divided for each age, rumors quickly spread through brothers and sisters.

Emily, whom my brother was dating, was the older sister of Mary, a sixth-grade student like me. When I was chosen as the main performer in a dance performance, Mary was jealous and tried to badmouth me behind my back. I hated Emily just because she was Mary's sister. I was sickened to see my brother, who either glared or lost his temper with me, smiling at Mary's older sister and even being nice to Mary. I threatened to tell Mom if they didn't break up, but my brother pretended not to hear. Of course, I didn't tell Mother, but only because I knew how disappointed she would be if she knew that her oldest son was dating a girl instead of focusing on the history and culture of Korea. My brother's first love came to an end when Emily started going out with a college student from the young adults' age group. He should have broken up with her when I told him to. That was what I thought at the time, but now I know it's not something where you can do as you wish.

Unlike my brother, I limited myself to dancing, and thus I was fulfilling the purpose for which Mom had sent me to the club. I learned Korean folk dances, such as the puppet dance, the basket dance, and the fan dance, from Mr. Park, who had recently come from Korea. In the name of cultural exchange, he also invited an indigenous Hawaiian dance teacher to teach us how to dance hula. I liked both Korean dance and hula. When I was moving my body to the music, it seemed that I was in a world other than reality.

The hula teacher taught us not only dancing, but also the spirit of aloha and the meaning of the lei. The word "aloha," which could be heard everywhere, was not just a greeting. It was a word meaning compassion, kindness, affection, and sympathy. It expressed the indigenous Hawaiian spirit of loving, caring, respecting, and sharing joy with each other.

When she talked about the lei, I was more interested because I was the daughter of a carnation farmer. The lei was also not just a flower necklace. In the Hawaiian language, it was anyone you loved enough to carry upon your shoulders. According to local customs, when you presented a flower lei you embraced the person as you rested the garland upon their neck. Lei has become so widespread a culture that there is even a Lei Day. I wanted everyone in Hawai'i to exchange leis as often as eating. That way, our carnations would sell well, and I would be able to dance to my heart's content.

It was when I started sixth grade that I had first became

interested in dancing. Not long after Auntie Rose and Charlie moved, they took me to a cinema to see a movie. They said that *The Great Ziegfeld* had been based on a musical that was famous on Broadway. I had no time to think about the story, because I was fascinated by the gorgeous costumes, the staging, and the pretty woman in the starring role. Even after the movie was over, the gorgeous, colorful dance scenes would not leave my head.

I was not very good at anything, but I excelled at dancing, and was praised for looking lovely. The compliments certainly encouraged me, but it was more correct to say that I enjoyed dancing for itself. Whenever I performed at the March First ceremonies, I liked having people watch me dance, but even more I liked using my body in motion to express myself. When I was dancing, I felt that I was becoming the real "Pearl."

Later, in high school, I was more into dancing than studying, until, without consulting me, Mom told my club teacher that I was not to participate in any more performances. It was something that parents should never do if they want to stop their children from following a path different from what they would like. I had my first serious fight with my mother and quit the club.

With my mother's opposition, my passion only grew, so that I went to the library to find and read books on dance. Among them, Isadora Duncan's biography was the most interesting. From the story of how she took off her ballet shoes and danced following her body, I vaguely glimpsed what kind of dance I wanted to pursue. From childhood, I had wanted my movements to express my heart and emotions freely like Duncan, who danced in the woods and at the beach. At the same time, I was aware of, and worried about, the reality of the modern American dance world, where it was difficult to make it unless you were white. I often wondered if there was a place for me, as an Asian-American.

I felt encouraged by Duncan, who, when America couldn't

accept her way of dancing, had left for Europe. After I went to college on the mainland, if I came up against a wall, I would just have to find a new path.

The University of Wisconsin was the only state university in the United States with a dance department. There were also departments at one or two private schools, but they were beyond our means and there was no guarantee I could receive a scholarship. I was planning to cover my own living expenses and pocket money, so long as tuition was paid from home, but my mother had already said she wouldn't. However, a mother doesn't have the power to determine the life of her children just because she has, she says, devoted her life to them.

Suddenly seized by anger, I struck the bed with my fists. At that, the box fell to the floor, photos and letters scattered out. It felt as if Auntie Rose's life were pouring out, so I hurriedly knelt down on the floor, afraid the box might be broken. When I picked up the overturned box, I saw two pictures stuck in a gap on the floor. One was facedown and one was a picture of three women together. I realized it must be Mom, Auntie Rose, and Songhwa, though it seemed as though it was from before they got married.

Sitting on the floor, I picked up the picture and looked at the three women, who must have been my age. The woman standing on the right, wearing a blouse and a long skirt, holding a folded parasol like a walking stick, was of course Auntie Rose. And the one on the left wearing a skirt and jacket and holding a bouquet must be Songhwa. The person sitting in the middle holding a fan would be Mother. When I realized that my face was similar to my mother's in her youth, I smiled. That's why my mother always insisted that I looked like her. I liked the mother I saw in the picture. Unlike nowadays, the young lady in the photo was looking somewhere beyond the camera.

I put that picture down and picked up the one that was lying facedown. Time had passed; the three women were with two children. At the bottom of the photo, I noticed that *Pearl's first birthday* was written in gold letters. This was a picture of my first birthday! At home, the only picture of my first birthday showed me alone.

I smiled as I imagined the scene with myself, the star of the day, being photographed surrounded by my boisterous mother and aunties. My brother was being held by Auntie Rose, and I was in the arms of my mother sitting in the middle. The woman sitting next to my mother and holding my hand must be Songhwa. However, when I looked closely, it seemed that the child my mother was holding was not me. Not only that, but the person holding the child looked like Mother, and the person sitting next to her looked like the woman I had taken for Mother in the picture I had just seen.

Then I saw the date Auntie Rose had written on the back of the photo. My heart skipped a beat at the figures I had only glanced at before. *May 27, 1923.* But I was born on June 4, 1923. On the day they took the picture of Pearl's birthday, I hadn't been born yet. So who was the Pearl in the picture, and who was the Pearl now looking at the picture? I suddenly felt a foreboding storm approaching.

I scanned the photos lying on the floor and found a picture of five couples. But the bride standing next to the youngest bridegroom wasn't the woman with the fan I had thought was my mother. That woman was standing next to the oldest man, looking somewhere beyond the camera even on her wedding day.

I began to look through the envelopes, struggling to think of something else. Among the letters in the box, I looked at those from Korea. I pushed aside the letters from Auntie's son and looked only for those bearing the family name An. I had heard that her brother lived in the same village as Auntie Rose, so if there was anything about Songhwa, it would be in his letters. The letters I found were like coded texts, a mixture of Chinese and Korean characters, written vertically, and with no spaces.

Auntie Rose received a letter from her brother about once every two or three years, mainly indicating that someone had died, been born, or gotten married. After struggling to read a few of the letters, I finally found the word "shaman" in one. Auntie Rose seemed to have asked for news, and he wrote that Kumhwa had died the previous year, and Songhwa, who had become a shaman, was managing the shrine. Japanese police had tried to smash and demolish the shrine, but there were many reports about how skillful she was, how she often celebrated shamanistic exorcisms for good fortune, and how she was taking good care of Auntie's omma and Willow's omma. It was short, but I could only understand it after reading it several times. At the end of the letter the date was written as a Sinmi year. I didn't know when that was, but when I looked at the postmark on the envelope, it was from 1932, nine years before.

I sat leaning against the bed for a while, then laid out the four photos on the floor in chronological order. The photo of the three women, the photo of the communal marriage, the photo of Pearl's first birthday, and a photo of Auntie Rose's wedding. They were in the same mother's arms, but Pearl as a baby and Pearl at the age of five were clearly different children. Even if children change as they grow up, eyes can be clearly distinguished. The Pearl smiling brightly at the age of five clearly had exactly the same mouth as Songhwa's elderly husband, who was smiling broadly.

I no longer knew who I was.

After an indeterminate while, I staggered up and went to the mirror. Like a puppet, the joints of my body seemed to be working separately, while the inside of my head was in a whirlwind. I looked in the mirror fearfully, as if I were standing at the gates of Hell. The nineteen-year-old Pearl's eyes, nose, large mouth, and slender chin resembled those of Songhwa. It was not Auntie Rose's life that had come pouring out of the box, but my own.

14

MY MOTHERS

"Pearl, get up." Auntie Rose woke me up.

When I opened my eyes, my auntie, who had changed into her outdoor clothes, was standing by my bed. It was bright outside. I had stayed awake until dawn, and then fallen asleep without even realizing it. What was going on? I wasn't fully awake yet.

"Get up quickly. We're going to your place."

I came to my senses and, at the same time, my heart sank. Suddenly going to my home? Was Auntie planning to talk about everything in front of the family? I wasn't ready yet.

"Wh-what's the matter?" I asked, tangled up in the sheet underneath the blanket. I was about to lie and say I was so sick that I couldn't get out of bed.

"This is no time to be idle. There's a big row going on. Jongho says he's joining the army."

Jongho, the army? A shock no less than the one I experienced the previous night hit me. My brother, who was majoring in accounting at UCLA, was due to graduate after one more semester, and was dreaming of getting a job on Wall Street, in New York. But all of a sudden, the army?

"Why aren't you getting up? If Jongho joins the army, it'll kill your mom."

She was right. No matter how much she loved Father, my

brother was the pillar holding her up. It sometimes made me sad and jealous, but it was undeniable.

I jumped up, rapidly washed my face, and put on a light blue dress. It was something Mom had made, and since it was baggy and with a high neckline, I never wore it if I had a date with Peter. It was probably because I wasn't thinking straight that my hand went to a dress that made my mother sad because I didn't like it.

I rushed down the stairs and got into Auntie's Chevrolet, parked in front of the restaurant. She was waiting with the engine already running, and started off before I even had time to shut the door. Her mouth was shut tight, as if talking would make the car go slower, and shot ahead, stepping on the accelerator and brake alternately. My auntie's skill in driving was no different from long before, when Mom said she used to get carsick.

I held on with both hands as I thought of Mother. How was she feeling now? My brother, who was an honors student throughout his high school years, received a full scholarship when he was accepted by the university. My brother, who had never been in trouble, was my mother's pride. I was too, but less so. The schoolteachers who remembered him did not believe that I was David's sister. We were alike in nothing. I had always thought it was fortunate that I wasn't like my brother or any of my family. I felt a pain as if my chest had been stabbed with an awl. We were coming close to my home, and I wasn't sure how I should confront the family I was about to meet.

I glanced at Auntie Rose. Would she remember what happened? The previous night, after seeing my resemblance to Songhwa in the mirror, I ran to her room and shook her awake, as she lay sleeping sprawled across the bed. She opened her eyes in a stupor and I questioned her like a detective interrogating a criminal.

"Rose, Songhwa was my mother? Right?" Each syllable emerging from my mouth turned into a sharp spear slashing at my heart.

". . . What are you talking about?" she muttered, as if talking in her sleep. Every time she opened her mouth, the smell of alcohol came wafting out.

"I know everything, don't try to deceive me." I shook my fist as if she were a criminal. She blinked bleary eyes.

"Heavens, is this a dream? . . . You're right. Songhwa's your mother," Auntie Rose replied with her eyes shut. My world shook to its foundations.

"Then, who was the Pearl you took to the beach? That's what you always said. That you took David and me to Sunset Beach. But at that time, I was still inside Songhwa's belly."

"That's right. . . . The baby who went to the beach was Willow's Pearl. That child died of pneumonia just after her first birthday. . . . Aigo, I can't distinguish between this Pearl and that Pearl."

The previous evening, she had said that Songhwa went back to Korea. She had left after giving birth to a child. And that child was me.

"Why did Songhwa leave? You said that in Korea, being a shaman is a low-class thing."

". . . She went back in order to live. Her mubyong was a lingering sickness and she was less and less able to live a normal life here."

"Then why did she leave me behind? She could have taken me with her."

By that time, she was fully conscious. She seemed surprised

to realize what she was talking about, but she still didn't open her eyes. That was better for me too. I didn't feel confident talking to her face-to-face. Auntie sighed. She slurred her reply as if to suggest that since she was drunk she didn't know what she was saying. "If she took you back to Korea, you would have had to live in a Japanese world as a shaman's daughter, and do you think she wanted that? When Songhwa was a child, everyone threw stones at her. I threw stones, your omma threw stones."

I closed my eyes tightly. I felt as if I were the child being stoned.

"Why did Songhwa give me to Mother? She could have given me to someone else," I barely dared ask. (Suppose I had grown up as Auntie Rose's child? I had often wished Auntie Rose were my mother.)

"You never know what's inside someone, do you? She had that special kind of insight so I suppose she realized there was some kind of bond between you and your mom. Anyway, Willow was in a desperate state after losing her child and raising you helped her recover. You saved your mom, and your mom saved you. Aigo, I've told you everything."

Auntie Rose turned over and began to snore again as if to suggest she had been talking in a dream. I didn't know if by the mother who had saved me she meant Songhwa or my mom.

After standing there in a daze, I returned to my room. The floor seemed to disappear, like I was floating in midair, so I sat down on the bed.

How could I have failed to notice? I had never once thought that my mother might not be my real mother, an idea that children all over the world have at least once while growing up. It wasn't until dawn that I brought the box back to its original place in my auntie's room.

Auntie hit the brakes and I almost banged my forehead on the windshield, but managed to regain my balance.

"Oops, are you all right? Last night, after drinking so much, I had all sorts of dreams. I talked a lot in my sleep, didn't I?" Auntie Rose glanced at me as she spoke.

My heart jolted. At that moment, I had needed to find out the truth, even if it meant digging deep, but now I didn't want anyone to know what I knew. I didn't want to give any more worries to my mother and father, who were already upset about my brother's plans. Indeed, I wasn't ready to accept this situation yet myself. I had thought about it until dawn, but I still couldn't decide what to do.

Whatever I was going to do, it was not for now. Like a child putting off homework she doesn't want to do, I decided to set my problems aside. I wouldn't feel comfortable until I'd dealt with it, but I wasn't ready.

"Why do you care so much about our family? Is there a reason?" After learning my great secret, I found everything suspicious. Auntie Rose had always been there, whenever anything happened to my family. When my father wasn't there, she and my mom raised us together, and even after moving, my brother and I were still indebted to her. Michael would also be staying at her house from next fall semester, when he entered middle school. And now, when Mother was in despair, she was the first person to go running to be with her. How was it possible to care that much?

"Although your mom and I didn't have the same mother, since we're both from Ojin Village, it's as if we're sisters from a single womb. Besides, if it weren't for your mom, how could I have endured such a harsh destiny, being married three times? Besides, it's not for your family's sake, it's to satisfy my greed. When I see you, you remind me of my son."

I recalled a letter from her son I had seen the previous night. I had only seen the first line, "Dear Mother," and set it aside, so I did not know the contents.

She hesitated for a moment, then said, "Songhwa is also like a sister to your mother and me. When she told us she was going back to Korea, we didn't try to stop her. Until then, Songhwa had always done as others told her to do. She came if told to come, went if told to go, lived with her old groom because she was told to. Going back to Korea was the first time that woman did something she decided for herself."

She said absolutely nothing about the child.

Koko Crater came into view. The car turned onto the road running between flower beds spreading like carpets. I had never felt so heavy-hearted on the way home. I couldn't imagine our home without my brother. In Pearl Harbor, in just a few hours the air raid had killed a huge number of people. Those people must have been somebody's child, parent, brother, and lover.

When my aunt pulled into the yard and stopped, Paul and Harry came running out. Both of them, now nine and seven years old, had been raised by me, feeding them and changing their diapers. My heart ached as I embraced my bright younger brothers. They said they were playing Monopoly with Michael and asked me to join them. Nothing had changed between me and my family. I wanted that to last forever. I entered the house with the boys, one on either side.

When I walked into the living room, my father and mother, who were sitting on the sofa, greeted me with expressions suggesting that they were walking through Hell. Michael, sitting in front of the Monopoly board on the floor, greeted me with a nod. The scar from when I had dropped him while carrying him on my back must still be somewhere on the back of his head. I tried hard to hold back my tears and asked nobody in particular, "And David?"

At other times, Mother would have scolded me, telling me to call him "Oppa," "older brother," but now she only sighed, and Father replied that he was in his room.

"Aigo, what's all this about?" Auntie, who had followed me in, pushed me aside, ran to my mother, and hugged her.

"Hongju, what am I to do?" asked Mother before she burst into tears.

Father said to Michael, "Jonggyu, take your brothers up to your room and play there. Then tell David to come down."

Michael looked discontented not to be involved in important family conversations, but without arguing, he went up to the second floor with Paul and Harry. I wasn't going to obey if I was also told to go to my room, but Mom wiped away her tears and asked me to bring in tea. That meant that it was okay for me to be there while they talked with my brother. Auntie Rose asked for black coffee. Going to the kitchen, I made milk tea for Mom and my brother, black tea for Father, and two cups of coffee.

I heard Mother's choked voice from the other room. "He said nothing at all for several days, then the evening before last, he said he had something to tell us, that he was joining the army."

"Down in the town, it's chaos, with all the young Americans saying they want to join the army. You should absolutely not let him enlist." Auntie always understood what we said better than Mother, and took our side when there was a conflict with our parents, but she spoke in a resolute voice.

When Mother replied, her voice sounded desperate. "Yester-day, we talked to him all day long. Nothing that I or his aboji said had any effect. Hongju, you try talking to him. He listens to what you say."

As Mother said, it was to Auntie he had talked about his first love affair and his broken heart. If Mom knew, she would be sad, but I understood my brother. We grew up seeing Mother suffering without Father. We thought that once Father came home, all her hardships would be over, but it was still Mother who had to bear the burdens of life. Mother being as she was, my brother would not have been able to tell her that he liked a girl or that his heart was aching because they had broken up. Just as Mom was utterly devoted to my brother, he always put her first.

Usually, my feelings toward them were divided. When my mother put him first, I felt sad and envious, and when she sent him to college on the mainland while saying that I couldn't go, I was unhappy. However, when I considered the expectations laid on my brother's shoulders as the eldest son, I felt I was fortunate not to be the top priority. Insofar as he said that he had to do as he had decided, my anxiety grew at the thought that his decision to enlist was not a mere impulse or bluff.

When I went back to the living room with the tray, my brother was just coming down the stairs. His face looked puffy. Father was sitting on a small sofa; Mother and Auntie sat on the couch opposite him. I put the cups down on the table and sat on the stool next to the couch. My brother stood for a while, then went to the sofa and sat down next to Father.

Auntie Rose spoke first. "Let's all calm down and drink our tea."

At that, everyone took a sip from the cup in front of them, like marionettes hanging from strings controlled by Auntie. The only sound to be heard in the room was the rattling of teacups and people drinking. Mother and Father were silent, hoping that Auntie would change my brother's mind, while he hoped that she would persuade his parents.

As if recognizing her crucial role, Auntie coughed a couple of times before she began to speak. "Jongho, I married Charlie, so I'm half American, too, but that's not the point. After only one more semester, you'll graduate and get a job, so why do you want to join in the American war? Do you realize how vicious the Japanese are? Look at the way they attacked Pearl Harbor. They're ruffians. Change your mind and stay at school."

My brother didn't answer. He had always been the same. While I screamed and expressed my emotions, my brother quietly did as he wished.

Mom summoned up her energy and said, "Do you know how my aboji died? He died fighting against Japanese soldiers when I was nine years old. My older brother was also killed protesting a Japanese policeman. If my mother sent me all this way to get married, it was so that I might have a quiet life, not under the rule of the Japanese."

It was the first time I had heard any of that. Mother had always told me that she was an only daughter caught between an older brother and younger brothers, like me. When she said that her older brother had died, I felt even more intrigued. Until now, quite honestly, I had been embarrassed that my mother was a picture bride. I hadn't asked for details because it seemed to me that a poor Korean woman had been sold for money. How many stories marked with scars were there in Mother's heart? But when she mentioned her hometown, I remembered Songhwa, who was living there. I quickly erased her image. Knowing that Mother had said she would never tell her painful story, Auntie intervened.

"Aigo, she came all this way, then your aboji went to join the Independence Movement. I know and Heaven knows the anxieties your mother experienced during those ten years."

Father looked away. Mother spoke again, looking firmly determined. "It's enough that my aboji gave his life for our country and my husband his leg. I can't send my children away too. Until the day I die, I can't."

Now Auntie Rose was crying. "That's it, David, you have to change your mind, to save your mother's life. I've heard how, even in Korea, the Japanese are sending young men to fight. Our Songgil may get dragged into the war. I can't bear thinking that you too might go. David, if you go to war, you and Songgil might end up fighting each other. Songgil is my son, and you too are my son. You brothers might end up shooting at each other. Could that ever be right?"

Mother wiped away tears. So that was the reason why Auntie had been so upset that my brother was enlisting. The eyes of my mother and aunt were focused on my father, who had not said anything. He was looking immensely conflicted.

My brother and my father had always had an awkward relationship. No matter what happened, there was little conversation between them. When Father returned home, my brother had been thirteen years old, a very sensitive age. At that time, my father was not in any state to try to understand or approach the hearts of his children who had lived separated from him for such a long time. As soon as we moved to Koko Head, my brother went to live in our auntie's house, so he didn't have time to close the gap with Father. My brother, who only came home once or twice a year after he started college, did not have the opportunity to feel compassion by watching his father from the sidelines, as I had done. Still, I wanted my father to say something, to stop my brother somehow.

As my mother, aunt, and I looked at him as if he was the last hope, Father reluctantly opened his mouth, paused, then said, "The reason I went to China, leaving you and your mother behind, was because I hoped to give my children an independent homeland. I thought that was more important and meaningful than taking care of my family and ensuring my own comfort. I am still bitter that I failed to achieve independence and returned home sick, but like your mother, I don't want you to sacrifice yourself for our country. As your aboji, I want you to enjoy a happy life."

It was very rare for my father to talk for so long, especially to my brother.

But with a sarcastic expression my brother said, "That's not why I want to join the army. It's not for Korea, nor for America. This is my chance. Do you think that we second- and third-generation people are fully American just because we have American citizenship? My parents' nationality is Japanese, isn't it? On the mainland right now, people are in an uproar telling Japanese people to go back to Japan. In the eyes of Americans, I am Japanese. In a case like this, I have to show that I am an American citizen and a patriot. That way, I can get a job and succeed, later on. I want to enlist for my own sake and that of my family, so that I can become the head of the family and fulfill my responsibilities."

I didn't know my brother was so good at Korean. Inside David's words, with their clear logic, there was a barb pointing at Father. I was angry at my brother for making Mother despair and putting Father down.

I spoke rapidly in English. "David, why are you so impossible? Is that any way to talk? Was it for his own sake that Father didn't look after our family? And you say you're joining the army in order to succeed? Don't you think about Mom? You know how much you mean to her. Do you think she can live if you ever get hurt?"

Mom wouldn't be able to understand what I said in any case,

and Father and Auntie wouldn't know what I was saying if I spoke quickly. But still, I couldn't speak the word "die."

My brother stared at me and said in English, "That's not what anyone planning to go to the University of Wisconsin should say. If I'm impossible, you're selfish. It's for my family that I want to succeed. If I succeed, I can relieve Mother's anguish. But what can you do for your family by dancing? You're only thinking of yourself."

I was speechless. Suddenly, the thought struck me that my brother might know that I wasn't his real sister. My brother was five when I was born. Just as I could remember Auntie Rose's wedding, my brother must remember the death of his younger sister and how I, Songhwa's child, had taken her place. I suddenly felt paralyzed and couldn't speak anymore.

When I lived in Wahiawā, David had been a strong guardian, protecting me both in the town and at school. Most of the time, if he got into trouble, it was because someone had made fun of me or made me cry. Even without a father, thanks to my brother I was able to live my childhood without being discouraged. Even in high school, the fact that I was David's younger sister meant that I received the attention and love of the teachers. If I ever heard him say, "What have I to do with you, stranger?," I felt that I would no longer be able to be part of this family.

Tears were about to come pouring out, so I got up quickly, collected the empty cups, and went out to the kitchen. The question of what kind of help I could be to the family by dancing remained stuck in my heart like a thorn. As my brother said, if I wanted to dance it was only for myself, in order to live as myself.

I want to dance in order to be happy. But what is there on a battlefield? Is there anything more than being wounded or dying? Even if you come back safely, there's nothing but wounds.

There was someone nearby to prove that: Father. He had come back after being wounded in a battle against Japanese forces, his health ruined. The anguish that Father suffered from was not only the result of coming back without achieving independence. Several times while we were living in the small house in Wahiawā, he woke up in the night, screaming. Even if the other person is an enemy, how can someone who kills or injures another person and sees many of his friends doing the same live with a healthy mind? Perhaps my father was suffering because he felt that even such feelings were sins against his country? I stayed standing there without going back to the living room, even after I finished washing the empty cups and put them on the drying rack.

"Father, Mother, Auntie. Please don't worry too much, because not everyone dies if they join the army. I will fight admirably, then come back."

My brother seemed to have no intention of changing his mind.

"There is no such thing as fighting admirably in this world," said Father, his voice strained.

Shells came flying. Flames soared up here and there, blood splattered, wounded people screamed. Father was limping away with one leg cut off. I cried and called, but when he looked back it was my brother. Songhwa appeared and hugged me, as I screamed and collapsed at the sight of my blood-soaked brother. She looked the same as in the photo taken before her marriage, so I didn't for a moment think that she was the person who had given birth to me. I simply felt that I was meeting a woman my own age. I wanted to ask if she was doing well, but I couldn't remember any Korean. When I spoke in English,

Songhwa couldn't understand. Songhwa put a carnation lei over my shoulders so it hung around my neck. The lei united us. We danced together. Songhwa danced a shamanic dance that united heaven and earth, while my dance united people with one another. I danced until I was exhausted, then woke up.

The room was filled with early-morning light; another day was beginning. Nothing had got any better since yesterday morning, when I was struck with shock and fear. Auntie Rose, having failed to persuade my brother, had scoured the cupboards and prepared a hearty dinner while Mother and Father watered the carnation field. Then she summoned the family to the table. It was the first time since last summer vacation that everyone was together.

"I'll eat today, then die. Why have you prepared so much?" asked Mother, looking at the table.

"At times like this, you have to eat to be strong. Everybody, eat well."

Thanks to Auntie Rose, and the talkative Paul and Harry, we began to breathe a little more freely. After dinner was over and tea drunk, Auntie stood up saying she would go home.

Mom held her back. "Why go back to an empty house alone? You can sleep in Jinju's room."

I was reluctant to share my room, but my aunt was the most comforting person for my family now. I also held on to her.

"Leave my house empty and crawl into Jinju's bed? No thanks!"

"At least take Jinju with you." Mom was worried that Auntie would be alone at such a moment. I was more worried about Auntie, who had been drinking until she was on the verge of tears, than Mother, who had recovered her usual form as if nothing had happened.

Auntie said to me, "No. You'll be starting school again in a few days, you should stay here with your family until then. No matter what, a daughter comes first to her mom."

Now was certainly a time to be with my mom.

Once Auntie Rose had left, the house was filled with a heavy silence, broken only by Father's intermittent coughing. I sent away Paul and Harry, still begging me to play, and went to bed before nine o'clock. I wanted to fall asleep quickly and escape from reality, but I didn't want to dream either, remembering the Songhwa I had seen in my dream the previous night. What did a dream of us dancing together mean?

The thought that it might be a revelation of the future was stronger than the thought that it was a dream I had simply because I liked dancing. A shaman's blood flowed through my veins too, so maybe I could also have visions of the future. What if it had been a premonition, the way Father with a leg cut off had turned into my brother? I shook my head vigorously.

When I heard that Mother's older brother had died, I felt it was rather fortunate that David was not my real brother. That thought had only lasted a moment, but the scratch left by my brother's words stung again. *What can you do for your family by dancing? You're only trying to do what you like doing.* It seemed to be a shame that I, who wasn't even a daughter of this family, should insist on dancing. I didn't even have enough self-confidence to fight with Mother, who was letting my brother go to the battlefield. Maybe it was the shaman's blood in my veins making me fond of dancing? Might that be why my mom hated to see me dancing? I remembered what happened when I was in tenth grade at a Fraternity Club activity.

After performing solo at the March First commemorative performance, I was intoxicated with the enthusiasm aroused by the dance. It wasn't enough for me to have danced for a while onstage. I went on dancing freely with fluttering sleeves, regardless of whether the staff saw me or not. I didn't even know that my mother was there.

"Are you out of your mind?" Mom had asked, and slapped me on the cheek.

My surprised eyes noticed the even more surprised expressions of the other children and the teachers. I looked at her. Her eyes were full of fear and embarrassment, as if she were the one who had been slapped. Humiliated, I ran out, and later learned that she told my teacher that I couldn't participate in the performances anymore because of my studies. At that time, I thought that my mother's slap and look came from her desire to make her daughter into a teacher.

Now it was clear why she was against me dancing. She was afraid that I might become a shaman like Songhwa. Maybe the reason that Songhwa being my mother was a secret was because being a shaman was contemptible in the Korean community's eyes. My very being was not something I had wished for. No one had asked me if she might bear me, if she might go away, leaving me behind, or who might raise me. It was my life, but everyone had made their own decisions, turned them into secrets that belatedly stabbed at my heart. They did all that, so why was it wrong for me to do what I wanted? I grew more and more angry, but there was nobody for me to shout at or accuse.

I sat up early the next morning. Looking out of the window, I saw that Mom was already in the carnation field. The field in full bloom was like a pink rug, while the field plowed was like an ocher rug. On the other side was a green carpet that had not yet blossomed. It was as beautiful as a picture. However, it didn't just look beautiful, I also knew how much hard work and care went into it. Compassion overwhelmed me. We were all pitiful—myself, of course, my mom, my father and David, Auntie Rose, even Songhwa . . . There was nothing in this world that I did not feel sorry for.

I put a cardigan on over my pajamas and left the room. My brothers' rooms were quiet. As I went downstairs, I saw Father preparing breakfast in the kitchen. I deciding to go outside. I wanted to leave him the comfort of preparing a good breakfast for his family, instead of pushing him out of the kitchen.

A cold, bracing wind struck me as I left the house. I saw the sea tinged red by the rising sun, and the raging waves. I pulled my cardigan around me and went to Mother's side. She stopped pulling weeds and looked up at me. Her tanned face was full of freckles, and her graying hair fluttered in the wind. Now she was forty years old, but looked sixty. The eighteen-year-old Willow overlapped with her in my mind.

My sight grew hazy.

"You should get more sleep. How come you're up already?" she asked as she scraped out weeds with a hoe.

Without a word, I squatted next to her and pulled at the weeds. The scent of flowers grew stronger as we worked. After a while, my mother put down the hoe and sat down on a bench on the bank. "Come and sit." Mother tapped the seat beside her with her palm.

I sat down by my mother.

"Jinju, go to the college you want to go to, but I can only pay the tuition fees. I have to educate your younger brothers, too."

She spoke calmly. I was so surprised that I couldn't say anything for a while. Had she given up on me because she spent so much energy worrying about David? *Doesn't she care what I do?*

"Why . . . why have you changed your mind?"

She sighed.

"I can't stop a child who says he's going to a battlefield where he might die, so why should I try to stop a child who wants to study something she loves? When you used to go jumping around the yard, you were as pretty as a fluttering butterfly or a hovering hummingbird." A smile lingered on her face as she seemed to be remembering it.

"Thank you, Mom." My throat was dry, I could barely speak.

"Relations between parents and children are like that. My mother sent me here so that I could live somewhere with no Japanese rule, but I came because I thought I could study. When I think back, I came here, leaving my mother and brothers behind, in order to live in a new world, so trying to force my daughter to stay with me would be greedy. For me, coming all this way was a great thing. Now, off you go, flying even farther than I did, in search of the world you dream of. Become someone precious, like your name. Even if you're far away, never forget that this is your home."

She spoke with frequent pauses, looking peaceful and cheerful. I held back my tears and nodded as hard as I could. She had come here, not sold because they were poor, not to live comfortably in a world without any Japanese, but in search of her dream, like me. Although she had not been able to achieve her dream, she had done her best at every moment.

Suddenly, I realized I was proud that such a person was my mother. Inevitably, two other people came to mind. I was happy that Auntie Rose was beside me. And I was grateful that Songhwa had given birth to me. Like the ends of a lei, my three mothers and I are united, as I am united with Hawai'i and Korea, no matter where I am. My heart grew warm.

As always, it suddenly began to rain.

"Lucky, because I've not been watering." Mother laughed.

We didn't shelter from the rain. If you live in Hawai'i, you simply let rain like this fall upon you.

Waves continued across the wide-spread sea, breaking relentlessly against the shore. The waves never pause, even though they know they will break. I will live like that. Like a wave, I will collide with the world with my whole being. I can do it knowing I will always have a home, and my mothers, like lei, to encircle me in their embrace.

Author's Note

I was reading a book about the hundred-year history of Korean-American immigration. One photo caught my eye. Three women wearing white cotton skirts and jackets were sitting or standing, holding either a parasol, flowers, or a fan. It said they were picture brides who had left a village together. It was the first time I heard about picture brides.

On January 13, 1903, the *Gallic*, carrying 102 Korean immigrants, arrived at the port of Honolulu, Hawai'i. Among them, only 86 people (48 men, 16 women, 22 children) were able to disembark after passing a physical examination. They had come to work on sugarcane farms and were the first Korean immigrants to Hawai'i in the modern sense of the word and the first official immigrants recognized by the Daehan Empire.

Those immigrants, who had come on the ship dreaming of a better life, had to work like slaves under the burning heat of the sun, among sugarcane with sharp-edged leaves, and with grim foremen wielding whips. There were 7,200 Korean immigrants to Hawai'i in the years up to 1905, when an immigration ban was imposed due to Japanese demands.

The majority of the single male workers chose picture marriages to start a family. It meant finding a spouse by sending a picture of himself back to his country. In the picture-marriage process from 1910 to 1924, when the Oriental Exclusion Act was passed, the men often sent photos taken when they were young, or they lied about their job or property status. Matchmakers did not hesitate to publish false advertisements about Hawai'i or the bridegroom.

There were over a thousand picture brides who took the risk of going to a distant land to support their families, or because they hated being ruled by Japan, or wanted to escape poverty and the bonds imposed on women, and even believing that once there, women could easily study. They were mostly young women in their late teens to mid-twenties. I did not forget the women in the photo that caught my eye, even after I finished reading the book. Rather, I felt more intensely touched by them.

How could women think of setting off for a distant place when it was difficult even to go to the local market? What made you risk your fate on a single picture? Where did that courage come from? What kind of people were the husbands when they arrived in Hawai'i? What was life like in a strange place? In response to my endless questions, the brides in the photo came alive as Willow, Hongju, and Songhwa, to tell their stories.

The picture brides who arrived in Hawai'i had to live their lives without a chance to mourn and lament over their broken dreams. They adapted to unfamiliar circumstances, built families, raised children, worked as hard as the men, improved their lives, and boldly devoted themselves to the independence of their country. Those women were pioneers and trailblazers.

The same is true of married migrant women living in Korea today. It must have been a great adventure for them, too, to leave their family, home, and country. It is hard to know how difficult it is for them to adjust to an unfamiliar language and environment. Whenever I hear bad news related to married immigrant women, it hurts just as when I saw the picture brides' photo from a hundred years ago. I hope that the stories of Willow, Hongju, and Songhwa will be a mirror for our present day.

Thanks are due to all the people who worked hard to produce this book. I hope it will be a small reward for the readers who always support and encourage me.

In the early spring of 2020

Lee Geum-yi

Translator's Note

The Korean name of the main character in this novel could simply be written "Bodeul," just as all the other names are transcribed without being translated. But she explains that "Bodeul" means "a willow tree" and that that very unusual name was deliberately given to her by her father, although she does not know why. Therefore, it seems better to call her "Willow" when telling her story in English.

Willow's family name is "Kang" but her mother is addressed as "Mrs. Yun" because Korean women do not take their husband's family name on marrying.

There are various ways of "romanizing" Korean, but in the time when most of this novel happens there was no official system. In this translation, the Korean names of people and places have been written in what seems the simplest, most accessible way, rather than adhering exactly to any one "official" system.

The three main characters all come from the same small rural village in southeastern Korea. The Korean text shows them speaking with a strong local dialect, not standard contemporary Korean. There is no convincing way of representing that in English; readers will just have to understand that a characteristic regional flavor is missing from the words the characters speak.

The Western name "Korea" has no Korean equivalent. "Choson" is the name that the characters in this novel use for their nation, which was not divided between North and South, but had been brutally annexed by Japan in 1910, and for whose independence they all long and some fight. In translating it seems easier to use the English name "Korea" throughout. The most important fact to remember is that at this time "Korea" is the name of an unwilling Japanese colony, not the name of an independent country.

The characters do not usually use the formal term "Ilbon saram" for "the Japanese" but call them "wae-nom," an insulting, belittling term very common in Korean, hard to translate.

Most of the secondary female characters in this story are never referred to by their given name but are always addressed and referred to as the mother of one of their children. The most important such character is known as "Julie's mother," and we also meet "Dusun's mother," "James's mother," while others are identified by their place of origin ("the Pusan Ajimae," "the Kaesong ajumoni"). In fact, many lower-class women were never "given" a name (a formal act by a father or grandfather) or as children might only be given a deprecatory nickname. Men, too, were commonly referred to by their son's name, even by their wives when talking directly to them. Korean does not have a general, neutral term for "you."

The three young women use their given names when talking to each other, since they are close friends, virtual sisters. In dialogue, they refer to their parents as "omma" and "omoni" (mother) and "aboji" (father). When addressing or talking about older women, they might call them "ajumoni"/"ajime" (aunt) or "halmoni" (grandmother); men, too, might be addressed as "ajosshi" (uncle) or "haraboji" (grandfather), with no implication of belonging to one family.

Koreans, Chinese, and Japanese at this time used two Chinese characters, 布哇 (pronounced "Powa"), when referring to Hawai'i, a name they found hard to pronounce. Honolulu was likewise called "Hohang." In translating, "Hawai'i" has normally been used, and "Honolulu" has been preferred throughout in order to avoid unhelpful confusion. The diacritical marks have been used in the spelling of the Hawaiian words, a practice more common now than in the plantation era but reflective of how the Hawaiian language remains alive.

Fall of 2020,
An Seonjae

Acknowledgments

It's always such a meaningful and heart-fluttering experience to have my work translated into another language and to get to the readers outside the terrain of my mother tongue. I send special thanks to my wonderful translator, An Seonjae, and the brilliant team at Forge—Robert Davis, Esther S. Kim, Anthony Parisi, Libby Collins, Ryan Jenkins, Greg Collins, and Kristiana Kahakauwila—for opening this door to a new, exciting world. I can't be happier to have one of my books published in English for the first time—my British son-in-law will finally be able to enjoy *The Picture Bride*!